BINDING SPELL

CHRISTINE POPE

Dark Valentine Press

BINDING SPELL

ISBN: 978-0-9883348-2-3
Copyright © 2013 by Christine Pope
Published by Dark Valentine Press

Cover art by Ravven
Book layout by Indie Author Services

To learn more about this author, go to
www.christinepope.com.

To Katherine, for always being there when I needed you

~ CHAPTER ONE ~

Of all the ways I might have imagined my day ending, assuredly none of them involved being stolen from one of the guest suites at my Aunt Laranel's estate, and then thrown across the saddle of a stranger's horse and spirited away in the middle of the night. While I do have my powers, carefully guarded and spoken of to no one beyond my immediate family, the gift of the Sight is one denied me. Because of this, I had no idea of what awaited me when I blithely bade goodnight to my aunt and my brother and looked forward to a restful night in the luxurious rooms that should have been occupied by someone of far greater rank than I—Lyarris, Crown Princess of Sirlende. But as the princess had taken ill at the last minute and could not travel forth to witness the investiture of the latest Duke of Marric's Rest, my aunt had decided that I, as the sister of the honoree, might as well enjoy the comforts of the suite.

What precisely woke me, I cannot say. Sleep had come to me easily that night, though I slept in a strange bed. True, I had spent far too many weeks on the road, first traveling from my homeland of South Eredor to the estate of Lord Senric Torrival, Duke of Gahm, where my brother Thani had spent the last seven years training at arms. From there, the Duke and Thani and I—and some forty-odd retainers and men-at-arms—had continued on to Marric's Rest, my Aunt Laranel's estate. Well, to be precise, the estate she had been keeping in trust for my brother, who rode forth to claim it as his own, now that he had turned twenty-five and reached his majority. At any rate, by the time I had tumbled into that heavenly feather bed, I had been on the road for the greater part of three weeks, and was more than happy to lose myself in sleep almost the moment my head touched the pillow.

For some reason my eyes opened in the deepest watches of the night, and I lay there in the dark for a long while, listening to the quiet of the house. The place was quite full, actually, what with all the men in Lord Senric's train in addition to my aunt's usual complement of servants. The house would have been even more crowded than that if Princess Lyarris had come to bear witness to Thani's investiture. Even so, the enormous building—in my eyes, even grander than the palace of King Vandor back in my hometown of Marestal—seemed full to bursting.

Although I had somehow awakened despite my weariness, I heard nothing save the long, mournful call of an owl from a tree outside my window, followed by silence once more. I closed my eyes then, telling myself I must go back to sleep, that a good deal of unfamiliar ceremony awaited me on the morrow. Easier said than done, however, for there came the faintest rustle from across the room, and I stirred, whispering, "Aunt Laranel?" Perhaps she had come to make sure that I rested easy in my strange bed.

But that rustle became movement, and a dark figure rushed across the room and clapped a hand across my mouth, then began to drag me from the bed. A scream rose in my throat, but the rough hand across my lips held in all sound save a muffled squeak. The first wave of shock passing, I recovered myself enough to squirm in his grip, then bite down on one of the fingers pressed against my mouth.

I was rewarded with the prick of a dagger in my side. My assailant whispered in Sirlendian, "Don't try that again."

His accent was strange and unfamiliar, as if Sirlendian was not his native tongue. True, it was not mine, either, but I knew it almost as well as the common tongue, well enough that I could tell if someone was unaccustomed to speaking it.

I could not see the intruder at all in the darkness, but I did not need my eyes to know that the arms which held me were brutally strong. Besides, even if I somehow managed to pull myself from his grasp, he would still be able to drive the dagger through my ribs before I got very far.

He then dragged me to the door, dagger tip still pressing into my flesh, and herded me down the long corridor and into the stairwell at its far end. At its base I saw two of my aunt's guardsmen slumped as if dead or asleep, but my captor gave me no chance to inspect them closely enough to know for certain whether they yet breathed.

The sight of those still forms sent an icy wave of dread through me, and I writhed in my captor's grip, thinking perhaps a knee to the groin might loosen that iron grasp on my arm. The dagger only pushed against me once more, this time with enough force that I felt rather than heard it penetrate the linen of my nightdress, the steel cold against my bare skin.

I sucked in a breath and went still, knowing I did not have the strength within to resist further, not when he could so easily run me through and leave me lying dead as he fled the building. How I wished then that I had command of those spells from the days gone before, when a mage could have turned such an attacker to dust with a few words. But such powers were far beyond me and the few meager skills I did possess.

We emerged through a small back door into the cold night air, which bit cruelly through my nightgown. I barely had time to note two more slumped forms just outside the doorway before my captor pulled me through the gardens and into a small pine wood.

"What do you want?" I gasped. I could only hope his sole motive was a handsome ransom.

His voice was a low, menacing whisper. "Quiet, girl, if you know what's good for you."

Whatever happened, I knew then that I must do what he told me if I wished to survive. It had to be a ransom. Otherwise, I would most likely be dead already. My aunt, I was sure, would pay anything to get me back safely.

I held onto that faintly comforting thought as my captor dragged me to a horse he had tethered in the wood and pulled me up into the saddle before him, my face pressed against his broad chest.

"Hold on," he instructed me in a rough mutter, and I was forced to cling to the coarse wool of his tunic as he spurred his horse to a gallop. We tore out of the wood in a scatter of pale leaves, and moved across open fields beneath the wan light of two half moons.

I hazarded a glance upward at the man who had kidnapped me and saw the dim moonlight catch in his golden eyes. I had never seen such eyes before, and wondered at first whether he was a true man or some evil spirit from a time now mostly forgotten. However, if one discounted those ochre-tinted eyes, he seemed human enough, although there was something wolfish in his aspect, in the lean weathered face and cruel set of his mouth. His left arm gripped me tightly, and I saw the glint of steel where he still held the dagger in that hand. Not that I would have considered jumping down—the best I could hope for after making such a leap would be a broken leg, or worse.

The miles flashed behind us as the night wore on, but I had no idea how long we rode, nor what time of night it had been when he seized me from my borrowed bed. As the sun rose, he guided the horse to a sheltered little dell where a pair of willows guarded a small pond.

My captor dragged me off his horse and pulled me over to one of the willow trees. He pointed at it, apparently indicating that I should take a seat at its base. Swallowing in trepidation, I did as he indicated. At once he produced a slender rope from his saddlebag and proceeded to bind me to the tree trunk.

Of course I struggled, but even I knew my wild flailings were more for show than anything else. Within the minute I was firmly anchored in place.

"You won't get away with this!" I cried out. "Once my family learns what you've done, they'll be after me for sure. And when they catch you—"

He shook his head at me, then pulled a somewhat grimy length of linen out of the saddlebag. "Quiet, or..." And he let the words trail off while he held up the dirty piece of cloth.

I knew it was going to end up covering my mouth if I didn't leave off. That prospect did not appeal at all, so I fell silent. Besides, there didn't seem to be another human soul in evidence. My cries of help would most likely go unheard, save by my kidnapper.

He nodded, as if satisfied that I appeared to be cooperative, and turned back to his horse, which he began to walk about the dell while murmuring low words in a language I'd never heard before. Somehow that rough monotone worked as a soporific, and I felt my head nod downward before I lifted it again with a jerk. Sleep? Was I mad?

Apparently I was, for after I struggled a minute or so more, my chin dropped to my chest, and my captor, his horse, and the willow trees faded into darkness.

How much time had passed, I couldn't be sure, but the sun was definitely high in the sky when the stranger woke me and offered me a few sips of stale water out of the skin he wore at his hip. Then he knelt and untied me.

When I stood, my legs trembled and shook. I stumbled, and my captor grasped me by the arm. It was not solicitude, however; he only hauled me back to the horse and pulled me up into the saddle once more. Then we rode again, this time at a fast canter and not the wild gallop of the night before. He shunned the roads, and instead guided his mount across fields and meadows, occasionally slowing to a walk when we entered a wood.

Clearly he was doing everything in his power to remain unnoticed, and with a sinking heart I realized he most likely would succeed. We might as well have been the only two people in the world. Clearly he intended to cover a great deal of ground in a short amount of time, or he would have waited for darkness to shield our progress.

Night came again, and still we rode on. From time to time he offered me a sip from his water skin, but no food seemed to be forthcoming. Just as well. Whether from worry and fear or merely the constant motion of the horse, the sour taste of nausea had risen in the back of my throat, and no doubt anything I tried to force down would only have found its way back up again.

After what felt like an eternity, we descended into a deep valley that cut through a series of rough hills. A stream wandered along the valley floor, while dark trees leaned over the water. Through those trees I saw the gleam of a few isolated lights, which came from a pair of torches standing duty outside a low stone building, apparently some sort of hunting lodge.

By that time I had settled into a sort of numb misery—I no longer even had the strength to invent interesting ways for my brother or my aunt to bring my captor to justice. The tears were long dry on my cheeks when the stranger pulled me out of the saddle and dragged me toward the flickering light of the torches. The dew-heavy grass dripped on my bare feet, and I began to shiver once more. During the ride I had not been so cold, since my kidnapper had shown me the rudimentary kindness of pulling his cloak across my shoulders, but now I had no such protection from the night's chill.

As we approached the lodge, a man came and stood in the doorway. For a second he turned to glance back over his shoulder, and the reddish firelight from within caught a golden gleam in those same strange ochre eyes. That, however, was the only real similarity between the two men; this new stranger was much younger, about my brother's age of five-and-twenty, perhaps a few years more, and his features were finer, sharp-drawn and handsome. The rich riding leathers he wore creaked faintly as he stepped toward us.

"*M'arynás, tellnoor s'braïyen?*" he said in the rising inflection of a question, and the man holding me replied in the same equally unintelligible tongue. Despite myself, I frowned. My father had introduced me to the dominant languages of the continent, but this was one I had never heard before. Not that this apparent gap in my scholarship was something that should have concerned me. I had far more important things to worry about.

My captor pushed me past the younger man, who stepped out of the way as I moved into the lodge's main room. A glorious fire burned in the hearth, and I stepped closer toward it, since neither one of them seemed inclined to stop me. After another brief exchange in the same incomprehensible language, the man who had stolen me from my aunt's house disappeared back outside, shutting the door behind him. Then the strange young man turned and looked over at me with a smile, which, while friendly enough on the surface, had something about it that made the skin along the back of my neck prickle.

"Welcome," he said, in perfectly accented Sirlendian, "and accept my apologies for whatever discomfort you may have suffered, your Highness."

Your Highness? I thought. *Who does he think...?*

The thought broke off. Cold inched its way down my back, despite the room's relative warmth, as I began to understand. The Crown Princess Lyarris and I were around the same age and of the same general description: dark-haired, tall, slender. And I had been sleeping in the apartments in my aunt's home that should have housed the princess. Whoever these men were, I realized then that they played a game whose stakes were almost unimaginably high.

I swallowed, thinking, *I don't want to be around when they discover their net has caught the wrong fish...*

The stranger regarded me with watchful golden eyes that seemed to reflect the fire's warm glow. He obviously expected a reply. Something about those eyes tickled at the back of my mind, some snippet of memory that I knew was probably important, but it escaped me at the moment. No matter. It would come to me in time.

I spoke then. I had to hope my voice was as steady and cool as I imagined a princess' should be, no matter what the situation. "My journey was hardly comfortable. I demand to know why you have brought me here."

"I don't think you are in a position to demand anything, your Highness," he replied, those golden eyes narrowing slightly as he looked me up and down. I could not help but be aware of how thin the linen of my nightdress was, or of how wretched I must look, what with the dried tears on my cheeks and my hair snarled and knotted by the ride into a mass of witch-tails. "Still," he went on, "let me attempt to make amends."

He indicated a low upholstered divan that fronted the hearth, and I sat. Despite my perilous circumstances, it felt wonderful just to sit down, to feel soft cushions beneath my abused muscles. The heat from the fire began to work its own magic on my numb hands and feet.

After I had seated myself, he called out something in his own language, and a moment later another strange man entered the room, holding a cup of glazed earthenware, which he handed off to me without a word before disappearing once more. I looked down into the cup with some suspicion, but from the smell it held nothing more dangerous than hot spiced cider.

Still, now that I was finally more or less comfortable, I could attempt some magic in my own defense. I murmured the quick words of the spell under my breath, but the liquid in the cup remained the same. If it had been tainted in any way, it would have turned black as the night outside.

So I lifted the drink to my lips and took a swallow, then another. The heat of it coursed through my chilled body.

"Better?" the stranger asked.

"Yes," I said, slanting a sideways glance at him through my lashes. He continued to watch me with that intent stare, but what precisely he was looking for, I couldn't hazard a guess. Surely he didn't expect even the Crown Princess of Sirlende to be at her best after the sort of journey I had just suffered.

Then he stepped around in front of me, blocking the light from the fire. In silhouette like that, his expression was difficult to see clearly, but it seemed to me he frowned, dark brows pulling down over the gleaming honey-colored eyes. After a few seconds he shifted once more so that the fire light shone full upon my face. His frown deepened as he stared down at me. For a few seconds he stood there, jaw clenched, and then he uttered something I couldn't understand but which probably was some sort of oath—and not the politer sort I'd heard my mother make when the cook burned a batch of bread. No, it sounded more like the profanity I'd once overheard down at the docks when one of our porters dropped a wine barrel on his foot.

I stared up at the stranger, uncomprehending, as he strode away from me to the door, which he opened at once. Apparently my erstwhile kidnapper had taken up guard duty just outside, for he peered in, eyebrows lifted. The young man snapped out an angry question. His subordinate hesitated, then made some sort of reply, looking very much like he wished to be someplace else. But something in his words caught my attention, unintelligible as they might have otherwise been. I was quite sure I caught the word *Arkalis* as a form of direct address. The family name of the Marks of Eredor? It came to me that this angry young man must be Kadar Arkalis, the ruler of North Eredor himself.

My eyes widened, and I looked down at once into my mug of cider so he couldn't see my expression.

After a few more heated remarks, he slammed the door shut once again and turned back to me. "Very well," he said, and although his tone was still taut and angry, he appeared to be back in control. "I know you aren't Princess Lyarris. Who are you?"

I wanted to ask him how he knew for certain, but obviously something in my face had given me away. No doubt Princess Lyarris' and my features were not terribly similar, despite our general resemblance to one another. Of course I had never met her, while it was possible he had actually seen the Crown Princess at the Sirlendian court once upon a time. I had heard that her eyes were dark, while mine were sea-grey, the same color as my father's. But I knew better than to let my curiosity get the better of me. I would have to tread cautiously.

Perhaps if I told the Mark who I really was, he would simply let me go. If he'd been angling to capture the Crown Princess, then ransom—at least of the ordinary sort—clearly wasn't his motive. I had not given any hint that I had guessed at his identity, so perhaps there was a chance, if however slim, of getting out of this unscathed.

"My name is Lark Sedassa," I said, after a perceptible pause.

The level brows lifted slightly, but his expression did not change. "The exile's daughter?"

I felt somewhat surprised he had heard of my father, or of me, but I only nodded. "Yes."

For a moment he was silent. He crossed his arms and then seemed to nod to himself. "Do you know who I am?" he asked at length.

I shook my head. "No, my lord."

He actually laughed. "You are a poor liar, Lark Sedassa. I saw your face as I was speaking with Lamakh. You may not understand the *corraghar* tongue, but you caught something."

The *corraghar*. Of course. The hill tribe of North Eredor, sometimes referred to as the "people of the wolf." This Kadar Arkalis' father had been one of them, and that was why the sight of Kadar's golden eyes had awoken a whisper of memory within me. I had never seen one of the *corraghar* in person before, although I had read about them.

Denials rushed to my lips, but I had a feeling they would be useless. So I faced him squarely and replied, "You are the Mark of North Eredor, my lord."

"Very good, Lark. So let me ask you another question. If our places were reversed, what would you do?"

"I'd let me go," I said at once.

That reply elicited another laugh. "No doubt you would. But if such a thing were not feasible?"

Despite the warmth of the room, another of those trailing fingers of cold ran down my spine. "You certainly have no need of a ransom."

His smile faded. "You might be surprised. Unlike Sirlende, my kingdom is not overburdened with wealth. However, that was not my intent, as you may have guessed."

"It would seem you are at an impasse, then, my lord," I remarked.

"Perhaps...perhaps not." He ran a thoughtful finger along his chin and gave me an appraising look. "Your family is very powerful."

"A family of wine merchants?" I asked, my tone all innocence. Of course I knew he could not be referring to the prosperous but simple folk on my mother's side of the family. True, my great-grandfather on that side had been the second son of a baron, but I doubted that mattered much to Kadar Arkalis.

"Don't be disingenuous. Your mother's kin are of no import, of course, but the Sedassas...the duchy of Marric's Rest is one of the greatest in Sirlende. And your brother has already ridden forth to take control of the Sedassa estates and titles?"

"You are very well-informed, my lord," I remarked, but I found I did not like at all where this conversation seemed to be heading.

"I make it my business to know things. So perhaps I gambled and did not win the prize I sought, but that does not mean I cannot console myself with a lesser reward."

The nausea of the ride reasserted itself. I swallowed the sour lump of fear before replying, "I fear I do not know what you mean, my lord."

"Do you not? If you would prefer that I spell it out for you, then I will do so." Kadar stepped closer and stared down at me, and once again I realized how thin my shift was. I had to fight to keep myself from crossing my arms over my breasts; I did not wish to attract his attention any more than I already had. "I sought to take the Crown Princess for my own, but fate seems to have deprived me of that prize. However, I have you, sister to the man who will soon become one of Sirlende's greatest lords. Who would willingly give up the chance at such a connection?"

Who indeed? I sat there, mute, fearing what was about to come next and desperately hoping he meant something else altogether.

"You are weary, and so we will pass the night in this lodge," he went on. "Have no fear—you will not be compromised. My guards will attest to the fact that I spent my night here in front of the fire, while you slept in the bedchamber."

The smallest sensation of relief crept over me. Perhaps my fate wouldn't be quite as terrible as I feared. But then my hopes crumbled into dust at Kadar's next words.

"After all," he said, "I want my bride's virtue to be unimpeachable. We will ride tomorrow for my capital, where we will be married. And then the great lords of Sirlende will be forced to treat with me as an equal."

I found I had no strength to reply. I could only continue to stare up at him, my mouth dry, and wonder what on earth I could do to extricate myself from this impossible situation.

Kadar was as good as his word. After our exchange, he showed me to the lodge's one sleeping chamber, whose door he locked firmly behind me. I saw little of use in there, although the low chest at the foot of the bed did yield a clean shift to replace my dirty one. A further search revealed nothing else, not even a gown or a pair of shoes. Surely he had known I—that is, the Crown Princess—would have come here directly from her bed and would need to be outfitted. But perhaps those items were being kept elsewhere, held until the moment of leave-taking.

No doubt he had supposed that a woman of high birth would not dare to make an escape attempt while wearing only her chemise.

He hadn't counted on me, however. I'd walk out of there naked if I had to. Not that I hoped things would come to such a pass. The Mark also hadn't counted on his captive having certain forbidden talents; much care had been taken over the years to ensure that knowledge of my magical gifts was limited only to my immediate family. True, I often wished I possessed more skill, and that the spells in my arsenal were more powerful, but oftentimes outright force is not necessary, when the same goals can be accomplished by stealth.

The sleep charm was simple enough, and used very little of my energy. I lay down on the bed, closed my eyes, and began the deep breathing exercises my father had taught me to center myself and collect the power I needed to effect the spell. Because I had to radiate calm for the charm to work, I thrust all thought of Kadar's intentions out of my mind, and instead concentrated only on the soothing solace of deepest sleep.

Still with my eyes shut, I let my consciousness move away from the room in which I lay, out to where the Mark of Eredor slept on the divan in front of the fire. I murmured the words, and his slumber deepened to the point where one would have to drop a heavy weight on his head to stir him. Then I moved on to where Lamakh stood guard outside the front door. Although awake, he was very weary from his long ride. It took little enough effort to work the charm on him as well. His eyelids drooped, and he sagged to a messy heap across the doorstep.

The last two men I found in the kitchen, and again it was but the work of a moment to increase their natural weariness to the point where they both succumbed as well. Both their heads fell with an audible crack against the kitchen table. Oh, dear. Well, they might have a few bumps and bruises in the morning, but otherwise they would awaken unharmed.

Once I knew the household would not be roused by my movements, I climbed off the bed and went to the door. Yes, Kadar had locked it, but it was a simple mechanism, and I knew I could bespell it with little problem.

"*Sorichar*," I whispered, and at once I heard a clink as the lock released and the door swung outward.

So far, so good. I moved out into the short corridor and then on into the front room, where Kadar's snores emerged from behind the high back of the divan. His high boots tempted me as they dangled over the worn upholstery. It was cold outside... so very cold. Even a pair of over-large boots would serve me better than to go barefoot in the freezing mud. In his spelled sleep, he would never know of the theft until long after I was gone.

I grasped one boot and began to tug...only to have a bronzed hand grasp me by the wrist. Kadar Arkalis sat upright and demanded,

"What, precisely, were you planning on doing with my footwear?"

❧ CHAPTER TWO ❧

I let go of the boot as if it had scorched my fingertips. Kadar sat upright, those odd golden eyes surveying me with a sort of amused suspicion. "Planning a little expedition, were you?"

"I—"

His gaze flickered past me to the bedroom's open door. "That was locked."

"It didn't catch," I lied. The last thing I wanted was for him to suspect me of possessing any powers out of the ordinary; he might have caught me now, but I refused to give up. My magic could still possibly help me...as long as Kadar didn't know anything about it.

"Indeed." He swung his still-booted feet off the arm of the divan and stood. "If you are so eager to leave, then we might as well set out now."

He couldn't be serious. "But your men have had no time to rest—"

"Your solicitude does you credit, but it is of no matter. They have ridden farther on less sleep, I assure you."

His raised left eyebrow mocked me. Of course he must know that my reluctance to set forth had absolutely nothing to do with the sleepless state of his servants and everything to do with my desire to delay our arrival in North Eredor for as long as possible.

"And what of me?" I asked—quite coolly, I thought. Or at least I hoped. "Am I to have no rest?"

"I believe your attempted theft of my boots proves that you require no further sleep."

I knew then I could say nothing to change his mind, so I only set my chin and looked away from him. He had fairly caught me. Why my spell had fallen so lightly on him, I did not know. Such things were never foolproof, even in my father's far more capable hands. Perhaps I had forgotten a syllable, or spoken the words too quickly.

Or perhaps Kadar Arkalis' will was simply too strong. According to my father, some people could be notoriously difficult to enchant; their spirits were not easily bent. I hoped that was not the case here. My future would be bleak indeed if it turned out my captor was one of the rare few immune to those helpful little charms.

He strode away from me and flung open the front door of the lodge, then prodded the prone form of his retainer none too gently with the toe of his boot. "A fine guard you make!" he snapped.

Lamakh rolled over and stared up at Kadar with bleary eyes. Realization must have set in, for after a second or two he scrambled to his feet, stammering what sounded like apologies.

"Enough," said his master. "We ride within the quarter-hour. Splash some cold water on your face and get moving."

At once Lamakh nodded. Without looking at me, he hurried off toward the kitchen, calling out something in the rough *corraghar* tongue.

"It would seem that your ride has wearied my servant," Kadar observed dryly. But the golden eyes narrowed a bit as he surveyed me.

"We did ride very hard and fast, my lord." Despite my present circumstances, it was only with difficulty that I kept my lips from quirking.

"Indeed." He sent me another one of those quick, sidelong glances before continuing, "You, of course, will require something a bit more substantial for the journey."

As I watched, he moved to a large chair pushed up against the room's far wall. I noticed that the chair was heaped with saddlebags, as if someone had dropped them there in haste. He pushed two aside, then undid the buckles on one and pulled out a wad of blue cloth.

"Perhaps not as fine as what you're used to, but it will keep you warm on the ride to Tarenmar. Come, take it."

I stepped forward and took the bundle from him. It turned out to be a gown of blue wool, plainly made, with no embroidery or trim to enliven the design. But the fabric itself felt soft and warm. I knew I would be grateful for it once I was back out in the cold air.

But I had no intention of thanking him for this small bit of courtesy. I only nodded and began to head back toward the bedchamber, where I could clothe myself in privacy. Kadar followed, and I paused at the doorway and inquired in acid tones, "Do you intend to watch me dress, my lord?"

"Not at all," he replied. "Only that, as the latch on this door seems to be somewhat unreliable, I felt I should stand guard here so that none of my servants might walk in on you by chance."

A very transparent ploy, but one I didn't feel inclined to protest. Without another word I went into the bedchamber and shut the door firmly behind me. As it closed, I heard Kadar let out a low chuckle.

How wonderful that I should be such a source of amusement to him. I scowled, but at the moment there was very little I could do save pull the gown over the clean chemise I had donned earlier. At least the borrowed dress had side lacings, and so I was able to fasten it myself. Perhaps a spell existed that allowed one to back-lace a gown without help, though I had never heard of such a thing. But I would have invented one on the spot rather than ask Kadar to assist me with the procedure.

Luckily, such lengths were not required. It only took a few minutes for me to be more or less properly attired, although I would have given quite a lot for a pair of stockings and some sturdy shoes. I guessed that my captor would be unlikely to grant such a request; no doubt footwear and escape attempts were already connected in his mind.

I had no hairbrush and no mirror, but I ran my fingers through my tangled curls and tried to sort out the unruly mess as best I could. If I'd had even a leather thong I would have braided my hair back to save it from further depredations on our journey, but I had a feeling that Kadar would not trust me with such a thing. Most likely he would suspect me of trying to use it on him as a garrote.

He gave me a mocking little smile when I re-emerged. "You are speedy. I appreciate that in a woman. The horses are ready—come with me."

As no other options presented themselves, I did as he bade me and followed him out of the lodge and into the freezing night. At once I wondered if he expected me to ride without the protection of a cloak, but it seemed he had thought of that as well. He approached a tall horse that was only a greyish blur in the dismal pre-dawn dark and pulled something from a saddlebag.

"You may have need of this," he said, and draped a heavy fur-lined mantle across my shoulders.

I said nothing, but only shrugged the garment into a more comfortable position so that its fur collar rode closely against my neck. It did feel good. I could almost ignore the icy ground beneath my bare feet.

Lamakh moved toward me, even as Kadar swung into the saddle of his dapple-grey. Only one other horse waited out in the cold, a dark shape that might be a bay in daylight. Was Lamakh not coming with us?

I understood why there were only two horses soon enough; the manservant took me firmly by the waist and planted me on

the saddle in front of his master. At once Kadar's arms tightened around me.

"What on earth are you doing?" I demanded, and began to
wriggle in his grasp so that I might free myself and drop safely
down to the ground.

But those encircling limbs might have been made of iron
for all the good my struggles did me. "You did not think, my
Lady Lark, that I would allow you your own mount? Not when
you've already proven that you are likely to flee at the earliest
opportunity?"

He must be mad. "I can't possibly ride hundreds of miles
like this!"

"It is not as far as you might think. You may wish to refresh
your knowledge of geography, once we are in my capital."

How he knew that impugning my education was the thing
that would infuriate me the most, I had no idea. In stony silence
I ceased my writhing, and his grasp eased somewhat. He said a
brief word in the corraghar tongue to Lamakh, and we set out
at a brisk trot.

Even with my sturdy gown and the fur-lined mantle, the air
felt as chilly as a grave. Or perhaps shock and exhaustion had
finally caught up with me. Back in the lodge my situation had
felt almost unreal, or at least something I might have the power
to change, but now...

...now every mile brought me closer to Tarenmar, the capital city of North Eredor, and to Kadar's stronghold. The little
magic I had learned could not help me here, for I knew no spells
that would allow me to strike at my captor. I had learned medi-
tation and protection, not the great magics that had sundered

Eredor north from south and which had led users of magic to be hunted almost to extinction. My gifts, which once had been a source of some pride to me, now seemed as nothing. I would have been better served to have my brother Thani show me a few tricks with a dagger.

Would Kadar at least show me the courtesy of a real wedding ceremony, or would he be content with a few quick words spoken in front of witnesses, followed by a bedding as soon as possible so he could lay claim to me forever?

At that thought tears began to sting at the back of my eyes. Or perhaps it was the wind. In any case, I blinked angrily and tried not to think of such things. But it was very difficult not to, with Kadar's arms holding me in place, and my legs bumping against his with every movement of the horse. This was far more intimate contact than I had yet had with a man. It didn't take much effort to go beyond those rough, almost impersonal touches to the even more intimate connection a husband and a wife would share.

But perhaps it would not come to that. Perhaps, despite his musings on the benefits of having a Sedassa wife, Kadar only desired a simple ransom, and the threat of marriage was merely that—a threat, and nothing more. After all, he had as much as admitted that his kingdom was not a wealthy one. But I knew better than to pin my hopes on such a meager promise.

I tried not to think of all the women throughout history who had been forced into marriage, whether by abduction or because of politics or simple greed. Indeed, I could count one such in my family tree, if I looked back far enough.

Seresa of Gathmir had been captured by a long-ago lord of Sedassa, in a time when many of the lands that bordered Sirlende proper had struggled to maintain their independence. Those small kingdoms were inevitably swallowed up by the burgeoning Sirlendian empire, sometimes through conquest, sometimes through diplomacy, and sometimes—as in Seresa's case—by abduction and forcible marriage.

When I first read an account of her life I had found it quite romantic, just the thing to stir the imagination of a young girl who found her own existence to be rather dull. For although Seresa had been taken by force, it seems she was treated with great courtesy by the Sedassa lord who captured her. Young and handsome, Daranic Sedassa had vowed not to make her his bride in truth until she could declare in all honesty that she loved him. As she did, over the course of time, taking his name and joining Gathmir's lands to his. In fact, she came to love her lord and her adopted homeland so much that in time she served as a protector for their estates when Lord Sedassa went off to war.

Now, how much of this was actually true, and how much of it had been embroidered upon by historians sympathetic to the Sirlendian cause, who could say? The passage of time tends to distort all tales, but I had always loved Seresa's story, and found myself glad that her blood flowed in my veins. I had never stopped to think how terrifying it would be to find myself in that situation, to be at the mercy of a man who saw me only for what my lands or family connections were worth. Somehow I doubted Kadar Arkalis would show me the same consideration Daranic had given his bride.

At least my captor exhibited little inclination for speech; the miles flowed away behind us, even as the sun rose to our right and the landscape became clearer. Under less miserable circumstances, I might have enjoyed my surroundings, for the land had a majesty altogether alien to my Southern-bred eyes. Mountains, snow-capped even in early autumn, reared their granite-grey heights before the rising sun, and great forests covered the horizon to the left. A wide river ran parallel to the road; I guessed it must be the Arandor, swollen from the snow-melt of the Opal Mountains.

Off to the northeast I saw a dark blur on the landscape that, as we approached, resolved itself into a large village. As we clattered our way across a bridge that traversed one of the Arandor's lesser tributaries, squawking geese and chickens announced our arrival.

Kadar slowed his horse to a walk, then murmured low in my ear, "We are now in North Eredor. These are my lands, and these are my people. You would do well to guard your tongue."

I hadn't thought he would ride so brazenly into a populated area if we were still in the hazy disputed border lands between North Eredor and Sirlende, but his admonition still irked me. Perhaps in the back of my mind I had thought I might be able to appeal to a stranger for help, but logic told me that no commoner would be likely to thwart the wishes of his own ruler. True, the Mark rode accompanied by only a single retainer, but he was safe enough within the borders of his own land. His late mother had been a beloved leader, and I had heard nothing to indicate that his people didn't feel the same way about her son...whatever my own feelings on the subject might be.

We approached a sturdy two-story building of grey stone with a dark-shingled roof. At the tether rail outside, Kadar stopped his horse and gave me a not-so-gentle shove so that I slid out of his lap and down into the dirt. I missed a dubious-looking pile by only a few inches and glared up at him.

But he gave me no time for recriminations, because he immediately dismounted and took me by the arm, leaving Lamakh to secure the horses.

Raised in a family who sold their wares to inns around South Eredor, I recognized the building's purpose at once. This establishment differed from those I had seen in my homeland in that it boasted a series of long, scarred oak tables rather than the round ones I knew, but other than that they were not materially different. A variety of patrons crowded those tables, their mugs probably filled with cider rather than ale, considering the early hour. From somewhere I smelled the familiar scent of frying bacon, and my mouth began to water. How long had it been since I last ate? Almost two days, at my best count.

Kadar called out to a tall, grey-haired man who had just emerged from behind the bar, his hands full with mugs. "Sirdahl, you old scoundrel! See the wife I've captured? She's a beauty, is she not?"

Around me the inn's patrons erupted into laughter, and hot blood rushed to my cheeks. No doubt his lordship thought my situation very good sport, but I was not amused at all by their merriment. I knew I was far from beautiful at that moment—what woman would be, after being stolen from her bed in the middle of the night and dragged hundreds of miles on horseback? I could have cheerfully driven my knee into Kadar Arkalis' groin and watched his laughs turn to groans. Instead, I only stood there, stony-faced.

Sirdahl, however, did not join in with the general merriment. He deposited the mugs on the tables of their respective recipients, and then turned to us and wiped his hands on the dark green linen apron he wore. "Whatever else, it appears to me that the young lady is in need of a proper meal."

The table closest to us was unoccupied, and he pulled out a chair. "If you would, my lady."

I sank down into it, grateful for this unexpected kindness from a stranger. I was also glad that the skirt of borrowed my gown was long enough to cover my bare and dirty feet.

To my relief, the rest of the inn's patrons returned to their food and drink once they apparently realized its owner would take no part in baiting me. Kadar remained standing, although he dropped his hand to grasp the back of my chair. Why, I wasn't sure. To affirm his continued ownership of my person?

"Sirdahl was one of my mother's retainers," he told me. "But he preferred to take his retirement here, for reasons no one has been able to explain."

"Perhaps he felt continuing at court in your service would prove detrimental to his health," I offered.

I didn't mistake the twitch at the corner of Sirdahl's lip that followed my comment, but he said nothing.

"She has quite the mouth, hasn't she?" Kadar remarked. Then he shrugged. "Ah, well, at least my future should be far from dull. Some cider, and bacon and eggs."

The older man nodded and moved off. After his departure, Kadar pulled out the chair next to mine and sat down. "You aren't afraid to speak your mind, are you?"

I shifted in my chair so I more or less faced him. "Not usually. At any rate, I see no reason to hold my tongue. You've already threatened me with the worst—what else do I have to fear from you?"

"'The worst'?" he repeated, and gave a short laugh. "That would be news to the noble daughters of my kingdom...and their parents. I've been dodging their matrimonial machinations for years."

That didn't surprise me at all. I guessed they would do much to secure such lofty status. At least Kadar was young and—if I forced myself to be objective about it—reasonably attractive. Many rulers often were neither.

The daughters of North Eredor were welcome to him, however. I could have no respect for a man who rode so roughshod over the rights of others. "Then far be it from me to deny them their prize. Would you not prefer a willing wife?"

He lifted his shoulders once more. "None of them offered the connections I desired. As to the rest..." A pause, while his gaze lingered on my mouth. "I wager you'll not be unwilling for very long."

"A wager you will lose," I retorted, but I held my tongue after that, as Sirdahl approached, bearing a tray of food and drink.

"It is plain enough fare," he said, setting a plate of bacon and eggs in front of me. "But I hope you will like it."

I smiled up at him. "It smells wonderful." And indeed it did, as hearty and toothsome as anything I might have gotten at home.

He put the other plate in front of Kadar, along with a pair of wooden mugs. "Let me know if you have need of anything else."

Kadar nodded. "This should give us strength for the road. But have a loaf wrapped up for us as well. And a few canteens of small beer."

"Of course," Sirdahl replied, and then departed for the kitchen.

Those words troubled me. It sounded as if, after this much-welcomed stop, Kadar intended to ride straight on for the rest of the day. At this rate, I'd be barely able to walk by the time we reached Tarenmar. Had I ever been so weary in my life? I felt I could barely lift my fork.

But lift it I did. Sleep had been denied me, and so the food was doubly needed. I kept my gaze resolutely away from Kadar as I made short work of the eggs and bacon on my plate. Perhaps guessing my mood, he remained silent as well, save for demanding a second helping once he had cleaned his plate.

"You?" he asked at last, pointing toward the few remaining scraps of my breakfast.

"No." Already the food had begun to bring on a sensation of lassitude. Over-indulging might lead me to fall asleep right then and there. Or worse, in Kadar's arms, once we continued our ride.

He broke his last piece of bacon in half and consumed that as well. Just as Kadar pushed his plate away, Sirdahl re-emerged with a napkin-wrapped bundle in one hand and two leather canteens slung over his other arm.

"Many thanks," Kadar said, and took the meager supplies.

The innkeeper hesitated and looked down at me. "Would you not rather spend the day here? Your lady seems wearied beyond endurance."

"Ah, she's tougher than she looks," Kadar replied, and clapped me roughly on the shoulder. I sat up straighter in my chair and glared at him.

Sirdahl appeared less than convinced, but he said nothing else. It seemed to me that while he might have been able to take liberties others would not, thanks to his long acquaintance with his lord, even he knew when to take a step back.

"Come, my Lady Lark. The day is wasting."

As there was nothing else I could do, I stood. "Thank you for breakfast," I told Sirdahl.

He nodded, but his dark eyes were still troubled. "A safe ride to you both."

"I have no worries on that account," replied Kadar with a negligent wave of his hand.

And he led me back out to the horse tether, where Lamakh still waited for us. I noticed he had a half-eaten sweet bun of some kind in his hand, so at least he hadn't gone completely without sustenance as he waited for us. All the same, I didn't think much of the way Kadar treated his servants. Had Lamakh slept at all since the night he abducted me, save for that bit of enchanted sleep I'd conjured the evening before?

Then again, I didn't know why I should care. These men were my enemies. Their well-being was nothing to me.

This time I didn't wait for Lamakh to hoist me up into the saddle, but grasped the pommel and hauled myself back into Kadar's lap. My dignity was already in tatters, but at least I could make some attempt at appearing as if I were partly in control of my destiny.

"So eager to be back in my arms?" he inquired.

"Oh, do leave me be," I retorted, and shifted a bit so that I didn't have his belt buckle digging into my hip.

I thought I heard the low rumble of laughter in his throat, but he said nothing as he turned the horse around and pointed us northward once more.

At some point the combination of weariness and a full stomach got the better of me, and I did fall asleep. So I missed much of that journey, and had very little awareness of my surroundings until I felt the horse slow to a walk. Then I opened my eyes and raised my head from where it had been resting against Kadar's arm.

"Back among the living, I see."

I forbore from replying, mainly because I was mortified that I'd slept all that time, and also because my neck was telling me that I had managed to kink it in a most painful fashion.

He continued, "Your timing is good, at least. Look—we have come to my capital."

By that time the sun was almost touching the western horizon, but it still cast enough light for me to see a low-lying city clustered around the edges of a dark lake with a stony shore.

We had come to the final crest of a series of hills, and below us the road wound gently downward until it met up with another, larger route that cut east and west. To the north, beyond the city, I thought I saw the dim edges of more forest.

Nothing about the scene seemed at all welcoming, but that could have had much to do with my worries as to the fate which awaited me once we were in Kadar's capital city. "It's lovely," I said, in sour tones that hinted I thought the exact opposite.

"No, it is not Marestal, with its white walls and seaport and warm winds," he agreed, then sent a roguish smile in my direction when I glanced up at him in surprise. "Yes, I have been to the South. Yours is a fair land, but soft. We are made of sterner stuff here in the North."

I did not reply. If he thought such speeches would appeal to me, he was sorely mistaken. While it had been an adventure to travel to Sirlende and to see the great castle in the duchy of Gahm, and the sprawling manor house my brother was to inherit, I realized I did prefer my white-washed city by the sea, with its flameflower vines and salt-scented air. Unfortunately, it did not appear that I would be returning there any time soon.

We began our descent. The light dimmed as we grew closer, so I could not see a great deal of detail by the time we entered the city proper. The buildings appeared to be mainly built of the native greyish granite, although some of the meaner dwellings on the city's outskirts were whitewashed stucco. Hard-packed dirt formed the bulk of the streets. And I realized Tarenmar was quite small, actually, smaller even than my native city, which, according to my father, would itself be swallowed up ten times over by Sirlende's capital of Iselfex.

Even so, it took our small party some time to pick its way through the streets to a walled castle that backed up to the southern edge of the lake. I thought it rather strange that no one seemed to note the passage of their lord, but perhaps he was not one to stand on ceremony and often traveled with little escort. Or possibly no one recognized him because now he traveled through the streets with no unnecessary pomp.

The city did not have the bustling energy of Marestal, my seaport home, but I still spied plenty of activity—farmers heading home after a long day at market, women laden with the fruits of a day's shopping, the odd drover with a gaggle of sheep or goats, scribes in dark robes, and players in the wild multicolors of their profession. It all looked quite normal, and not unlike what I would have seen in the streets of my native city. At least it was a far cry from the dark and dangerous stronghold I had worried would greet me at journey's end.

The guards at the castle entrance recognized Kadar, of course. He did not even have to call out a greeting; as soon as he approached on his dapple-grey, they hurried to open the huge barred iron door. He raised a hand, as if giving thanks for their alacrity, but he passed by without greeting.

We entered a courtyard crowded with more guards, the hurrying shapes of servants in dark livery, and other people whose occupations I could only guess at. An ostler came to take Kadar's horse by its bridle, and I slipped out of the saddle, hoping that my quivering legs would hold me up long enough for me to get inside. Lamakh dismounted and began to lead his horse away—to the stables, I supposed. Apparently he was not to accompany us inside the castle proper.

I did not have to trust my shaky limbs for very long, as almost at once Kadar was at my side, his hand firmly on my elbow. "This way," he murmured, and guided me toward a set of tall double doors that opened even as we approached.

"Welcome back, my lord," said a tall individual who appeared a few paces in front of us. His gaze settled on me, but aside from an eyebrow lift that came and went so quickly I wasn't sure I hadn't imagined it, he showed no reaction.

"Althan," Kadar acknowledged. "This is Lady Lark Sedassa, my affianced bride. See that she is well taken care of." He turned to me and lifted one of my hands to his lips before I could think to pull it back. "Neglected business awaits, my sweet. I shall call on you as soon as I am able."

And with that he released my hand, then strode off down the corridor, bellowing out what sounded like another of the odd corraghar names.

I stood where I was, looking after him, mouth slightly agape. So now that he had me safely trapped within his castle, I was of no immediate interest to him?

"My lady," Althan said. He sounded resigned, as if he were all too used to the peculiarities of his master's character. "If you would come with me?"

All I could do was nod and then follow as he led me down another hallway and up a narrow flight of steps. While it was certainly nowhere near Lord Senric's castle in terms of opulence, I saw at once that Kadar's keep was well built and furnished, with bright hangings on the walls and cleanly scrubbed stone floors. While I couldn't claim to be exactly reassured, I did feel somewhat less low. Or perhaps that was merely relief at being out of Kadar's presence for the moment.

My spirits lifted even more when Althan ushered me into a very comfortable suite of rooms, with Keshiaari carpets on the floor and a charming fireplace of carved stone in the main sitting room. More hangings covered the walls, and the furniture was of heavy dark wood with invitingly plump upholstery.

"I must apologize, my lady, for not having made any preparations for your arrival." Althan paused by the fireplace, a diffident expression on his lean features. "I hope you find these chambers adequate."

"Very," I replied. The rooms were more than adequate, and offered the comforting side benefit of obviously being guest chambers, and not Kadar's private rooms. So perhaps I would have enough breathing space to see if I could find some way out of this mess.

Althan asked delicately, "And your baggage...?"

"I have none," I said, not bothering to temper the bluntness of my words. "I come to you as you see me now." Resisting the impulse to lift my skirts so he could see my dirty bare feet, I added, "A hot bath would be most welcome."

He bowed. "Of course, my lady. It will be seen to immediately. I will gather what items I can to lend you comfort for now, but of course tomorrow I will have seamstresses come in to provide you with a suitable wardrobe."

"Thank you, Althan."

Again he inclined his head, before taking his leave of me and shutting the doors behind him. I waited for a moment, then crossed the sitting room and tried the lock. It wouldn't turn.

So for all his courtesies, Althan was disinclined to trust me...or somehow Kadar had managed to convey more information to his steward about my situation than I had thought. For all I knew, the attitude of mild bemusement Althan had assumed at my arrival could have been false.

Well, locked doors were certainly not enough to hinder me, but a castle full of people loyal to Kadar was. I could escape the suite, but I doubted I would get more than a few feet before being marched straight back to my rooms. Besides, I was exhausted and dirty and barefoot. It seemed obvious enough that Kadar Arkalis had no intention of coming in and ravishing me in the immediate future, so why not allow myself a bath and a good night's sleep in a real bed with sheets and pillows and blankets? I would be much better prepared to face whatever came my way on the morrow.

Thus having reassured myself of the wisdom of my decision, I sat down on the chair closest to the fireplace and awaited the arrival of the bath. It was only weariness, after all, that led me to feel the first heat of unshed tears in my eyes and a curious constriction in my throat.

I swallowed, and told myself to take heart. My world had not yet ended, and the next day would offer its own possibilities. I had to satisfy myself with that.

~ Chapter Three ~

To my surprise, I did feel better upon awakening the next morning. For one thing, I had spent so many nights in a row in strange beds that it took me half a moment to realize I was not at the Sedassa manor house in the Black Hills, or even one of the inns I had patronized during my journey from South Eredor to Sirlende. My muscles still had the faintest ghost-trace of weariness about them, but other than that I felt remarkably refreshed.

But then I sat up and looked about me, and remembered that this comfortable chamber was located in Kadar Arkalis' castle, and that I was no better than his prisoner, no matter how luxurious my cell. I pushed myself off the tall bed and made my way over to the window so I might get a better view of my prison.

My suite appeared to be located in a tower at the rear of the castle. It did afford a fine view of the lake, which I had to admit looked somewhat more inviting in the morning light. While a few high clouds traced their way overhead, the sky was a deep, serene blue, that same hue reflected in the waters below me.

As far as I could tell, the city followed the curve of the lake to the east and almost halfway to its more northerly banks, but its western edges remained wild and free, the trees there showing the first flame-colored hues of autumn. The dark shapes of fishing boats dotted the lake itself; apparently some sort of freshwater fish were to be found there.

A knock came at the door, and I hurried back over to the bed. Although from somewhere a clean sleep chemise had been found for me, I had not been provided with any sort of dressing gown. And while Kadar had already seen me in my chemise, I preferred to avoid a repeat of that experience. At least in bed I could pull the covers up to my chin.

But after I called out, "come in!", the door opened, and the same woman who had brought the chemise and the bath and my supper the night before stepped in. She carried another tray, this one laden with a large slice of some sort of pie and a steaming mug of tea.

"Your breakfast, my lady," she said, and brought the tray to me in bed.

I took it from her and settled it on my lap. "Thank you."

She bobbed her head. "The Mark wishes for you to eat and then dress. He will see you within the hour."

Her words made the food before me smell far less appetizing, but I made myself pick up the fork and scoop out a good portion of the pie. It appeared to be some sort of egg and cheese mixture, dotted with small pieces of green onion and ham.

I lifted the forkful of pie to my mouth and chewed. At least the food was excellent. "Am I to go see his lordship in my chemise?"

Her dark eyes widened. She was a round, comfortable-looking sort of woman, although she appeared far from comfortable at the moment. "Of course not, my lady! Althan is sending up a gown, although you will also meet with the seamstresses later today."

"Very well," I told her, and she bobbed a curtsey and departed.

There was nothing for it except to finish the pie and drink the tea—which wasn't true tea, but some tisane tasting of rose hips and chamomile. Still, it was refreshing enough, and my stomach seemed relieved that it had finally gotten enough to satisfy it.

Along with the chemise, I had been provided with some necessary toiletries the night before, and I went to the little mirror above the side table and combed my hair before using the washstand to clean my face and teeth. If I must be forced to face Kadar Arkalis so soon after breaking my fast, at least I could do it while looking as respectable as possible.

I had just finished my ablutions when the servant woman reappeared, this time carrying a length of deep wine-colored velvet that proved to be a quite elegant gown trimmed with pale fawn-gold embroidery. She also provided a clean chemise and other underthings, finely knitted wool stockings, and— wonder of wonders—a pair of low indoor slippers.

In a brisk, no-nonsense fashion, she helped me into these items, then produced from her apron pocket a pair of finely carved combs, which she used to pull some of my hair back from my face, although she left most of it loose.

"Thank you..." I trailed off, realizing I had never asked for her name.

"Beranne," she supplied. "Never mind that, though. He is waiting for you."

Her brisk tone told me she would allow no delaying tactics. I had none in my arsenal, anyway. My face was clean, my hair done. At any rate, I found myself wishing to get this over with. Once I knew of Kadar's immediate plans for me, I would be in a better position to craft a counter-attack.

With that thought to buoy me, I followed Beranne out of my suite and down the stairs, through a long corridor filled with servant girls, couriers, men-at-arms, scribes, and others I couldn't begin to identify, and then finally up a set of wide, shallow steps. Although we faced a pair of double doors, Beranne opened only the one on the right and stepped aside. Her meaning was clear enough: I was expected to enter alone.

Which I did, head high and chin up. The gown was a good enough fit for me, if a trifle large. The slippers pinched my feet, and I hoped a replacement pair that actually fit would be provided at some point, but for the moment I would endure the discomfort. At least now I felt as if I looked like a lady and a Sedassa.

These rooms were grander than my own, the ceilings higher and with intricate coffering instead of the plain beams of my own chambers. Rather than hangings, painted frescoes of hunting scenes covered the walls. To my surprise, one wall boasted a large bookcase filled with a number of volumes in varying shapes and sizes. The Mark of Eredor had not struck me as a reading man, and I wondered whether someone else had put that impressive collection together.

At the far end of the space, the main chamber narrowed into what was obviously another tower room. Arched windows similar to those in my chambers let in another view of the lake, although from a different perspective. From here one saw only forest and water, with no trace of the town visible. Standing silhouetted against those windows was Kadar Arkalis.

He turned as I approached, and gave me an appraising look. "You appear recovered from your journey."

"Sleep does have amazing restorative properties."

"So it would appear."

He seemed to make no attempt to hide the admiration in his gaze, and I found it difficult to keep from glancing away. I did not want him to admire me. I wanted him to let me go.

Perhaps he noted my discomfiture. Whatever the reason, he moved past me to a large table that was scattered with pieces of paper. A pen of chased silver rested in an inkwell, and he leaned over and picked it up.

"I've been composing a letter," he said. "After all, your relatives should know that you are safe."

I raised my eyebrows. "Apparently the word 'safe' has a different meaning in North Eredor than where I am from."

He paused, pen still clasped in his fingers. I noted that he appeared to be left-handed. "Are we to continue this game?

What is the point? In all true meanings of the word, you are safe. You are fed, and clothed, and housed under my protection."

"One might say the same for the prisoners languishing in the gaol beneath the Imperial palace in Iselfex," I retorted. "But I daresay if you stopped to ask their opinion, they would not tell you they were *safe*."

His only reply was a snort. Then he asked, "Is Lark your full name? It seems a bit...unusual."

In point of fact, it was not; the nickname I had taken for my own was a shortening of Larkhenna, just as my brother Thani went by something infinitely more manageable than his given name of Sorthannic, which he had always hated. But I saw no reason why I should provide Kadar with such information. "Lark will do," I told him.

It was his turn to raise an eyebrow at me, but he said nothing, and only pulled out the chair that faced the table and began scratching away on the parchment. Although I dearly would have liked to see what he was writing, I forced myself to feign indifference. As I waited, I began making a surreptitious survey of my surroundings.

The suite appeared to have only the one main entrance, but there were all those windows. Breaking the leading that separated the panes would be no easy task, although I guessed it could be accomplished by hurling a chair through them. Of course, that would make quite the racket, one that someone would be sure to investigate, but I knew of a sound-deadening spell which might work. I wished I could go closer to inspect the ground beneath those tower windows, for from this angle it looked almost as if the lake came right up to the building.

That would never do. I could swim, as could most citizens of my seaside town, but the water in that lake looked dreadfully cold.

A doorway on the far side of the chamber led into what appeared to be Kadar's sleeping quarters; I spied an enormous green-hung bed through the partially open door. More windows in there, probably, and perhaps ones that didn't directly overlook the lake. But of course it would not do to show any interest in his bedchamber, or that might lead his thoughts in undesirable directions.

I began to sidle toward the bookcase, only to have his voice stop me.

"Should I send this to your aunt, do you think? Or to your brother?"

"I cannot say for sure," I replied, then crossed my arms and faced him. "It depends."

"On what?"

"On whether the investiture went on as planned, even with my kidnapping. If my brother now is the Duke of Marric's Rest, then it should go to him, of course. But I fear I have been rather out of touch the past few days."

Kadar set the pen back in its inkwell and considered me for a moment. Now, in the shelter of his own castle, he had discarded his riding leathers for a long doublet of fine wool in so deep a brown it appeared almost black, and his dark straight hair, which for the ride had been pulled back away from his face, just brushed his collarbones. His mother had supposedly been a great beauty in her day. It did not take any great effort for me to see echoes of that beauty in her son's face, in the high cheekbones and straight, sculpted nose. What a pity his soul did not match his handsome countenance.

"The wisest thing for you to do," I went on, "would be to write them both and ask for whatever ransom you deem fit. I have no doubt that either of them would agree to any amount you request, as long as it is not completely out of reason."

"Back to that, I see." He smiled, but no warmth touched his eyes. "A temporary solution at best. No, I think my plan the better one."

Thinking quickly, I said, "Why settle for the sister of a duke, when you might yet make a royal connection? I have heard the daughters of the King of Purth are quite fair…"

"…And promised to various princes from the cradle, none of them me, unfortunately. But thank you for reminding me."

I retorted, "It was your choice, my lord, to attempt to make do with what is a poor substitute at best." I didn't much like referring to myself in such a fashion, but it was the simple truth.

To be sure, I didn't know exactly how much a connection with me would even bring him, save perhaps a measure of security for his borders. He should have been content with the knowledge that at least the Sirlendian Empire hadn't decided to gobble up his country along with all the others it had swallowed over the centuries. Its ongoing independence did owe something to the ferocity of its warriors, but rather more to the reality that North Eredor was a poor country with very little to offer a conquering empire. It had no mineral wealth beyond a few tin mines in its extreme northeast, and it did not produce crops beyond those which fed its own people. Why fight a war over such negligible scraps?

I guessed the Mark would not like to hear such reasoned arguments, even if they were based on cold truths. Somehow he had convinced himself that marrying me would bring him status and connections he did not currently possess, and I was beginning to realize even the most logical assertions to the contrary would most likely be ignored.

He had shot me a sharp look at the phrase "poor substitute," but his tone was mild enough when he replied, "One learns to make do."

How those words were any less insulting than the ones I had applied to myself, I wasn't sure, but I refused to allow him to upset me. I had a long way to go before I achieved the true stillness of spirit my father said magic required, but I hoped that what I had acquired so far would aid me in my dealings with Kadar Arkalis.

I added, "At any rate, you should be glad you missed your mark in this...enterprise. While I believe the Emperor will not trouble himself on my account—he will no doubt expect my family to take care of the situation—I cannot say the same would have happened if you had actually succeeded in kidnapping the Crown Princess. He would have been sure to send some force against you."

"For what?" Kadar laid down his pen and sprinkled some sand over the document he had apparently just completed. "Can an army restore a woman's virtue? The shell on that egg would have already been broken. He would have had to make the best of the situation, as so many other relatives in similar situations before him have."

"Indeed?" I allowed myself to smile. "Your intelligence is lacking, my lord, if that is your measure of Torric Deveras. He is not, I am led to understand, the type to endure what he would most certainly see as a slight against his house. He would surely retaliate, even though such an act would do nothing to restore the Crown Princess's lost honor."

Kadar pushed back his chair and stood, then lifted the now-dry letter from the tabletop. "And do you know him so very well?"

"Not at all," I admitted. That was no more than the truth, as all I knew of the new Emperor were a few chance comments from my aunt, who appeared to have no great regard for the man who now occupied the throne. However, I had heard enough to guess that he was a difficult man, haughty, quick to see slights even when none had been intended. "But the little I do know seems to indicate he is not the sort of man to calmly make the best of a bad situation. You may have dodged an arrow by taking the wrong woman."

"Your concern for my welfare does you credit."

I raised my eyebrows and gave a small, bitter chuckle. "Do not flatter yourself, my lord. I have very little concern for you...but I would hate to see innocent people lose their lives in a conflict over something so poorly planned and ill-conceived."

"Poorly...?" For the first time I saw a true flash of anger in those golden eyes. The sooty lashes almost obscured their feral gleam as he shot me a narrow look. "As far as I can tell, the whole scheme was managed well enough. It is not my fault the lady in question fell ill at the last moment, or that you occupied the chambers which had been intended for her."

"And precisely how *did* you gain such knowledge? The details of my visit were not known to those outside my aunt's household staff."

"North Eredor is a poor country, but my meager resources are still enough to buy a few well-placed spies."

To that I had no real response. I supposed I was being naïve if I thought all servants in all noble households were above taking bribes. Quite likely they viewed such dealings to be an accepted way of supplementing their wages, and it was entirely possible they believed the information they passed on to be of no real significance.

Kadar smiled a little at my silence, as if pleased that he had been able to best me on at least that one point. Still smiling, he held out to me the letter he had just written. "What think you of this? I will make a second, addressed to your brother, if you think it necessary."

I looked down at the paper and saw he had written the missive in perfect Sirlendian. My estimation of his scholarship increased slightly, although I could not say the same for his character.

Lady Sedassa, it said, *I am pleased to inform you that your niece, Lark Sedassa, became my wife on the fifth day of Octevre. The suddenness of these nuptials may surprise you, but rest assured that the violence of our regard for one another required a speedy ceremony. She is safe, and well, and content, and hopes that her family will wish her happy.*

I remain, his Highness, Kadar Arkalis, Mark of North Eredor

"'Violence of our regard for one another'?" I repeated. "I suppose it is only a slight stretching of the truth, as I must confess that I do find myself overcome by a violent desire to slap your jaw for concocting such a pack of lies. And better that it go only to my aunt, for I fear if my brother were to read it first, he might ride forth directly to seek your head."

His smile broadened somewhat. "You do have an interesting turn of phrase, my dear. No matter. I will send this by courier today, as I would not wish your family to suffer any more worries on your account than are necessary."

I scowled at his use of "my dear," but decided to let it go. I had more important battles to fight. "And what do you think my aunt's reaction will be? Why, once my father hears of this..." And I trailed off, for I realized that even if my aunt sent the fastest couriers in Sirlende to my parents in Marestal, still it would be at least a fortnight before they learned of my fate.

"He will be surprised, no doubt," Kadar said calmly. "But once faced with a feat already accomplished, I assume he will make the best of the situation."

"A feat already accomplished?" I echoed, even though I knew all too well exactly what he meant.

"The wedding will take place tomorrow evening. I thought you should have some time to prepare yourself. Besides, even if I send my riders forth with this letter today, your aunt will be unable to respond until well after our marriage is a fact."

Tomorrow. Something inside me constricted at the word, and I swallowed. So little time to find a way to escape.

For once I could think of nothing else to say. Legend told that in ages past messages could be sent back and forth between mages as fast as thought, but now time and distance constrained us all. Perhaps Kadar believed he was being magnanimous in allowing me some time to grow resigned to my situation, but I knew one day would make no difference when it came to hope of an outside rescue. The result would be the same even if he married me this very morning.

In this, I could only rely on myself.

As promised, the seamstresses appeared later that morning, and all was organized chaos for a few hours. At some other time, I might have been thrilled at the prospect of acquiring a wardrobe of new gowns, most of them far more lavish than I would have expected, considering Kadar's comments about the state of his country's treasury. But now I could only nod and feign some sort of enthusiasm as fabrics and trims were matched up, and the seamstresses debated the merits of embroidery versus bullion or wool velvet as opposed to silk.

If any of them noted my lack of excitement about this process, they were too well-mannered to show it. The senior of the group—I never did catch all their names—held up a length of exquisite silk of the palest grey, all woven with silver thread in subtle patterns, and said, "We thought this for your bridal gown, my lady. So few could wear this color, but you will look lovely."

I summoned a smile and thanked her. It was not her fault, after all, that Kadar was forcing me into this marriage. And truly, I did not envy them the task of churning out so many garments in such a short amount of time. If all went well, I would have no need of those new gowns, and their efforts would be for naught.

Eventually they left, taking their fabrics and trims and chatter with them, and I was left alone. At the noon hour Beranne brought me a tray; I was thankful that apparently the Mark did not expect me to share my meals with him. I ate, though I had little appetite, for I hoped to be free of the castle by nightfall and knew I needed all my strength.

After she had gone, taking the empty tray with her, I sat down in one of the overstuffed chairs by the fireplace and began the breathing exercises my father had taught me. This was the first step to centering my thoughts and gathering the concentration necessary for my next move.

It was hardly a spell at all, but rather a way of focusing the consciousness and sending it outward. I must confess that my thoughts skipped and danced like a coracle in a heavy current, but at length I found the stillness at the core of my mind, the dark pool that dwelled in the very center of my being. I breathed in, and sent my mind forth.

Two men stood guard only a few feet away on the top step directly outside my chamber. It appeared his lordship was taking no chances. And beyond them were two more flanking the end of the hallway, where it opened into the wide corridor that seemed to run the length of the building. From there I could sense only a confusion of many minds and many thoughts, and I pulled back within myself, considering.

I did not possess the ability to turn myself invisible, but I did know one spell that shielded the caster by having those in the vicinity look away at a key moment, or by drawing them away on some remembered errand. I had tried it several times back in Maristel, with varying degrees of success. It was the sort of thing that worked better in large crowds where more distractions existed, and I had no idea whether the spell would get me past four armed guards whose only purpose was to make sure I didn't escape.

Still, I had to try.

Once again I drew in a breath, and then another. Beneath the calm lay the acid nausea of panic, and I swallowed. No time for that. No time for anything except peace and darkness and the words of the spell.

Ahl sar ostair, met fahl sar andaire.

I felt no different, but as this was a spell directed outward to the observer, I never did. Holding the shape of those words in my mind, feeling their strength pulse along my veins, I rose from my chair and went to the door.

It was locked, of course, but that was one spell I knew I could perform in my sleep. "*Sorichar*," I whispered, and put my hand on the handle.

Luckily the door was the type that swung inward, and so at least I avoided hitting the guards with it. I ghosted out into the hall, light as I could be in my soft borrowed slippers. The two men who had stood on the top step were now on the hallway floor proper, staring up in apparent great interest at the tapestry hanging from the wall there. Perfect.

The other guards still maintained their position at the end of the corridor, but one of them was busy picking at a loose ring in his mail shirt, and the other had taken off his helmet and was occupying himself with polishing it on the hem of his cloak. Neither man looked up as I drifted past.

Despite my best attempts at remaining calm, my heart had begun to pound in my chest. My success surprised even me. Surely it couldn't be this simple?

But apparently it was. I mingled with the crowds in the main corridor and followed the flow of bodies out to the courtyard. No one paid me any mind, although whether that was because my spell still held, or whether I, dark-haired and fair-skinned—a coloring shared by most Northerners—blended that well into the crowd, I had no idea. At the moment I didn't much care, as long as I could get myself far away from the castle as soon as possible.

What I would do next, lacking money, supplies, a horse, or any of the other necessities required for a successful escape, I didn't know, but I told myself I could work that out once I was safely off the castle grounds. If nothing else, this same spell might aid me in procuring some of the items I required. My father would be most displeased if he ever learned I had turned my gifts toward picking pockets or stealing horses, but I guessed he'd be even more upset if I were forced into marriage with the Mark of North Eredor. One must have one's priorities.

With that thought to strengthen my resolve, I fell in behind a group of women carrying baskets—most likely off to do the marketing for the castle's kitchens. They wore gowns much plainer than mine, but I blended in with them far better than I would the squad of men-at-arms who exited the castle gates directly ahead of them. And none of the women seemed to notice me, which appeared to indicate that my spell was still doing its work.

Feeling a bit more at ease, I glanced around me. The day held fine, the sky deep as the lapis inlays in a hair clasp my mother sometimes wore. The sun warmed me, although the air had a bite behind it that did not bode well for my further travels unless I could procure a cloak somewhere.

We approached what looked to be some sort of farmer's market, where the street widened into an area filled with wagons and stalls and the odd vendor selling his wares out of a wheelbarrow or a hand cart. My escort broke up as each woman went her own way, apparently intent on gathering her necessary supplies.

Which seemed to be my cue to do the same. A cloak, of course, and a sturdier pair of shoes, food, water—the list seemed almost endless. I hated what I was about to do, and vowed to take careful note of the people from whom I took supplies so that I could try to send them some sort of compensation once I was safely back in Sirlende.

The shoes and cloak were easier than I had thought. At the edge of the market stood a vendor with a table full of what appeared to be secondhand boots and mantles, and while he was occupied with another customer I sidled up to the table, cast a quick eye over its contents, and snagged a pair of low boots that looked close to my size. The mantle I pulled off a peg as he bent to sort through a box of laces under the table.

Then, heart racing, I dashed down an alley and pounded my way through some muddy puddles until I was certain no one followed. No one had raised an alarm, apparently; I heard nothing except the normal rise and fall of voices out on the street, and the rumble of wooden cart wheels.

I nodded to myself, and bent and unlaced the uncomfortable slippers I had been wearing and replaced them with the stolen boots. Those proved to be slightly large, but better that than the opposite. Then I shrugged the mantle around myself, shoved my now-unneeded slippers behind a couple of empty wooden packing boxes, and went back out to the street.

Kadar and I had entered through the southern precincts of the town, and so that was where I headed. To the north lay only the lake, and to the east the wild lands that abutted the shoulders of the Opal Mountains. I must head south and then west, and hope I could find an outlying farm or small estate where I might steal a horse and some supplies. Perhaps I could have procured them here in Tarenmar, but I found myself wishing to leave the city as soon as possible. Every second I lingered within its walls seemed like tempting fate.

And so I slipped once more unnoticed into a crowd, only this time moving through the streets toward the city's southern edges. Although it had been almost dark the evening before when I entered Kadar's capital, I thought I recognized the meaner dwellings that surrounded me now, the ones which formed the outer districts of the city. Good. The last thing I wanted was to go in circles.

A jingle of harness seemed to ride over the noises of the crowd. Around me, people began to move aside. I shifted along with them, then lifted my face to see what had caused everyone to give way.

Golden eyes bored down into mine. Kadar Arkalis rode at the head of a troop of armed men, all of whom wheeled to a stop as he paused his dapple-grey only a few feet away from me.

"Going somewhere, my Lark?"

∾ Chapter Four ∾

Kadar said nothing to me during the ride back to the castle, nor once we were inside. I could sense the anger within him, though; his lean body was taut as a bowstring. Althan took charge of me as soon as we crossed the building's threshold, and I was marched back up to my rooms and deposited therein. Almost at once I heard a shuffle of booted feet outside and knew the guards had taken up their positions again. In my agitation I could have miscounted them, but I thought this time they numbered at least eight.

I knew there would be no more escapes that way. I also knew I had to will myself to stay calm, or I would be of absolutely no use to myself. While part of me would have very much liked to curl up into a ball on the divan and cry my eyes out, I realized I didn't have the time for such indulgences.

Instead, I went to one of the windows and peered outside. Unlike Kadar's rooms, my suite did have solid ground directly below—at least twenty feet down, unfortunately. And even if

I somehow managed to reach the ground safely, it would have done me no good. Another clot of men-at-arms stood underneath my tower rooms, more of Kadar's measures to ensure that his would-be bride remained just where she was.

Perhaps now it was time to weep. I could think of nothing else to do; my magic certainly would not allow me to sprout wings and fly away, or turn myself both invisible and inaudible. I had exhausted my limited repertoire.

Rage against the idea I might, but it appeared clear to me that, come this time tomorrow, I would be Kadar Arkalis's wife.

My sleep that night was restless and nightmare-ridden. I tossed and turned, dreams haunted by voices and faces—my father's pale features, my mother's serene countenance, even a young woman I had never met but who looked too much like me for comfort...my dream-envisioning of the Crown Princess Lyarris, no doubt, as I certainly did not know what she looked like in actuality. I would wake, and rage that I should be in such a situation, I who had only wished to accompany my brother as he went to claim his inheritance. This was none of my doing. Why, up until a few months earlier, I had had only a very hazy idea of how important my father's family actually was.

My father had left his homeland when he was younger than I, vowing that he would never be lord of Marric's Rest, not afflicted as he was with his white hair and skin, and ice-grey eyes. He had concealed the truth of his magic, gone forth into the world to find someone who could train him. And so he had, in perhaps the most unlikely of places—the warm, friendly land of South Eredor, where he met the man who helped him learn how to control the power rising in him. Before he had gone, though, my father had promised his older sister—my Aunt Laranel—that if he were to have a son, one day the boy would inherit Marric's Rest, and come home to Sirlende.

Such a promise had seemed simple enough to make; my father had not thought any woman could ever love him. But the white hair and pale skin that made him such an outcast in his homeland were not quite so striking in South Eredor, where flaxen heads were common enough, and my mother ended up proving him wrong. Thani came along a few years later, with me following some five years after that. We both inherited our mother's dark hair, as her own mother was Sirlendian, and raven-haired and dark-eyed, but my grey eyes were almost as silvery-pale as my father's.

To both our parents' relief, Thani showed no sign of possessing any magical powers, whereas I...well, I was a slightly different matter. But my father taught me as best he could, showing me the simple spells most all users of magic could use, even as he told me that every mage-born soul had his own particular talent. My father was gifted in weather control; more than once I had seen him watching the harbor, lips moving as he conjured a charm to keep the fog away from the coast so the sailors might come safely into the port at Marestal.

What my particular gift might be, we had not yet been able to determine. Perhaps I had none at all, and would be forever doomed to the minor charms and cantrips I'd already been taught. This happened sometimes, according to my father—or, more accurately, according to Lhars, the mage who had trained him. But more than that we did not know, as Lhars had died the year I was born, and far too much of his knowledge passed with him.

Even those small skills I did possess had been kept secret, for magic-working was still met with suspicion and hatred. Memories were long when it came to the destruction the mages had wrought so many centuries ago. Foolish prejudice, really—I doubted my ability to unlock a door or always know where I had left an item was all that dangerous. And certainly these minor talents had been of no help to me in my current situation.

And so I lay awake, and brooded, and rolled onto my back, and then my side, and realized it didn't matter what I did, for I could not escape my current situation. Somewhere toward dawn I fell asleep again, although again nightmares haunted me, visions of hands grasping me, pulling at my hair, my dress, dragging me down into darkness.

The morning which followed was not much better. Oh, they did not neglect me—quite excellent meals were brought up at the proper times, and Beranne bustled in and out at regular intervals as she gathered together all the items required for a splendid turnout at my impending nuptials: slippers of silvered leather, stockings with the sheen of real silk, a truly lovely collection of jewelry—earrings and necklace and intricately wrought crown—all in silver set with gleaming grey river pearls.

"It belonged to the late Mark, rest her," Beranne said, and made an odd little gesture with her middle and forefinger toward the center of her brow. "His lordship wanted you to wear it for the ceremony."

Oh, did he? It was on my tongue to make a sharp remark as to the current Mark's wishes, but what would have been the point? Beranne only did as she was told.

As, apparently, did I.

The afternoon wore on, and another woman appeared to dress my hair, Beranne's services apparently not deemed skillful enough for such a momentous occasion. Then at last the seamstresses appeared, bearing my wedding gown.

Truly it was beautiful, the rich patterned fabric set off by bands of plain silver trim around the low squared neckline and the separate sleeves, which tied on with lengths of silver cord. At another time I would have gladly worn such an exquisite creation, but now I looked on it as something very akin to a funeral shroud. Still, I could do nothing but allow Beranne and the seamstress to draw it on over my fine new silk chemise and let them lace up the back and tie on the sleeves. Finally Beranne set the delicate pearl and silver crown on my head, and fastened the necklace around my throat.

"Beautiful," she said, and behind her the other women murmured their assent. "The North hasn't seen such a bride since his Highness's mother was wed. He will be pleased."

No one, of course, had bothered to ask whether I would be pleased. Perhaps my continued stony silence throughout these preparations told Beranne all she needed to know about my own feelings regarding the situation. Truly, the whole process had taken on the feeling of a bad dream, as if my nightmares of the evening before had bled over into the daylight hours.

Surely I must awaken soon.

Something in Beranne's dark eyes softened, and she reached out and made a minute adjustment to one of the curls hanging over my shoulder. "It is time," she said quietly.

I didn't bother to argue. Nothing would stay this execution, so I might as well go to it with my chin held high. After all, was Kadar not marrying me because I was a Sedassa? I would not whimper and weep and plead—at least, not in his presence.

She opened the door, and the guards waiting outside stepped out of the way so I could exit the suite. As I descended the stairs, they fell in behind Beranne and me, and formed a silent escort as we moved through the castle's main corridor and on into a wing I had not yet seen. Here the ceilings were loftier, with carvings of leaves tracing delicate spirals around each doorway. Here also were concentrated clusters of onlookers who whispered and watched as we swept by.

I did not bother to decipher the content of those whispers. Did they know I had tried to escape, that I was an unwilling participant in this farce? Or did they whisper merely because I was a novelty, an unknown who had somehow snatched away the matrimonial prize they had desired for their sisters or their daughters? Somehow I did not care to find out.

My little party approached a pair of enormous doors, easily three times the height of a man and carved with more of the twining leaf patterns, this time accented by the graceful forms of leaping deer. Outside those doors stood four men-at-arms, two of whom reached out to open them in a single controlled motion.

"You must go on alone," Beranne whispered in my ear. She stepped to one side and gave me an encouraging nod.

I swallowed, and forced myself to put one foot in front of the other, even though each movement was so ponderous I might as well have been walking through thick mud. My steps dragging, I entered a great hall, one filled on either side with those who must constitute the upper echelons of Northern society. A runner of dark green covered the grey stone floor between those watching ranks; I knew this because I kept my attention focused on it as I inched my way forward to the dais at the end of the hall and the man who waited for me there.

How I wanted to run, to gather up those gleaming skirts and flee on my silver-shod feet as if death itself followed me. But there was no escape, not with guards at every door, not with all the nobles of the land watching me with curious eyes. No, I would have to play this game to the end.

Kadar was not alone on the dais; an older man in the dark-grey robes of a disciple of Inyanna stood there with him. While I was a follower of the One, I had studied the religions of the continent and knew a little of their ways. The priests of Inyanna, goddess of the hearth and home, presided over weddings and naming ceremonies and most of life's impor-tant way-posts...save one. The acolytes of Thrane, lord of the land beyond death, were the ones who guided the souls of the departed to the next world.

This world and its concerns were quite enough for me at the moment, however. I grasped my glinting skirts in both hands and mounted three shallow steps, and paused at last next to Kadar. His face as he glanced down at me was impassive. Probably he had not yet forgiven me my escape attempt.

He nodded at the priest, who stepped forward. I noticed that he held a length of plain white linen in his hands.

"Lark Sedassa," he said.

I had no idea how I was supposed to respond, and so only nodded mutely.

"Give him your hand," Kadar instructed. A curl at the corner of his lip told me what he thought of my ignorance.

Not that I cared. While I had studied something of the religions of the continent, their respective marriage rituals had not been included in my reading. I certainly had never thought I would require such knowledge.

Although I hated to do as Kadar said, I knew I had no choice. I raised my left hand, and at once the priest draped one end of the linen strip across my wrist, then brought it underneath and around the other side so it rested lightly against my skin like a loose bandage. Detached as though gazing at someone else's appendage, I noted that my hand shook as if I were afflicted with palsy.

"Kadar Arkalis, Mark of North Eredor," the priest intoned.

Kadar raised his right hand and held it directly above my left. The priest then took the loose end of the linen and wrapped it around Kadar's wrist, binding the two of us together. The significance of the gesture was not lost on me. His hand was heavy against mine, although the pressure of it did ease my trembling somewhat.

"The goddess bears witness to your joining. As you are one now with hands fast, may you be so in all the days of your lives. This bond is a holy one, not to be taken lightly." Was it my imagination, or did the priest's pale-grey eyes narrow at me for a moment? Perhaps Kadar had been telling tales after all. After an infinitesimal pause, the priest said, "What the goddess has brought together, no power on this earth can sunder. Honor her, and honor one another."

Not bloody likely, I thought with sudden viciousness. How I wished I had the courage to tear that ridiculous piece of linen from my arm and let the watching company know that I didn't think much of a goddess who would sanction a forced union such as this.

The priest then unwrapped the linen, and brought it to his forehead and his mouth before gesturing that I should do the same. I lifted the fabric to my lips and saw with some satisfaction as I drew it away that the cosmetics Beranne had applied earlier left a reddish stain.

Kadar repeated the movements. If he noticed the lip print on the sacred cloth, he gave no sign. Then he handed the linen back to the priest, who folded it with utmost care into a small triangle before placing it in a small brazier that stood off to one side. At once the fabric blazed up and emitted a billow of pale grey smoke that smelled of some sort of aromatic wood. Cedar, perhaps.

"A good omen," the priest said, smiling. His teeth were crooked but very white. "Your union will be blessed with passion. So let it be."

Wild laughter bubbled to my lips, but I had no chance to let it out, for Kadar had grasped my hands in his and turned me to face him. "Try not to bite," he murmured, even as he bent his head toward mine and pressed his lips against my mouth.

Truth be told, he took me by enough surprise that I merely stood there, staring up at him. The kiss lasted for only a second or two, most likely just long enough to satisfy convention. Then he turned me toward the watching nobles.

"I give you my consort!" he announced.

As one they surged to their feet and began to clap. From various points in the hall, the more boisterous members of the crowd hallooed and whistled, some even stamping their feet. Apparently Northerners did not tend to stand on ceremony.

Still holding my hand, Kadar led me down the steps and through the noisy ranks of onlookers. I concentrated on keeping my chin high, but something in me seemed to break as I fully comprehended for the first time what that firm grip on my fingers meant.

There had been no last-minute rescues, no divine intervention. For better or worse, I was now wed to Kadar Arkalis.

Of course I would not be allowed to retire quietly. No, a great feast and celebration was held in the castle's main hall, where I found myself marveling a little at the household staff's ability to put together such an important event in so short an amount of time. Perhaps by the loftier Sirlendian standards the feast might have been considered meager, consisting as it did of only three courses, and there was little in the way of flowers, although garlands of autumn leaves decked the high table and the doorways and windows. Still, all in all it was quite a respectable show.

I sat next to Kadar and forced myself to smile and nod as well-wishers approached to offer their congratulations. While

I wanted nothing more than to plead a headache and disappear, I knew the Mark would never accept such an excuse. At least he was so occupied in responding to the outpouring of felicitations that he paid scant attention to me. As was to be expected, I supposed. Now that he had accomplished his nefarious goal, I probably held little interest for him.

The food might have been good, but I would have been hard-pressed to say for sure. It all tasted like sawdust. And although the wine tempted me with its promise of easy oblivion, I forced myself to take only measured sips. I would never forgive myself if I somehow missed a chance at escape simply because I was too intoxicated to recognize it at the time.

Escape. What a foolish, vain thought. For now I was Kadar Arkalis' wife, and he had every right to come after me and imprison me in his castle. Even if I should somehow find the means to slip away, any freedom I gained would be short-lived at best. I was his property now.

I thought then of the doomed Soraya, Duchess of Donrath, who had flung herself from the highest tower of her husband's keep the night of her own forced marriage. Hers made a suitably tragic tale, perfect for songs and poetry, but I knew I would not have the strength to do such a thing. No, I would meekly lower my head and allow Kadar to...

A tremor passed over me, and I reached for my wine glass and took a bigger swallow than I had intended. I knew something of the relations between men and women, since my mother, in her particular no-nonsense way, had been rather frank on the subject. No blissful, girlish ignorance for me. I knew all too well what awaited me once this feast was over.

At least my doom would be somewhat delayed, as the festivities showed no sign of abating once the meal was done. No, the dishes were cleared and the tables whisked away, while a group of musicians took their places at one end of the hall.

"If you will allow me?" Kadar said, extending one hand.

As I could hardly refuse, I laid my hand on his and allowed him to lead me to a spot a few paces away from the musicians. I noted that there were viols and drums and an odd, flat device with strings stretched across it and which its master appeared to manipulate with a small set of hammer-like instruments.

The wedding guests fell into place below us, forming a long line with men on one side and women on the other. Indeed, there were so many who wished to dance that a second set formed a few yards away. I watched in some trepidation, as the dances I had learned back home from my friend Maris's dancing master were of the Sirlendian style, which meant they were performed in circles, not in lines. No doubt I would make a complete fool of myself trying to keep up with the unfamiliar steps.

"They always start out slowly," Kadar told me. His eyes glinted with amusement...at my discomfiture, no doubt. "The musicians know they must needs give the guests time to digest."

"Thank goodness."

After a bit of preliminary plucking and tuning, the musicians struck the obligatory chord for everyone to honor their partners, and then launched into the first piece. It appeared Kadar had been telling the truth—this particular dance was slow and stately, with a good deal of walking and a few circles with the two couples in each set holding hands, but nothing more complicated than that. Once I understood how our progression down the hall worked, there really was nothing to it.

The other couples around us laughed and chattered, but I remained silent throughout the piece. Perhaps Kadar and the rest of the dancers attributed my taciturn behavior to my unfamiliarity with the dance...perhaps not. At the moment I did not much care one way or another. And as Kadar did not seem inclined to press me for conversation, I managed to survive the dance without embarrassing myself.

Afterward he led me back to my seat at the high table, the only table that had not been cleared away to make room for dancing. "You may rest here—it is known that you are not familiar with our dances, and so I think you will be able to sit quietly."

"And you?" I inquired. Certainly I was in no mood for celebrating, but I also didn't much relish the thought of sitting alone the whole night.

"Oh, I'll come reclaim you from time to time," he replied, purposely misunderstanding me. "But I intend to make merry this evening."

With that he left me and went to claim as his partner a pretty, pert young woman with curls almost as wild as mine and a brilliant smile one could see from halfway across the hall. I doubted she was one of the young noblewomen whose matrimonial hopes had been dashed when Kadar took me as his bride, or she wouldn't have been grinning so broadly. But she looked to be a lively partner, one far more appealing than I knew I was at the moment.

Of course no one approached me, and so I had to pretend it suited me to merely watch the dancers. The next piece proved to be more spirited, with couples weaving and twisting in and around each other as they progressed through the line. Most likely I would have been lost if I had attempted such a thing, and I tried to tell myself that being a wallflower was not so bad. For some reason I kept looking to see with whom Kadar danced next, whether she was pretty, and whether he seemed to be enjoying himself. In every case, the answer to both those questions seemed to be yes, and I fought a losing battle to keep a scowl from my face.

Sitting and watching also meant that I had little to do save take small sips from my goblet and try not to think about what would happen once the music was over and the guests had departed. The food I had managed to eat rested uneasily in my stomach. I swallowed against the sour taste that rose in my throat and wished to be someplace very far away.

At length Kadar either decided to take pity on me, or perhaps he realized that to leave his new bride sitting alone for too long would invite questions. He approached and said merrily, "Are you rested enough to try the next one? I will warn you that it is rather lively."

"I'm sure I can manage," I told him. "Even though I do confess that I am rather weary."

The dark brows lifted. "Weary? After only one dance?"

"I fear I did not sleep well last night."

He said nothing, but gave me one hard glance before taking my hand in his and leading me out to the new line that had begun to form. To my surprise, he did not bother to claim his place at the head of the line but fell into position halfway down.

"Remember," he said. "Lively."

"I'll be fine," I replied and lifted my chin, mentally vowing to acquit myself well even if it killed me.

And truly, when the dance began I thought Kadar must have been making a joke at my expense, for the steps seemed simple enough, merely basic movements right and left and a few one-hand turns. But then we finished the first verse, and the musicians increased the tempo of the song. Just a little, but enough for me to realize that by the end of the dance I would have to be moving very quickly indeed.

I shot Kadar a glare of annoyed comprehension, and he grinned back at me. After that I had no time for remonstrances, because I was far too occupied with not falling over my own feet—or those of the other women who shared the line with me—to tell him what I thought of his little joke. Several times I bumped into my neighbors, but they did not seem to mind and only laughed at the silliness of it all until I found myself laughing along with them. By the time the dance was over, I was both gasping and giggling, and did not feel overmuch inclined to struggle when Kadar took me by the waist and led me off the dance floor.

"Ah, so you can smile," he said, after helping himself to a reviving draught of wine. "I had begun to wonder whether your continued dour expression was an attempt to hide missing teeth. I am glad to see I was wrong."

Missing—"My teeth are all very well, I do assure you," I retorted. "But perhaps you should have checked that before you brought me here."

"Perhaps. Then again," he added, looking thoughtful, "I fear if I had attempted to open your mouth to inspect those lovely teeth of yours, you most likely would have bitten my fingers off."

Despite myself, I smiled. The silly dance had worked like a tonic on my mood, and if I just concentrated on the lively music in the background and the quite fine vintage in my cup, I could almost forget the reason why I was here in the first place.

I didn't want to admit it, but it seemed that some part of me enjoyed the verbal sparring with Kadar. It reminded me of the practice swordplay rounds back in the courtyard of my home, when Thani and my father used to spend hours trading blows. Just before Thani had departed for Sirlende to complete his training in Lord Senric's household, my brother and my father had been evenly matched, and most of the time there never seemed to be a clear victor. Neither of them seemed to be bothered by the situation overmuch, and somehow I didn't mind the back and forth with Kadar quite as much as I probably should have.

"Another smile!" Kadar exclaimed. "Truly, a momentous occasion. I must have the scribes make a note of it."

"I'm sure they've been diligently recording all of the day's great activities."

As soon as the words left my mouth, I wished I had not said them at all, for Kadar's expression grew thoughtful. He gazed down at me for a moment, then looked away to the revelers, who had continued with their dancing and drinking and talking. No one seemed to be paying us much attention.

"But this day, like all others, must come to an end at last." He set down his wine goblet and reached for my hand. I almost snatched it away and stopped myself just in time. Despite my reluctance to face what must inevitably come next, I did not want to make a scene.

And so he led me from the hall, away from the light and color and music. The corridors of the castle seemed ominously dark to me in contrast, for low candles burned in sconces at large intervals, thus providing barely enough illumination to show the way.

I could not yet pretend any great familiarity with the building's layout, but at length I did recognize the corridor through which he led me, as well as the wide shallow steps leading up to the double doors of Kadar's suite. Two guards stood there, and one opened the right-hand door for us.

The servants had been busy here as well; more of the autumn garlands decorated the mantel, the window arches, and even the top of the bookcase. Candles smelling of sweet beeswax flickered from every corner. If the circumstances had been different, I might have found it all very lovely.

As it was...

Kadar let go of my hand and strode to the fireplace, then grasped a poker and stirred the logs—quite unnecessarily, I thought, as the fire seemed to be blazing away quite well without his assistance. Perhaps he was not quite as at ease as he would have liked me to believe.

After he finished with the fire, he replaced the poker in its wrought-iron stand and moved to a small table a few feet away, where a squat decanter made of heavy greenish glass sat, along with two small cups of what appeared to be etched silver.

He poured a small measure of pale gold liquid into each cup and handed one of them to me. Despite my efforts to moderate my intake of wine at the revel, by this time I felt just the smallest bit light-headed, and the thought of drinking anything else did not seem particularly wise. I could think of no way to refuse, though, so I took the cup from him. But I only held it, and did not raise it to my lips.

"Share a drink with me, Lark," he said.

Perhaps I should have poured it away, or flung it on the fire to show Kadar what I thought of this forced marriage and his transparent attempts at currying my goodwill. But I was alone with him now, with no watching nobles to temper his actions. I found I did not wish to rouse his anger.

"What is it?" I asked.

"A brew we make here in the north, of wildflower honey. Most find it pleasant enough."

Whether he meant that statement as a challenge, I did not know, but I decided the drink sounded harmless enough. That is, until I took my first sip and had the sweet fire of it burn its way down my throat. I coughed, and Kadar smiled.

"You will be glad enough of it when winter comes," he said, and helped himself to a swallow far less timid than mine.

I didn't know about that, although I did admit to myself that once the initial heat had worn off, the drink left behind a mellow warmth somewhere in my midsection. Not wishing to be thought a coward, I drank again.

"Good girl." He tossed back the rest of his cup's contents and poured himself some more.

His actions set off a tremor of doubt within me. For while he seemed in control for now, I knew the drink must be quite strong. What would he be like after three or four measures of the heady liquor?

"I suppose I should put your mind at ease." He drank once more and then placed the half-empty cup back on the table next to the decanter.

I looked up at him and fought to keep a questioning frown from my brow. "At ease?"

Kadar smiled, but I saw little of humor in his expression. Perhaps he had noted my disquiet. "I am not the sort of man who takes pleasure from forcing unwilling women."

"You—you aren't?" I stammered, then felt a complete fool. But his comment had taken me by surprise, and I had responded without thinking.

His teeth showed again. "I suppose you may be forgiven your low opinion of me, considering our current circumstances. Know then, Lark, that while I made this marriage for political reasons, I have no intention of taking you against your will. I will not lie and say I do not hope that this can be a true marriage in time, but until then—" He shrugged and extended a hand toward the divan that faced the fireplace—"I will sleep here."

To say I was relieved would be an understatement. I stared at him, letting the import of his words sink in. So might an innocent man sentenced to die feel when given a last-minute reprieve at the gallows. Until that moment I hadn't realized how dreadfully I had feared this night.

Apparently my shocked silence discomfited him, for he went on, "We will share these rooms, for we must keep up the appearance of a true marriage. Your things have already been brought here. May I have at least your cooperation in this?"

"Of course," I agreed at last. If he wanted to perpetuate such a fiction, I saw no harm in following along.

He didn't relax precisely, but I did see some of the tension leave his shoulders. "My thanks for that. As it is late, I believe we should retire for the night. I'll just retrieve some blankets from the wardrobe in the next room—"

With those words it finally sank in that he really did intend to sleep in here on the divan. I had a sudden recollection of his long legs dangling over the arm of a similar piece of furniture back at his hunting lodge and felt compelled to say, "Oh, no, you mustn't!"

A startled lift of the level dark brows, followed by the dawning of a certain terrible hope in his eyes. Oh, dear. I hadn't intended for him to think that.

"I mean—that is, I am much smaller than you. I should be the one sleeping out here on the divan."

"I would not ask a lady to do such a thing."

"But you're not asking. I'm offering."

Apparently flummoxed, he looked from me to the divan and back again. Then he said, "You continue to surprise me, Lark Sedassa. Well, my back does thank you, even though honor tells me I should protest a bit more."

"Go ahead, if it makes you feel better." Relief made me giddy, and I laughed. "But it won't make me change my mind. Really, the divan looks entirely comfortable, and I am not so tall that there is any worry as to my feet hanging off the edge."

He shook his head, even as his mouth twisted in a grin. "Truth be told, you will probably be much warmer out here, as the bedchamber lacks a fireplace."

"Well, there you have it."

Still shaking his head, he left me to fetch the promised bedclothes from the sleeping chamber. After he returned, I took the sheets from him and covered the divan's cushions as best I could, then spread a heavy wool blanket over everything.

Even with separate sleeping arrangements, some awkwardness ensued when I had to use his wash basin to clean my face and teeth for the night, but I told myself that the situation was a hundred times less unpleasant than it could have been, given what I had feared would transpire this evening. I retrieved my sleeping chemise from the drawer where Beranne or one of the other servants had stowed it, then bade Kadar good night. His golden eyes gleamed in the dimly lit room as he watched me go, but he said only,

"Sleep well, Lark."

I replied with a muffled, "Good night," then went out to the main room and my makeshift sleeping accommodations. I had to struggle with the lacings of my elegant gown, but the last thing I wanted was to ask Kadar for help with the recalcitrant cords. Eventually I got them loose enough that I could pull the gown over my head, followed by the silk chemise. I climbed into my much warmer nightwear, and then sank down on the divan and pulled the covers up to my chin. The last thing I saw as I drifted off into a much more peaceful slumber than I had expected were the dancing flames in the hearth.

So passed my wedding night.

~ Chapter Five ~

Aknock at the door woke me. I sat upright, clutching sheets and blankets to my breast as I blinked at the unfamiliar surroundings. At first I could not think where I was, but then my focus sharpened on the last bit of glowing coals in the hearth, the dim shapes painted on the frescoed walls. Kadar Arkalis' chambers. From behind the heavy figured wool curtains I saw faint traces of daylight, although the room itself remained quite dark.

"Your Highness?" came a tentative female voice I did not recognize. "I've brought up your breakfast."

I knew then if I wanted to maintain the fiction that Kadar and I had spent any kind of normal wedding night, I must remove myself from the divan immediately. Hurriedly I gathered up my borrowed sheets and blankets and bolted for the door to his bedchamber. As I approached, it opened, and I ran straight into him.

"Easy," he said, reaching out to catch me by the shoulders. "It is far too early for such haste."

"There's someone at the door," I replied. I tried to avoid looking at the expanse of tanned throat and chest the deeply slit neckline of his sleeping tunic exposed. At least he was not completely bare-chested. "I thought—that is, I guessed perhaps the servants shouldn't find me on the divan."

"How thoughtful of you. Do come in, then."

He stepped out of my way and spread a hand in the direction of the bed. As there didn't seem to be time for anything else, I paused by the chest at the foot of the bed and quickly stuffed the sheets and blankets I carried inside, then awkwardly clambered onto the green-hung bedstead and pulled the covers up to my chin.

From the doorway Kadar called out, "Come in," then returned to the bed and climbed in next to me. The frame creaked and shifted with his weight. I bit my lip and gazed up at the green damask canopy above me so I would not have to look at him.

A moment later I heard the same unfamiliar woman's voice. "I trust it is not too early, your Highness."

"Of course not. My bride and I could hardly lie abed all day." Kadar chuckled, and added, "Or perhaps we could, but the kingdom would not thank me for it. Would it, my love?" And he leaned over and kissed me on the cheek.

Hot blood rushed into my face, and I opened my mouth to retort that I could think of about a thousand other things I'd rather do than be in bed with him. Then I remembered our audience, and instead summoned a wobbly smile before sitting upright, the bedclothes still clutched firmly against my breast.

A young woman wearing the same plainly fashioned dark brown garments as most of the other household servants stood at the side of the bed, a wide tray balanced on her hands. From it came the delightful scents of new-made bread, and hot tea, and two of the same delicious egg pies I had consumed just the morning before.

For some reason she seemed to find a spot on the floor uniquely fascinating, and kept her gaze fixed there as she murmured, "Should I set this on the bed table?"

"Do, Narenna. Thank you."

She moved a few candlesticks out of the way to make a space large enough to accommodate the tray and set it down. "Anything else, your Highness?"

"No, that will be all."

She nodded, dropped a quick curtsey, and then hurried out of the room before closing the chamber door behind her. As soon as she had gone, I swung my legs off the edge of the bed and began to slide out.

Kadar drawled, "So eager to leave?"

I refused to let him bait me. "I've never cared for eating in bed."

Chin lifted firmly in the air, I stalked around the foot of the bed and over to the table that held our breakfast. Still without looking at Kadar, I poured myself a full mug of tea, and cut myself a slice of bread and spread it with honey.

"That looks good. I think I will join you."

He stood and came over to the table. I watched as he helped himself to some tea as well, though he opted for a plate of pie rather than the bread. His arm brushed against mine as he reached for a fork, and I had to force myself to stand still and not flinch at the contact.

"Does the Mark of North Eredor always take his morning meal with so little ceremony?" I inquired, more to gloss over the awkward moment than because I actually cared about his reply.

"Sometimes. It depends on my schedule for the day."

"Schedule?"

Those golden eyes seemed to mock me over the glazed brown rim of the mug as he blew gently on its contents. "Sadly, my day is comprised of more than planning kidnappings, or dancing with my new wife. Occasionally a land does require its ruler to actually rule."

"Well, of course it does," I snapped, nettled that he would think me such a simpleton. "I was not questioning the fact that you had a schedule, my lord, but rather expressing polite interest as to what it might contain."

"Ah. Then I do beg your pardon for the misunderstanding. Perhaps it was merely surprise that you should be interested in anything to do with me."

As I recognized his comment for the taunt it was, I kept my expression blank and went back to sipping my tea.

He did not appear concerned by my lack of response, and went on, "Unlike Sirlende, North Eredor is not known for its week-long revels. It is back to business as usual today, although

I thought perhaps this morning we could go for a ride so that I might show you some of Tarenmar's environs."

"How delightful," I said, although the prospect did not fill me with much joy. Perhaps one day I might feel more at home in the saddle, but at the moment I could only think of the inevitable aching muscles which would follow yet another bout on horseback.

Kadar smiled. "Anything to please you, my lady wife."

I sighed. It was going to be a very long day.

My band of seamstresses must have worked through the night; little as I wanted to spend the morning riding with Kadar Arkalis, at least I was able to do so in the smart riding suit of burgundy wool they produced for me. Several other articles of clothing were also placed in the large wardrobe of Kadar's bed-chamber, awaiting the time I would require them.

"And the rest by the end of the week, my lady," Beranne assured me as she coiled up my unruly hair and topped it with a fetching little cap of brown velvet decked with several jaunty pheasant plumes.

I murmured a few words of thanks and shot a sidelong glance out the door in the direction of the sitting room. Kadar sat at the large table where he had composed the missive to my aunt several days earlier. Now he scribbled away at some kind of document, although I could not tell if it was another letter or not. Whether to spare me any further awkwardness, or simply because he was the sort who did not care to waste time in his morning preparations, he had dressed quickly while I waited out on the divan, then went on to his writing as Beranne came to prepare me for the ride.

"There now," she said, sticking one last carved bone hairpin into the knot at the back of my head. "I trust we didn't keep his lordship waiting overlong."

"Not at all, Beranne. Thank you."

Because she seemed to expect it, I smiled at her, even though I had little heart to put into the expression. I knew I should be feeling some relief; after all, I had survived my wedding night with little amiss save a slight stiffness in my neck from sleeping on the divan. Things could have been so much worse.

However, I could not help but quail a little at the thought of the hours and days ahead, of all the time I must spend in the company of the man who was now my husband. True, he must needs leave me alone for long stretches while he tended to the care of his kingdom, but we still would be thrown together a good deal of the time. How long would he be content to let me sleep apart, despite his assurances about not forcing me?

I had no answer to this question, of course. All I could do was dismiss Beranne, who bobbed a curtsey and exited the suite. I left the bedchamber and went out to meet Kadar. He placed his pen in a silver inkwell and stood.

"Ready?" he inquired, and I nodded. He gazed down at me for a few seconds and shook his head. "No need to look quite so stricken, my pet. It is only a ride, not a trip to the gallows. And it is a fine day outside."

If my thoughts had revealed themselves so plainly on my face, then I knew I must do something to keep such a thing from happening in the future. If Kadar could somehow guess what I was thinking...

I lifted my shoulders and said, "My youth in Marestal did not provide much opportunity for riding. That is all."

"We can change that soon enough. My grooms have found you a good riding mare, very biddable." His lips quirked. "Quite unlike her mistress."

I could think of no reply to that, so I settled for sending him a stony glance. He did not appear discomfited, but instead took my gloved hand in his and led me from the room.

It felt odd to see the people within the castle's halls bow and curtsey as Kadar and I passed. On more than one occasion I had to stop myself from curtseying in return. As Kadar returned their obeisances with a simple nod of the head from time to time, I attempted to do the same, even though I felt an embarrassed flush creep up my cheeks as I did so. Somehow it seemed strange that I, whose mother was engaged in trade, should be the center of such fawning attention, even though I knew they were bowing to the new consort of the Mark and no more.

At length we reached the courtyard, where several grooms waited with our horses. I recognized Kadar's dapple-grey at once, and guessed the pretty black mare beside him was my mount. Their glossy tack gleamed in the bright morning sunlight, a good match for the shining coats of the horses. If nothing else, it appeared the Mark's servants took very good care of his horseflesh.

I was helped up into the saddle while Kadar mounted his own horse. A half-dozen other men were already astride and waiting for us—our escort, I presumed.

"Raven will follow my lead," Kadar told me, as he wheeled his dapple-grey around. "Just give her her head."

That sounded like dubious advice, but I did as he said and allowed the reins to lie more or less limp across the pommel. At least here in North Eredor they seemed to be sensible about women and riding; the suit I wore had a voluminous split skirt so I could ride astride, so much easier and more practical than the Sirlendian side-saddle.

We rode out of the castle gates and through the streets of Tarenmar, where the crowds parted to let us pass. A fresh breeze caught the banners carried by our escort, rippling the scarlet and silver silk.

Despite myself, I felt my spirits rise along with the breeze. It was much more difficult to be downcast in the face of such a glorious morning. Perhaps I had been more oppressed by the confines of Kadar's castle than I had thought, especially as I had had no reason to believe I would escape its walls any time soon.

Not that this was an escape, I told myself, as I watched Kadar's back rise and fall with the motions of his horse. For the ride he had pulled back his hair, so there was nothing to obscure the fine lines of his shoulders, or the sword-straight posture. He looked as if he had been born to the saddle.

Which he probably had, that and sword-fighting and all sorts of other manly pursuits. I knew he was an only son, and so of course all possible attention must have been lavished on him. Unfortunate that he had turned out to be such an arrogant bastard.

At that moment he turned in the saddle to look back at me and smiled, his teeth flashing in the bright sun. "We'll go by the lake and westward to the woods there. It is a fine ride."

I nodded, trying to ignore the pang of remorse I experienced at thinking such things of him when he obviously was making an attempt at civility. Then I told myself not to be a fool and waste such emotions as guilt on him. If anyone should be feeling guilty, it should be Kadar, for stealing me from my family and forcing this sham marriage on me. At the moment, however, it appeared he hadn't a care in the world. I could not say the same for myself.

We had ridden westward, away from the town. Here I at last saw where the lake met its grey, pebbled shore. The water itself, however, was almost as bright a blue as the sky. Boats bobbed up and down in that water, although they were clustered near the town, with not many occupying the section of lake we now passed.

At least Kadar did not seem inclined to conversation, but led the group away from the water's edge and into the outer reaches of the woods I had spied from the castle windows. Autumn had already brushed the trees' leaves with scarlet and orange and gold, a shimmering panoply that surrounded us as we passed into the forest proper. But it was no wildwood; I saw several paths cross ours, and although leaves carpeted the ground, our way was clear enough.

At length we paused in a clearing with a stream crossing its western edge. Kadar brought us all to a halt, and the little mare I rode dutifully stopped with barely a signal from me.

He dismounted and came to me, arms outstretched to lift me down from my saddle. I knew I could not decline his assistance in view of our escort, and so I allowed him to place his hands on my waist and lower me to the ground. From the glint in his eyes, I guessed he knew precisely how much I disliked having his hands on me...which of course was why he had done so in the first place.

"I thought we might have some refreshment," he said, and gestured toward his escort, who began unpacking saddlebags.

In no time they had spread a blanket over the fallen leaves, and assembled an assortment of delicacies for us: cold roast pheasant, more new-baked bread, cheese, what looked to be a pear tart. And with it a jug of wine, accompanied by a pair of earthenware goblets. I guessed Kadar hadn't wanted to risk the rare and expensive glassware we used in the castle.

"It looks wonderful," I said, then took matters into my own hands by immediately kneeling on the blanket and crossing my legs so he would not have time to assist me.

He smiled, but I thought his expression looked a little strained. But he said nothing and sat as well, and poured me a goblet of wine with his own hands. "You may take up a perimeter," he said. At once our escort melted away into the forest, forming a silent barrier between us and any possible intruders.

"Are these woods so dangerous?" I asked, my tone all innocence. "For if that is the case, then I wonder why you would bring me here."

"This forest is no more dangerous than the central market in Tarenmar—less, possibly, as at least here there is no danger of being swindled." He poured some wine for himself and drank. "No, rather that I would not have prying ears listening to our conversation."

"Is what you have to say to me so private?"

His eyes narrowed. "Perhaps. Does that frighten you?"

"Frighten? Hardly." I sipped at my wine, hoping that I looked sufficiently casual. "At any rate, your behavior of the past few days suggests that, while you may have the morals of a tomcat in heat, you do not appear to intend me any direct harm. So what is it you have to say to me?"

At my remark about the tomcat, he scowled, but then his features relaxed into the sardonic grin I knew all too well. "Ah, I shall not debate you on that. And apparently you must have some concern for my reputation, or you would not have acted so quickly to hide the details of our sleeping arrangements."

I did not bother to tell him that I had done so more to preserve my own hide. The last thing I wanted was him angry with me because his people had discovered that I did not share his bed. I cut myself a piece of bread, spread some blue-veined cheese on it, and took a bite.

He appeared somewhat nonplussed by my lack of response, but continued, "I will not bore you with an account of my country's history, but I will say that to be the consort of the Mark of Eredor means a life of service, of involvement. We have no use for pretty figureheads who appear at state functions to serve some decorative purpose and then go back to embroidering pillowcases or whatever it is that highborn Sirlendian women do."

"As to that, I wouldn't know, either," I interjected, "as I am neither full-blood Sirlendian nor highborn."

"You may continue to deny your birthright if you like, but it does not change the fact that your father's family is one of the greatest in Sirlende. No amount of hawking wine in the marketplace can change that."

I didn't bother to point out that, while my mother had carried on with managing the vineyards she'd inherited, she employed people to take our wine to the great market in Marestal. However, I also chose not to mention that I'd taken over some of her bookkeeping, once I'd proved myself to have a good head for figures. "I had never intended to be a figurehead, pretty or not, so if you are trying to provoke me in some way, you are definitely taking the wrong tack."

He frowned a little at those words. Perhaps, coming from a land-locked country as he did, he was unfamiliar with sailing terms. But, being who he was, he did not appear to be put off for very long. "I am glad to hear that, for this afternoon I shall sit in my audience chamber and hear the grievances of my people—and you will sit there with me."

The swallow of wine I had just taken seemed to sour in my mouth. Or perhaps it was simply that the thin Northern vintage didn't measure up to the richer wines produced by my family's vineyards. "I'll what?"

"The consort always accompanies the Mark on audience days. I see no reason why you should be treated any differently."

I could think of several hundred reasons why I should be treated differently, starting with how I was in North Eredor under duress, and therefore not someone inclined to offer an overly sympathetic ear to the grievances of its people. None of these arguments would work, though. I knew, as I watched Kadar's false smile grow again, that I would be forced again to suffer yet another of his charades.

The audience chamber was located in the same wing as the great hall where we had feasted and danced only the night before. Somehow that evening already seemed very far away, as if it had happened to someone other than myself. This room, I noticed as Kadar led me to the pair of high carved thrones on a dais at its far end, was smaller and narrower, with long benches arranged on each wall—presumably for the watching audience.

I took my seat, grateful for the new gown of green cut velvet Beranne had brought to me. The grey pearls that had belonged to Kadar's mother circled my throat and crowned my head; I thought perhaps I looked like a consort, even if I didn't feel much like one.

Once we were seated, the guards began to let in the observers. I hoped, as I watched the throngs enter and jostle for places on the benches, that they did not all have grievances to present, or we would be there for a very long time. Perhaps some of them had merely come to catch a glimpse of the new consort.

This thought made me sit up a little straighter in my chair, and I took in a deep breath. Beside me, Kadar looked impressive enough in a high-necked doublet of black wool, a band of silver set with a single faceted garnet holding his heavy dark hair back from his brow. He nodded to Althan, who stood at the foot of the dais. "We may begin."

I had worried what my role in these proceedings would be, but apparently while my presence was required, my counsel was not. Several people came forth and stated their cases, which tended to be simple enough disputes over land ownership, or claims of grievances in various business dealings. Kadar listened to all the parties involved, asked more cogent questions than I had expected, and in all cases but one delivered the same judgment I would have given—had I been asked.

Not a figurehead? I thought, considering my current role as a silent observer. *Perhaps he and I have different definitions of the term...*

But then two men approached, one in the simply cut doublet and high boots that seemed to be the standard male garb in North Eredor, the other in a long tunic of a style that had been out of fashion even in the South for at least a decade. He had mid-brown hair and eyes, and was not as tall as most Northern men.

The Northerner bowed to Kadar and said, "Your Highness, I did not wish to approach you with such a petty matter, but the other party involved has proved so intractable that I had no choice but to bring my case to the Hall of Grievances."

Kadar nodded. "Go on."

"Highness, this man and I entered into a business dealing, but he has conspired to cheat me at every turn. Now I only wish to recoup my original investment, but he will not allow me even that much satisfaction."

During this speech the man in the tunic had remained silent, but his brow had twisted and an expression of angry bewilderment crossed his features. Finally he burst out, "No cheat! Not—deal—" And he trailed off into a flood of incomprehensible syllables.

...Incomprehensible to both Kadar and Althan, that was clear from the puzzled looks on both their faces. But I found I understood the brown-haired stranger well enough, once those first words awakened in my mind a vocabulary I had not used for some time.

"He says he is not the cheat," I broke in. "He says that Master Haddimer here cheated him, and tried to renege on their deal."

If I had suddenly sprouted wings and flown out of the chamber, I do not think I would have evoked a more astonished reaction from the Mark. His eyebrows lifted, and the incredulity was clear in his tone as he remarked, "'He says'— how do *you* know what he says?"

"Because he is speaking Selddish," I replied calmly, then added in an undertone, so only he might hear my next words, "If you had bothered to learn anything about me, save who my relatives are, then you might have known that I have been schooled in many of the languages of the continent, along with mathematics and history and geography. At any rate, as we can now hear both sides of the story, I think we should continue."

For a few seconds Kadar continued to stare at me, as if really looking at me for the first time. Then he nodded. "Yes." He leaned forward. "Tell him to proceed."

Perversely pleased I had been able to offer the Mark something of value besides my family connections, I turned to the man and asked in Selddish, "Can you tell me what happened?"

Which he did, launching into a lengthy and impassioned speech about how he had found himself overburdened with flax seed following the plague that had swept Seldd only the year before. In Marestal we had been able to escape the ravages of the disease, save for a small outbreak near the docks, but we had heard it devastated the lands east and north of us: Purth and Farendon and Seldd. As Seldd's main export was its fine linen, I could see how, with more than a third of its population lost to the plague, there would be an excess of flax seed.

So this merchant, one Dhirne, had loaded up his pack animals and undertaken the perilous trek through the Opal Mountains' one safe pass to bring his seed to North Eredor, where he might at least get enough money for it to see his family through the winter. He had met with Haddimer, a seed merchant, and struck as good a deal as he could, considering the language barrier. But when the day of payment came, he was given copper instead of the silver he was promised. The resulting row had gotten both men thrown out of the tavern where they were conducting their business, with the proprietor telling them to take their argument to the Hall of Grievances, or he'd set the City Watch on them.

I related all this to Kadar, who listened with narrowed eyes. As I concluded my translation of the Selddish man's woes, Haddimer cut in angrily and said, "And you believe this, your Highness? It's a pack of lies from beginning to end!"

Kadar straightened, mouth tight. I knew I would not have wanted to be on the receiving end of the glare he directed at the other man. "Are you calling the Mark's consort a liar?"

Haddimer blanched. "No, your Highness—that is, I am certain her translation is accurate, but that Dhirne is lying to her."

"Do you think he is lying?" Kadar asked me. He sounded as if he genuinely wanted to hear what I thought.

Here was one situation where I could use my magic, and do so quickly enough that no one need know what I had done. Again, it was a quiet spell, one that only required a few seconds of mental preparation; anyone watching me would have merely thought I closed my eyes to consider the question more deeply. But in that small space of time I was able to mouth the words without speaking them, uttering the spell that would reveal any falseness clinging to either of the two men. And so I saw in my mind's eye the cool blue of truth enveloping the man from Seldd, while Haddimer's outline bristled with the spiky yellowish hues of falsehood.

"No, he is not," I said, after I reopened my eyes. "But Haddimer most definitely is."

"You sound very certain."

"I am."

A considering expression on his face, Kadar turned away from me, back to the two men who awaited his verdict. For a long, uncomfortable moment he said nothing, and I swallowed against my unease. He had asked for my opinion, but that did not mean he intended to act on it. Besides, this was a case of the word of his subject against that of an outlander, a man from a country widely despised because it still practiced slavery, even in this enlightened age. How could I trust Kadar to believe me and rule against one of his own people?

Finally he spoke. "Haddimer."

The merchant's pale blue eyes gleamed. "Yes, your Highness?"

"You have taken advantage of a man who attempted to trade with you fairly, someone who has already suffered through more hardship than you can possibly comprehend. You will pay him every silver crown you owe him, as well as a penalty of twenty percent above and beyond the original price. And you will pay him by the end of the day tomorrow. You've already wasted enough of his time; I do not want him delayed so that he cannot get home before the mountain passes close for the winter."

Haddimer's mouth opened, as if he very much wanted to protest. He shut it without speaking as I began relating to Dhirne in rapid-fire Selddish what the Mark had just decreed. A look of terrible relief passed over the man's face, and he dropped to his knees and touched his forehead to the ground directly in front of the dais, even as he began to praise Kadar's wisdom and my cleverness.

"Erm, he says thank you," I told the Mark, whose lip twisted.

"I rather gathered that."

Althan somehow managed to pry Dhirne off the floor, and usher both him and his erstwhile adversary down the aisle and out of the room. That seemed to be the conclusion of the afternoon's grievances, for immediately afterward the spectators left their seats on the benches and exited the chamber as well. Kadar and I were left alone, save for the two men still standing guard at the entrance.

"What were you saying to yourself back there?"

A tremor of unease passed through me. I thought I had barely moved my lips while invoking the truth spell, but Kadar must have seen something. I hoped he did not notice my slight hesitation before I replied, "I was praying."

That seemed to surprise him. His eyebrows lifted, and what might have been the beginnings of a smile touched the corners of his mouth. "I had no idea you were so devout."

"Even those who do not think of themselves as devout may ask for assistance at certain times. God is always listening, even if you and I might not always hear what He has to say in return."

"Ah, I had forgotten you most likely would be a follower of the Southern heresy."

I didn't bother to correct him. True, ages ago both North and South Eredor had shared a pantheon along with a name, and worship of the One was regarded as heresy. But the Great Cataclysm had sundered the beliefs of the two lands just as irrevocably as it had broken them north and south, forever separate. South Eredor had suffered the least from the effects of the mage wars and the Black Time that immediately followed. Acolytes of the One had prayed incessantly to be delivered from the darkness, and their prayers had been answered. Ever since, we in the South had turned away from the old gods and followed the One. Whether or not divine intervention was responsible for our salvation, I truly did not know. It seemed as good an explanation as any.

At any rate, better to confess to praying to a god Kadar despised than admit to casting a truth spell. "Whether it was God working through me or not, I did see the truth of the situation."

He nodded, his expression thoughtful. Then his expression cleared, and he said, "You did very well."

"I did, didn't I?"

He laughed then. "And modest as well. Then again, what need for modesty in a lady as wise and lovely as you?"

"Are you such a dreadful flatterer with everyone?" I inquired in arch tones.

"Not at all." His expression sobered, and once again I had that impression of him truly seeing me. "I believe, my Lady Lark, that in the end not kidnapping Princess Lyarris was a stroke of great good fortune."

For him, perhaps.

I knew I could not say the same for myself.

~ Chapter Six ~

If someone had told me on the morning of my wretched wedding day that I might become used to being the consort of the Mark of North Eredor, and would actually come to enjoy certain aspects of the position, I most certainly would have laughed in their face. The truth of it was, awkward living arrangements notwithstanding, I began to find my new life engaging in ways my old one had not been. Yes, I missed my studies with my father, and I missed him and my mother even more, but even though I had lately reached my twenty-first year, they still treated me very much like a child in some ways.

Here I was the lady of the land, and although perhaps I did not have quite as much freedom in my movements as I would have liked, still it seemed most of my wishes were obeyed without question—not that I asked for anything more untoward than venison for dinner one night rather than yet another round of lake fish, or requested much beyond some additional books to supplement Kadar's quite extensive library. I could even leave the castle as long as I had sufficient escort with me, and so was able to familiarize myself with Tarenmar's muddy streets, its central market and the surprisingly good playhouses that crowded its eastern border.

I did wonder at the lack of response from my family; two weeks had passed since Kadar brought me to his capital, and that certainly allowed enough time for my aunt to have received his letter and for her to have sent word on to my father. Not that I expected to see the armies of Sirlende sweeping down upon Tarenmar to avenge my wronged honor, but the absence of any sort of reply had begun to send small threads of doubt through my mind. Kadar had said he sent the letter, but I had not used the truth spell to verify his actions. For all I knew, he had thrown the paper into the fire, and my family thought me dead, lost forever.

As one might expect, this prospect dismayed me a good deal, but I could not think of how to remedy the situation. I did not yet have the courage to confront Kadar openly about his letter. While he seemed to treat our separate sleeping arrangements with a sort of weary good humor, I could not help but wonder how long his patience might last. Not forever, certainly, and though we got on better than I could ever have expected, considering our rather rocky start, still I had no desire to share his bed.

My presence was not required at all of the Mark's audiences; he met with his lords separately, in the same chamber used for the Hall of Grievances. During those times I usually stayed in our apartments and read, or journeyed forth to the marketplace if the weather was fine. This particular day, however, a chill rain fell, one which drove the bright leaves from the trees and hinted at the harshness of the coming winter.

Restlessness sent me from my rooms, Beranne my faithful shadow. Within the castle I was not required to have more than a single retainer as an escort, and though I had already thoroughly explored much of the stronghold, I thought perhaps I could revisit the hall where some very fine old tapestries were hung, or walk again through the long corridor on the east side of the castle that functioned as a sort of informal portrait gallery. Anything rather than remain in the apartments I shared with Kadar.

Because of the weather, the castle seemed unusually crowded, with knots of men standing about talking instead of being outdoors on one of their regular hunting expeditions, and servants finding all sorts of indoor tasks to occupy them rather than hanging laundry in the kitchen yard or going to market to purchase supplies. More often than not people got out of my way, even when I was accompanied only by Beranne, but then I rounded a corner and almost collided with a young woman of about my own age, someone who clearly hesitated before she stepped aside.

She stood out in the dark-garbed crowd not only because of the sky-blue wool gown she wore, almost the color of her eyes, but also because she was quite outstandingly lovely. Her hair was sleek and black as a raven's wing, her skin very fine. Long lashes swept down over those startlingly blue eyes, and I almost heard a sniff as she made her curtsey.

Then we had passed her by, but the resentful expression in her eyes stayed with me long after she had left my sight. After we had rounded a corner, I turned to Beranne. "Who on earth was that?"

"Who, my lady?"

I stopped and crossed my arms. Here, on the edge of the portrait gallery, the hallway was empty save for my maid and myself. "That woman in the blue gown."

"Oh, her."

"Yes, *her*. Well?"

Beranne hesitated. Her pleasant, round-cheeked face was not made for distress, but she looked quite anxious. "I can't imagine what she was doing here—his Highness sent her away weeks ago—"

"Beranne!"

"She's Tanira Banaris, my lady." Her eyes would not meet mine. "She is—that is, she was the Mark's mistress."

Well, I supposed that would explain the young woman's apparent hostility. At the same time, I felt an odd little twinge. So Kadar had a mistress, did he? I told myself the situation wasn't that odd; highborn men had been known from time immemorial to keep mistresses. It had nothing to do with me. Frankly, I should be glad the Mark had someone to keep him occupied. No wonder he was so remarkably unruffled by my continuing presence on the couch rather than in his bed.

Apparently unnerved by my silence, Beranne said, "Not anymore, my lady. As I said, his Highness sent Lady Tanira away some three weeks ago, before you were even brought here."

"Oh, it's *Lady* Tanira, is it?" I asked, and was a bit surprised by my own sour tone.

"Yes. Her father has holdings up near the northern border. Very little wealth, I've heard—she's like to be married off to the owner of one of the tin mines, if Lord Banaris has his way."

"And how does the lady feel about that?" While I certainly had no reason to love this Tanira Banaris, if what Beranne had told me was true, still I was more than a little sensitive on the subject of forced marriages.

This time it was Beranne's turn to sniff. "What more could she expect, with everyone knowing of her relations with his Highness? She all but threw herself at him, and what could anyone expect him to do? She is very beautiful—but no more so than your ladyship, of course," she hastened to add.

"Of course," I murmured, and felt my mouth quirk. Truly, it mattered very little whether Tanira Banaris was lovelier than I. Kadar had married me, not her...more's the pity. If only he had been the kind of man to be swayed by a pretty face rather than impressive bloodlines, he could have wed the young woman and left me to my fate. But ambition had apparently out-ruled lust in his case.

Why Kadar's erstwhile mistress had returned to the castle, I did not know, but I had the sudden impression he would be less than pleased to learn she was here.

I heard the shouting when I was still a few paces away from the double doors to the apartments Kadar and I shared. Beside me, Beranne stopped, one hand going to her mouth.

The guards standing just outside the doors exchanged a grin. "Not the best time to go inside, my lady," said the guard on the left, whose name was Thran.

"Indeed?" I replied, my hands on my hips. "These are my chambers, are they not? Why should I not enter?"

He exchanged a quick glance with Beranne, as if silently asking her to make me see reason. "His Highness is occupied at the moment."

"I can hear that." I paused long enough for a woman's voice to cry out something about a lying bastard. Kadar's reply was muffled, so I could not make out any individual words. But he sounded quite angry indeed. "Perhaps he would be glad of an interruption."

And I strode past Thran and raised the latch. Out of the corner of my eye I saw him lift one hand and then subside, as if he had realized that attempting to restrain the Mark's consort against her will might not be the wisest course of action. I chose to ignore him, and swept into the sitting room before closing the door behind me.

Kadar and Tanira faced each other in front of the fireplace. His back was to the entrance, and so he could not see me. She, on the other hand, spied me at once, her blue eyes widening as I squarely met her shocked glare.

"Who is this, Kadar?" I asked. "I must say she appears to be a trifle upset."

At my words he turned to face me. Oh, yes, he was angry; color burned high on his cheekbones beneath the last remnants of his summer's tan, and the golden eyes fairly snapped with fury. "Lady Tanira," he said deliberately, "was just leaving."

"I was not!" she retorted, and stamped her foot. Despite myself, I wanted to grin. I had read of people stamping their feet in anger, but I had never actually seen anyone do such a thing until that moment. "Is *this* what made you discard me— this meaching little Sirlendian baggage? I can't say I think much of your taste!"

"I find myself questioning it as well," he replied, with a sharp glance in Tanira's direction. There could be no possible way to misinterpret his remark, and I saw her scowl as the barb found its way home.

I looked toward the doorway. Perhaps I shouldn't be enjoying this as much as I was, but then again, I was not disposed to think kindly of someone who called me a "baggage."

"Should I call the guards?" I asked.

"I don't think that will be necessary. Will it, Tanira?"

Full mouth pursed into an angry pout, she glared at Kadar and then at me. "You should not have treated me thus."

"What, the dowry of a thousand silver crowns I sent home with you wasn't enough? I should think that would have been sufficient for your tin merchant to overlook your rather... sullied...status."

The crack of her hand hitting his cheek was shockingly loud. I flinched, and waited for the explosion that surely must follow.

But it did not. Instead, Kadar made her a mocking little bow, then pointed toward the door. "I think you know the way out."

She turned a most unbecoming shade of red and gathered up the folds of her forget-me-not-colored skirts before lifting her chin in the air and storming from the room. The slam of the door was almost as loud as the slap she'd delivered a moment earlier.

For a few seconds Kadar and I were both silent. Then he cleared his throat. "I am sorry you had to see that."

"Indeed? I must confess I found it rather entertaining."

"You—" He paused and shook his head. "Most women would not care to be confronted by their husband's mistress."

"True. But you and I do not have what could be called a precisely conventional marriage, and it seemed clear enough to me that you wanted nothing to do with her. Anyway," I added disingenuously, "Beranne had already told me that you had tried to rid yourself of this Tanira person some weeks ago. I don't believe it would be fair to blame you for her bad behavior."

Again he was silent. The hooded lids dropped to partly conceal his eyes, and so I had a difficult time attempting to read his mood. His mouth tightened and then somehow relaxed into a smile. Before I could think to react, he stepped toward me and touched my cheek briefly before letting his hand drop back to his side.

"I recall telling Sirdahl that life with you would be far from dull. It appears I was correct in that assumption."

Then he turned from me and left the room. As he shut the door, I could hear him begin to give Thran and the other guard a dressing-down for allowing Tanira entry in the first place.

I stood there for a long moment. Almost unconsciously I raised my hand to feel the spot on my face where Kadar had touched me. I should have stopped him, and yet...

...and yet somehow I was glad I had not.

Oh, dear.

Almost a week later Kadar rode out in the company of his guards, on some errand whose purpose he did not reveal to me. I told myself I should be glad of the separation. We had spent too much time together these past few weeks, and it was obvious I was not thinking clearly. For why else would I continue to feel the pressure of his hand against my cheek, even though I had washed my face quite vigorously the night he had touched me?

Beranne, always my source for the latest information within the castle, told me that Tanira had been sent packing soon after she stormed away from our chambers, so I knew it was no assignation of that sort which drew Kadar from his stronghold this morning. He did leave the castle several times a week on a variety of business, from following the progress of the fortification of Tarenmar's walls to overseeing a special project of his involving the creation of a central exchange to expedite the flow of goods coming into the country.

But none of those tasks should have elicited the aura of barely suppressed excitement that surrounded him this morning. He had seemed almost absent as he bade me farewell and went to join his party. I watched him go, surrounded by a smaller escort than usual; only six men accompanied him this time. Wherever he was headed, apparently security was of no great concern.

During my time in the castle I had also discovered what must once have been a music room in one of the building's forward towers. Apparently Kadar's maternal grandmother had been quite musical. A green-muffled harp still stood against one wall, and a tall cabinet held a variety of carved flutes. A small chest contained age-faded papers covered with musical notations in barely legible ink, but the shelves in the room were quite bare, just waiting to be filled with books.

So I had placed some of my recent purchases there, and took over the chamber as my own private sanctuary within the castle. Surely Kadar knew I had made it my impromptu study, but he never said a word to prevent me from going there. While our apartments were more luxurious, I found I preferred the little tower room, not merely because of its atmosphere of quiet peace, but also because it provided an excellent vantage point for me to see everyone who came and went through the castle's main gates.

This was how I saw Kadar return late in the afternoon, his party now numbering nine instead of seven. The rain had returned, and all the men had turned up their hoods as protection against the wet. I could not see the faces of the additions to their group, only that one of them presented an oddly shaped outline, as if he had some sort of pack muffled under his cloak. He seemed to have difficulty staying in his seat; he swayed in the saddle as if he were intoxicated or perhaps ill, yet he did not fall.

What became of this newcomer, I did not know, for even though I left my tower room soon after under the pretense of greeting Kadar as he entered the castle, I saw no sign of the other man. But the Mark appeared in high spirits, meeting me with a grin.

"Do you know what day this is?"

I shook my head.

"Why, it is my birthday. I am told the cooks have prepared a great feast. And we will have dancing again. I hope this time you will be more inclined to stand up with me."

He appeared the very picture of a man without a care in the world, but something in his manner almost seemed forced. I could not exactly put my finger on why, save perhaps for a certain tautness to his jaw and a tension in the lines of his throat.

It seemed best to play along. "I think that can be arranged. You are remiss, though, my lord."

"Remiss?"

"If you had provided me with some warning that this was your birthday, I could have gotten you a gift. As it is, I have nothing to give you."

His smile widened. "As to that, you are gift enough for me." He took my hand and brought it to his lips. "Wear something festive."

And with that he left me to watch after him, until the crowds in the corridor obscured him from view. I frowned, wondering where he had gone, and who he had brought back with him. I guessed I would not soon know the answers to either of those questions.

We stayed up into the small hours of the morning, Kadar urging the musicians to play dance after dance. It was a good thing by this time I possessed a pair of properly fitting slippers, or

I would barely have been able to put one foot in front of the other by the end of the evening. The company consumed far more game meats and wine than I thought wise, considering we looked to be headed into a harsh winter. Then again, they knew this land far better than I. No doubt Althan and the other household retainers had already calculated the supplies necessary to see us all through the cold months.

As promised, I did stand up with Kadar many times, though I took my turn on the floor with others as well. I thought it prudent to keep him from monopolizing me too thoroughly. Just as well, for as the evening wore on and I drank more wine, I began to enjoy our dances together a little too much. He danced well, but it was more than that. I found myself looking forward to the feel of his fingers against mine, the weight of his hands around my waist as he spun me into place.

The glow in those odd golden eyes as he looked down into my face.

No doubt he thought the evening a great success, my open demeanor one step in a softening process that would eventually lead to my being his consort in more than just name. But as I lay down on the divan and shut my eyes, I berated myself for my weakness. Surely my resolve couldn't have begun to melt after only a few weeks in his presence?

I drifted off to sleep, no doubt assisted by the wine I had drunk earlier that evening. But at some point my eyes flashed open, as an odd thrill moved through my body.

Someone in the castle was using magic.

In the past I had been able to detect this sort of thing whenever my father cast a spell. The closest I had ever been able to come to describing the sensation was to say that it felt like standing on the deck of a ship floating on a calm sea, only to have a swell lift you up from underneath and shake your balance.

Only this swell was stronger than anything I had ever experienced before. My father's powers were greater than mine—or at least he had a great deal more practice and control—but the tidal surge of magic that swept over me now made his efforts feel small as ripples in a mill pond compared to surging ocean breakers.

I sat up and clutched the blanket against my breast as the world seemed to rock and sway around me. I had never conceived of such power, never believed it could exist in the present day's pale remnants of magic.

Somehow I swung my shaky legs over the edge of the divan and stood. The flow of magic called to me, pulled me toward it with the inexorable strength of an unfettered rip tide. I took a few tottering steps toward the door before the surge of power disappeared. With its absence, my sanity returned. What on earth had I been thinking? I wouldn't have gotten a foot past the doors to our apartments without one of the guards halting me.

I paused in the middle of the sitting room, the only break in the darkness the last glowing embers in the fireplace behind me. My breaths sounded unnaturally loud, as if I had just raced up a steep hill instead of taking a few steps across a level floor.

Who could have been summoning such powers in the blackest hours of the night? Surely no one I had yet encountered in the castle; I would have felt their abilities within a few seconds of meeting them. My thoughts cast back to that afternoon, to the oddly muffled stranger who had ridden into the stronghold with Kadar and his men. It had to have been him.

But whence he had come, and how he possessed such powers, I of course had no idea. Neither did I know what sort of spell he had cast. And as much as I longed to go forth and find the stranger and see what he had wrought, I knew that was impossible. I had gotten past the guards once, but ever since that day four men kept watch on the doors to our apartments, with more stationed at the entrance to the corridor beyond. There would be no more escapes by the Mark's consort.

I gritted my teeth and returned to my makeshift bed. Sleep was the furthest thing from my mind at that moment, but I knew I could do little else but try to reclaim my lost slumber. Whatever powers had shaken the castle that night, I would have to wait until the next day to discover their origin.

Of course I could make no mention of what I had felt to Kadar. So far I had managed to keep him blissfully unaware of my own small abilities, and I wished for matters to stay that way. At any rate, even if I had been inclined to discuss the situation, his actions prevented such a thing; he only nibbled at his breakfast before uttering a hasty farewell and leaving me alone and still engaged in front of the bedchamber mirror as Beranne finished dressing my hair.

Well, if he had a mage of unknown power secreted somewhere in the castle, I could understand his eagerness to be about his business, but his behavior still nettled me. However, I tried to maintain an aspect of airy unconcern as I rose from the dressing table and told Beranne that I wished to take a turn through the corridors. This was not so unusual a request, since the rain had kept up through the night and a trip to the market-place was quite out of the question for anyone not wishing to be soaked to the skin. And I wondered then if Kadar did know anything about the mage, or whether he was as unaware of the magic that had surged through the castle the night before as everyone I saw around me.

I could not decide which possibility was worse.

So I roamed the hallways of Kadar's stronghold, not sure quite what I was looking for, but knowing even as I went from wing to wing that my search would most likely be futile. After all, I did not expect the mysterious stranger to have been housed in one of the empty apartments reserved for visiting dignitaries, and neither did I think he would be loitering in the audience chamber or dining hall. I knew beneath the structure lay a complex warren of storerooms and what used to be a prison, although according to Beranne nothing more danger-ous than casks of wine and bags of dried peas was housed there these days.

At length I retired to my quiet tower room, where I picked up the hammers for the little dulcimer Kadar had given me and picked out a tune in a desultory fashion. While I was far from musical, the mechanics of the dulcimer fascinated me, and the Mark had seen to it that I should be given lessons several times a week. I saw no harm in the occupation. If nothing else, my attempts at mastering the instrument provided some diversion to fill up my time.

Beranne took a seat near the harp, where she pulled a piece of darning out of her pocket. She seemed to show infinite patience with my clumsy playing, but I had to admit it was difficult to make the dulcimer sound truly bad. As I plinked away, my thoughts kept worrying at the sensation of magic I had felt, and what on earth I should do about it. I didn't even know if Kadar had left the castle on some other business, or whether he was still here somewhere with his unknown guest.

From the courtyard outside there came the sound of sudden shouts, accompanied by a jingle of harness and the unmistakable staccato beat of many horses' hooves. At once I abandoned the dulcimer and went to the window to see what the commotion might be.

A large company rode into the courtyard, their banners brave even in the driving rain. I saw the silver and sable of the Sedassa family colors, accompanied by sky-blue flags of truce and another set of banners in green and gold with a device that looked halfway familiar, although I couldn't recall in that moment whose it was. I did, however, immediately recognize the tall figure who rode at their head.

My brother Thani had come to North Eredor to rescue me.

~ CHAPTER SEVEN ~

He had not come alone. The green and gold banners were from the house of Gahm, and Lord Senric himself rode at Thani's side.

Their arrival threw the castle into a frenzy, as I found when I descended the stairs from the music room, my heart pounding. Already servants had begun to run to and fro. Naturally such a large party would require accommodations, and it would be on the servants' heads if those accommodations were not ready when called for.

It seemed Kadar had not gone so far after all; he almost collided with me as I exited the staircase and began to step into the corridor. I must confess I was rather preoccupied, and not paying much mind to my direction. Of course I had hoped to hear from my family, but I had not expected my brother to come here, especially with Lord Senric in tow. What his presence meant, I couldn't begin to guess. True, Thani had been part of his household for some seven years, and the Duke had accompanied him to Marric's Rest so he might be witness to my brother's claiming of his inheritance, but that somehow didn't seem explanation enough.

Kadar caught me by the arm. "What are they doing here?"

I lifted innocent eyes to his face, which had flushed with anger. "As I have had no communication with my family, my lord, I cannot say. I'm sure if we go meet them, they'll be more than happy to explain the exact nature of their visit."

He let go of me and muttered something in the rough *corraghar* tongue under his breath. I had noticed that whenever he desired to swear he invariably did so in the language of his father's people. Perhaps he meant only to spare my delicate ears from his invective, but I found his attempts amusing, considering I had grown up on a working vineyard and so had been introduced to some of the more colorful curses at a fairly tender age, thanks to the seasonal workers who came to harvest the grapes. But no doubt Kadar did all he could to ignore my rather plebeian beginnings.

As they had arrived under the blue flag of truce, there was little Kadar could do save meet my brother and Lord Senric in the audience chamber and see how matters progressed from there. While their company had appeared large—some fifty men or so—it was not of a size to offer any real threat. Most likely their number had been chosen to give an impression of how much more Sirlende could throw in North Eredor's direction if provoked.

Kadar led me down the aisle to the two high seats on the dais. His hand was a firm weight on my forearm, a not-so-subtle reminder to both me and our visitors that whatever they might have to say, I was still legally his wife.

That he had chosen the audience chamber for this confrontation was not lost on me. The simple courtesy due a member of his wife's family and an exalted guest such as Lord Senric normally dictated a more intimate meeting in one of the smaller receiving rooms, where we could have sat down and taken some refreshment. Moreover, both my brother and the Duke were still soaked from their ride through the rain, their wet hair plastered to their foreheads and their cloaks dripping on the stone floor.

But such niceties had apparently been ignored in the face of the Mark's displeasure. If either Thani or Lord Senric was annoyed by such high-handed treatment, they did not show it. My brother looked a little grim, but I could see no emotion at all in the correct, impassive lines of the Duke's face.

"My lords," Kadar said, after a significant pause.

Both Thani and Lord Senric bowed—if not very deeply. Kadar's mouth thinned.

My brother spoke. "Your Highness, I have come on behalf of the Sedassa family, and indeed the Imperial court itself, to right the wrong that has been done my sister."

"'Wrong'?" The Mark sat up a little straighter and cast a look of practiced confusion in Thani's direction. "What wrong is this of which you speak?"

I saw my brother set his jaw and couldn't help but wince a little. I knew that expression all too well; it meant he was angry and likely to grow much angrier, even though he was doing his best to conceal those emotions.

He said, "I will leave aside for now the injuries done to Lady Laranel's retainers, as they suffered nothing more than a few bumps on the head and are fully recovered. But if you think that the Sedassas will countenance such an affront as the kidnapping of one of their own from her bed in the middle of the night, only to force her into an unlawful marriage—well, then, I think you do not know much of us at all."

Truthfully, I had not expected Thani to state the matter quite so baldly, but if nothing else the exalted presence of Lord Senric seemed to indicate my family had a good deal of support in Sirlende for attacking Kadar on his own ground.

"I fail to see what is so unlawful about it," the Mark replied, his tone indicating nothing but puzzlement at Thani's strong words. Part of me wanted to laugh at his disingenuousness. I wondered briefly if he had been taking lessons in acting from some of Tarenmar's players. "Perhaps we have been a bit precipitate, but love is often impetuous, is it not?"

Thani looked directly at me. "You're very silent, Lark—which is quite unlike you. I would like to hear what you have to say about the situation."

I opened my mouth to speak, only to find my throat dry, the plea I had thought I would make for Kadar to release me from this ridiculous marriage somehow strangled within me. I felt the weight of Lord Senric's dark eyes on me, puzzled yet concerned. Why could I not say the words I had been practicing for the past month?

Beside me Kadar shifted in his chair. His hand closed around mine, warm and heavy. Was he trying to warn me...or was he attempting to offer some sort of comfort?

My brother did not miss the gesture, I could tell. His voice somewhat harder, he remarked, "I can see my sister fears to speak her mind freely in front of you. Understandable, I suppose. Very well. Then let me be blunt, your Highness. The Sedassa estate is prepared to turn over the sum of ten thousand gold crowns for her safe return. I believe that should compensate you for any inconvenience you might suffer at the loss of your consort."

A gasp I couldn't quite hold in escaped my lips. I had known the Sedassa estate was one of the richest in Sirlende, but until that moment I hadn't quite understood the magnitude of the wealth my family had at their disposal. Especially since my father had steadfastly refused to touch any of that money, and throughout my childhood our fortunes had depended on each year's harvest, not the Sedassa riches.

Kadar's fingers tightened on mine, but he kept his gaze fixed forward. "A lofty sum for used goods, don't you think? Even if I did agree to send her back with you, what man would want her now?"

"I would." Lord Senric stepped forward to stand shoulder to shoulder with my brother. His gaze was level, direct and unflinching. "I would be honored to take her for my wife—if she will have me."

It would have been difficult to say who was more dumbfounded by this pronouncement, Kadar or myself. He released my hand as he abruptly stood, while I could only remain rooted in my chair, amazed that one of the greatest lords in Sirlende had offered the disgraced Sedassa daughter an honorable way out of her predicament.

"I would like a word with my wife," Kadar said, placing particular emphasis on that last word. "You are wet, your lordships, and no doubt wearied from your ride. My servants will see that you are settled."

"That is not an answer," my brother replied, and crossed his arms.

"No, it is not. But I would advise you to see to your comfort. It would not do for you to catch a fever because you lingered too long in those wet clothes."

He clapped his hands, and Althan appeared as if by magic, bowing and pointing toward the wing where the guest chambers were located.

I finally found my tongue. "Do go," I said. I could not quite meet the Duke's eyes. "It's silly to stay in those wet things. We will talk more later."

"Eminently sensible, as my lady always is," Kadar chimed in. "You are in good hands with Althan here. We will send word when we desire a further audience."

And he took me by the arm and raised me from my seat, then led me away from Thani and Lord Senric, both of whom appeared as if they couldn't quite understand what had just happened. Kadar seemed disinclined to make the full trek back to our apartments, and instead took me into a nearby chamber whose main purpose appeared to be storage for furniture that hadn't found a home anywhere else in the castle.

As he shut the door behind us, I said, "It's a princely sum. Probably far more than I am worth."

At once Kadar came to me and took my hands in his. "No, it is not, not even if it were ten times as much."

I somehow doubted that, but somehow I found I had little strength to protest. Still, I deliberately untwined my fingers from his before clearing my throat. "Surely you cannot hope for any future cooperation from the Imperial court if you turn down this offer. What good would I be to you then?"

He did not respond immediately, but moved a few paces away, as if our proximity had become painful to him. Golden eyes hooded, he asked abruptly, "What is this Lord Senric to you?"

"The Duke?" I repeated, taken a little off-balance by the brusque question. "I—well, that is, we were in one another's company as we traveled from his lands to my family's estate. And my brother has been part of his household for the past seven years."

"And?"

"And nothing." Perhaps I should have told him I was as startled by the Duke's offer as he. Oh, he had been gracious and kind during our journey, and I had fancied that several of the glances he'd sent in my direction were more than a little admiring, but that had been the extent of our interactions. Surely it seemed a great leap to go from exchanging pleasantries and comments on the weather or the roads to offering marriage.

"Did you have hopes of marrying him, this lord who is twice your age?"

"I don't see how that is any concern of yours."

"It is my concern because I have made it so. I want to know why Lord Senric, a widower who could have had his pick of many other more eligible ladies, decided to make this magnanimous offer."

I frowned at Kadar, who matched me scowl for scowl. Surely I was flattering myself to think he might be jealous. "Then I think you must ask him, for I fear I can give you no satisfactory answer."

"I believe his Grace would not be inclined to confide in me."

"Then I suppose you must be doomed to ponder the matter yourself."

The room was dim, lit only by one small window. In the half-shadow Kadar's eyes gleamed, feral as the hunting cats that roamed the hills on Marestal's borders back in my homeland. "You think I should take the settlement."

Persuading him to accept the ransom seemed the most reasonable solution. True, the Duke was much older than I, but he was one of Sirlende's greatest lords, honorable, kind, handsome in his own fashion. Again, though, I experienced that odd dryness in my mouth, that unlooked-for hesitation. After weeks of longing for nothing more than my freedom, why did I now want to clutch my prison's bars more closely to me?

And then I recalled that swell of power from the night before, the rich surge of magic being performed. How could I ever bring myself to leave with such mysteries yet unanswered? No one with mage-born blood could willingly turn away from such a puzzle.

"You hesitate," he said. "Why?"

Another pause, while I waged war with the conflicting desires in my heart. Oh, why had Thani come today of all days?

Why not tomorrow, or even a week hence? Perhaps then I would have had enough time to discover the identity of the mage who had sent that ripple of power across my consciousness.

Of course I could never confide in Kadar, and so I knew I must come up with a plausible reason to turn away from the prospect of freedom. I managed a brittle laugh and said, "Do you think I am eager to trade one set of chains for another? One husband I do not love in exchange for another? I fail to see the bargain in that."

His lips thinned at my words. Surely he couldn't have deluded himself into thinking I was in love with him, but even so he probably was not pleased to hear the truth stated so baldly. "You would be closer to your home and your family if you went with the Duke."

"Some of my family," I admitted. "But my true home is in South Eredor, and an almost equal distance separates Duke Senric's lands from the city where I was born. One exile is like enough to another, I should think."

A measuring stare then, as if he were trying to use those wolfish eyes of his to penetrate my very soul. What he saw, I could not say, but after the space of a few heartbeats he said, "There is something you are not telling me, but no matter. I daresay I will learn the truth of your decision soon enough— and in the meantime I will admit that I am glad of the choice you have made."

If only I could tell him he had figured in that decision very little. But such a comment would have wounded his pride and only led to questions I did not wish to answer. I met his gaze as squarely as I could and said, "I think I should speak to my brother now."

At least Kadar had shown the proper respect for Thani's rank as the Duke of Marric's Rest and had housed him in the finest of the castle's guest chambers. Here, as in my own apartments, the walls were painted in bright frescoes. Warm draperies of wool velvet blocked out any wandering drafts, while a cheery fire blazed in the hearth.

My brother had changed out of his wet things into a formal doublet of deep wine-colored wool, and his damp hair was combed back off his forehead. These improvements in his comfort seemed not to have enhanced his mood, however; he frowned as I entered the room and said without preamble, "What on earth were you thinking, Lark?"

His disapproval hurt only a little less than my father's would have, but I said mildly enough, "Things are not as clear-cut as you might think."

"Indeed? Perhaps you should enlighten me. Are you saying Kadar did not have his men kidnap you from your bed?"

"Erm...no."

"And that he did not marry you against your will?"

"Well, I—"

Thani turned away from me to grasp the fireplace poker, then jabbed at the logs with unnecessary force, as the fire was burning away quite happily. Perhaps he was stabbing the logs because he couldn't do the same to Kadar. "So if he did kidnap you, and did force you to marry him, then perhaps you can explain to me why you could not speak up for yourself, urge him to abandon this madness and let you go free."

I made a helpless little gesture. "It is not so easy as that." Once we had been very close, close as a brother with a sister more than five years his junior could be, but he had changed a great deal during his time in Sirlende, and I felt I did not know him as well as I used to. Surely it was that awkwardness which tied my tongue now.

His face flushed a little. He appeared to find a small section of the carpet particularly fascinating as he asked, "Am I to understand that you are no longer a maid?"

For a few seconds I couldn't quite grasp what he was asking. Then I shook my head, even as a rush of blood heated my cheeks. "No, that is not the situation at all. That is—he has not touched me."

My brother's expression cleared at once, and he straightened. I could almost see the burden lifting itself from his shoulders. "Then he has no claim on you at all. The marriage will be dissolved. We can leave this place tomorrow, if you will but convince him to take the settlement and let the matter go."

His tone left little room for argument, but argue I must. I did not recall him being this high-handed, but he was now a duke, a man of great power. Be that as it may, I knew I must state my case as persuasively as possible.

Perhaps some small part of me still longed for escape. I knew, however, that I could not go without learning who had cast that spell the evening before, or discovering how Kadar had somehow managed to bring a person of such abilities into his service.

I said simply, "Thani, someone here is using magic."

My words brought him up short, as I had expected they would. His eyebrows lifted, and he took a few strides toward me before demanding, "How do you know this?"

"Because I could feel it, just as I always sensed when Father cast a spell back home. Only this is stronger...so much stronger," I added, in a voice barely above a murmur. Even to recall the swell of that magic now was to shock me with its power. Indeed, I wondered how the other inhabitants of the castle had been able to ignore the strength of that magical wave, blind to such things as they might otherwise be.

"Good God," he said, his face paling.

"You see? How can I leave now, without knowing who might be wielding these powers, and why?"

"Because it's far too dangerous! We must get you out of here, tell someone—"

"And whom would you tell? The Emperor, who like as not would put me to death once he learned I possessed magical powers myself?"

He gave an impatient shake of his head. "I could go to Father."

"Because he could do more?" I stepped closer to my brother and laid a beseeching hand on his arm. "Thani, do you not see what a unique position I occupy here? It must have been obvious to you that Kadar has no desire to let me go. As his consort, I have a far greater chance of discovering who this wielder of magic is, and how he came to be in the Mark's service. If I leave, then we will be as much in the dark as we are now, and worse, because we will have incurred Kadar Arkalis' enmity. Do you really want to be at odds with someone who has a mage of such power at his disposal?"

"How much power?"

"I do not know for certain. But what I felt was certainly more powerful than Father. More powerful than Father and I put together and doubled, I think."

Again my brother shook his head, only this time in wonder and worry. "I cannot leave you in such danger. To have my sister be a spy—"

"Who else?" I asked. However precarious my position, however great the chances I might be discovered, I knew I had to find out who this mage was and try to learn what Kadar's plans for him might be. A man who did not scruple at kidnapping the Crown Princess of Sirlende might have very little to restrain him once he had control of powers beyond those that any other leader on the continent commanded.

"Who else, indeed." Thani ran his fingers through his still-damp hair and sighed. "I don't like it at all. But I see you are not to be dissuaded."

"If it were someone else and not your own sister, you would see the logic in the situation. If there is only one person suited to a particular task, you let them do it. Correct?"

"Correct."

He looked very weary then, and I realized he must have been riding through the rain all day to reach Tarenmar by nightfall. I reached out and gave his hand an encouraging little squeeze. "Come, you must be hungry, and I know the cooks are preparing quite a feast for you. We can fetch Lord Senric on the way downstairs."

"The Duke," my brother said heavily. "And what are we to say to him, after he lent his support to this venture, and went so far as to offer for your hand?"

My heart quailed a little at the thought of facing Lord Senric and informing him that I had chosen to stay in North Eredor, but I knew it must be done. He deserved that much, even if I could not tell him the entire truth. For while my brother might discuss magic in a somewhat rational fashion, as one who had grown up with it around him, I did not trust the Duke to do the same, no matter how kind and sensible he might otherwise seem. He was Sirlendian, and so raised in the same prejudices and blind hatreds as the rest of his countrymen.

"I shall talk to him," I told my brother. "It's the least I can do."

As feasts went, I cannot say it was the most comfortable of evenings, although the cooks had done their best, given such short notice. A pang went through me as I saw how Kadar's eyes lit up when I entered the hall, my brother on my right side and Lord Senric on my left.

I summoned a smile for Kadar, as all were watching us and such behavior was expected of me. Somehow, though, I wished I could take him aside, tell him what I had felt the night before, and ask for the truth of the situation. Oddly enough, I had little appetite for the lies I knew I must tell this night and in the coming days, even though logic told me he was not to be trusted, not a man who would steal a woman from her bed in the middle of the night and force her into marriage. Never mind that he had treated me honorably since then, had shown himself to be a good and steady lord to his own people.

No, I could not allow myself to think such things, or I would surely say more to him than I ought.

We took our places at the high table. I sat at Kadar's left, with my brother next to him on the right and Lord Senric one place beyond. Despite my current unsettled state, I was amused to see that the Mark wished to keep some distance between the Duke and myself, although what he thought we would have done or said, there in plain view of everyone, I couldn't begin to imagine.

At least Kadar seemed to be on his best behavior. Perhaps my assurances I would remain with him in North Eredor had helped to mellow his mood. Whatever the reason, he managed to converse quite cordially on that year's wheat crop and to speculate as to the harshness of the coming winter, and in general behaved so unexceptionally that several times I saw my brother's eyebrows assume a puzzled tilt. Perhaps Thani had been expecting a bit more ranting and raving. Some would have called Kadar mad for attempting to kidnap the Crown Princess of Sirlende, but I knew he was not mad. Ambitious, certainly, and ruthless when necessary, but even in our brief time together I had come to realize a quick, restless intelligence lay behind all his actions.

At length servants came to clear away the remnants of the roasted elk and meat pies and honey-laced tubers. There would be no dancing tonight, but musicians did play quiet tunes in the background as stronger after-dinner drinks were brought out to supplement the wine we had consumed with our food.

I allowed myself a few sips of the strong honey-flavored methlyn—to give me strength, I told myself. I knew I must speak with Lord Senric, and this seemed to be the most likely time for it. Turning to Kadar, I murmured, "I would have private speech with the Duke."

His brow darkened. "Why?"

"Because I know I must refuse his generous offer, and I do not wish to keep him waiting for my answer."

At once Kadar's face cleared, and I felt him reach under the table to touch my hand. His fingers wrapped around mine for a few seconds before he released them and nodded. "Now?"

"After the hall is cleared, and everyone has gone. Ask if he would stay behind and speak with me."

He said, "Of course," and leaned over to my brother and spoke a few brief words to him. Thani's mouth tightened, but it appeared he did pass the message on, for he said something under his breath to Lord Senric, who gave one brief nod.

At length Kadar gave the signal for the hall to be emptied, and everyone rose from their seats and made their way to the exit. A few curious glances were cast in my direction as I lingered in my place and Kadar left me behind, but of course no one dared to inquire why I should stay there without him. At length only the Duke and I remained in a hall that felt larger and draftier than it had a few minutes earlier. He stood, and I did the same.

"So," he said.

"So," I replied. Perhaps I should have waited to have this conversation. That way I would have had more time to devise a kinder way to refuse him.

"You are staying."

I glanced up at him in some surprise. His face wore only a weary sort of resignation, with none of the surprise my brother had betrayed when I told him I wished to remain in North Eredor.

"Am I so transparent, then?"

He smiled, albeit a little grimly. "I am not blind, my lady. I see how the Mark looks at you. Such a man would not easily give up his prize."

Was that how they all saw me—as a piece in a game of Castles, to be captured or traded or sold off as it pleased them? Even the Duke, for all his pleasant mien, seemed to think nothing of asking for me as one might a piece of shopworn goods that nevertheless still held some value.

My tone was perhaps a little harsher than I intended as I replied, "You seem very certain that I had no say in this decision."

For the first time he appeared less than calm. The lines around his eyes deepened, and he stared down at me as if at a stranger. Then again, did he really think his brief acquaintance with me was enough to inform him of my character?

"Did you?" he asked, his tone gentle enough, though the words were not.

Did he consider my decision a blow to his pride, that the sister of the man he had taken into his household chose to remain with the barbarian who had kidnapped her? It was a question I would never ask. "You may not understand me," I said, "but yes, I did ask to remain in the North."

A flicker in the dark eyes then, before he looked away from me, his jaw hard. "I will not pretend to understand what has happened here, but it is not my place to comment further. If you have made your peace with the situation, then there is nothing more to be said."

The cold anger in his voice helped to coil the excellent dinner I had just finished into an uncomfortable knot in the pit of my stomach. I wished there were something I might tell him to mend the rift my words had caused, but somehow I knew there was nothing I could say. Still, I couldn't help blurting, "Your Grace, I—"

"We have said enough, I think. Thank you for your hospitality, my lady, and thank your husband as well for the accommodations he has provided."

Lord Senric bowed then, and left me alone in the hall. I stood in one place for a long time, as the candles burned ever lower and the servants returned to remove the last of the glasses and wipe down the long tables. I saw no point in remaining there any longer, and so I made my slow way back to the apartments I shared with Kadar.

He sat at his work table, a clutter of books and papers around him, but as I entered the room it seemed clear enough to me he hadn't been paying much attention to any of them. His chin was propped on his hands as he stared off into the distance, and he stood at once as I shut the door behind me.

"Everything settled?"

"As well as it can be," I replied, and again I felt that worried knot in the depths of my stomach. The puzzled anger in Lord Senric's eyes haunted me, and I no longer knew whether I was doing the right thing by remaining here. Perhaps I should have followed Thani's counsel and allowed our father to sort out the business of Kadar's unknown mage.

He came to stand a pace or two away from me. "There will be no further trouble?"

By the narrowing of his eyes, I guessed he was concerned by the apparent alliance between my brother and the Duke, and what it might mean for North Eredor. The northeast marches of Marric's Rest were not so very far from the border. For some reason I felt compelled to put his fears at rest, and said, "If by 'trouble' you mean my relations interfering, then no, I doubt there will be any more trouble. My brother thinks I am mad, and Lord Senric is less than pleased to have been led on this snipe hunt, but I misdoubt that is a cause for war. If I had to predict the future, I would guess they will have a most uncomfortable ride back to Sirlende, one in which my brother will wish to expound at length upon the folly of younger sisters, and the Duke will desire to comment upon my questionable judgment. But because they are both too well-mannered to say such things to one another, they will instead spend most of the return journey being studiously silent."

This speech elicited a hearty laugh from Kadar, who then said, "Much would I like to be there to see it, my lady, just to verify your judgment of their character. But I do find I have more important matters which tie me to Tarenmar."

His gaze lingered on my lips as he said this. Rather than being alarmed by such attention as I might have been only a fortnight ago, instead I only felt a deep wave of weariness. I did not want to bandy words with him. I wanted only to go to sleep and forget this day had ever happened.

My silence must have told him something of my mood, for his expression sobered. His tone quite formal, he said, "But it seems my lady has had a trying day. Shall we retire for the night?"

I nodded, thankful he had not attempted to continue the conversation. It was not until I had laid myself down on the divan some time later and drawn the covers up to my chin that I reconsidered his previous statement. There had been a ring of truth in his words when he said he had important matters keeping him here in his capital. But was I really to be counted among those concerns...or had he been speaking instead of the mage who even now must be sequestered somewhere in the castle?

I knew better than to ask.

～ CHAPTER EIGHT ～

Thani and Lord Senric rode out the next morning, at an hour just late enough not to be construed as overtly rude. Their leave-taking was awkward at best. The Duke barely bowed to me, and Thani gave me a quick, rough hug before murmuring in my ear, "Write to Father."

I knew I wouldn't; for one thing, a letter was too chancy a means of communicating such vital information. Perhaps my brother, now used to life in the Duke's household, had forgotten that not everyone had access to private couriers who could be trusted not to tamper with the contents of a letter. Kadar had his own couriers, of course, but I would no sooner give them such a note than stand up in the Hall of Grievances and announce to everyone there that I possessed magical abilities.

But I only nodded at my brother, and smiled, and lifted a hand in farewell as his company wheeled their horses about and rode out through the castle gates. The rain of the day before had stopped, but the morning light was still chancy, sun and shadow fighting for supremacy in a sky that shifted from blue to grey and back again.

Kadar took his leave of me almost at once, and I soon knew why. No sooner had I gained the sanctuary of my tower room than magic surged through the castle once again. This time I stood near a table and was able to grasp its edge to steady myself, but even so Beranne cast an askance look in my direction.

"Is there something amiss, my lady?" she asked, and made as if to set her mending aside and rise to her feet.

Of course there was, but I could never tell her that. I shook my head and summoned a wan smile. "No, not at all," I replied. "I suppose it's just that I miss my brother already."

"Ah." Her expression appeared to reflect ready sympathy, if somewhat mixed with puzzlement. "All this way, and only to stay one night? Well you should miss him."

No doubt she was attempting in her gentle way to learn exactly why Thani and Lord Senric had left so abruptly, but I worried anything I told her would only be fodder for servants' gossip. During my time in North Eredor I had grown to be quite fond of her. That fondness, however, would not allow me to loosen my tongue.

"They could spare no more time away from Sirlende," I said shortly. "My brother wished merely to reassure himself that I was well and healthy and happy."

She only said, "Ah," and returned her attention to the torn chemise which lay in her lap.

Just as well, for another pulse of magic swirled around me. I sucked in my breath and tried not to fight it, but instead to feel its strength and ride with it, the way the sailors back home would allow the breakers to bring their small boats safely to shore. That did seem to help somewhat; at least I could walk more or less normally to the chair by the window and then sit down without Beranne apparently noticing anything amiss in my movements.

Outside the sky darkened, as the clouds that had appeared on their way to breaking up somehow coalesced once more. Within the minute heavy rain began to fall, followed by a crack of thunder so loud Beranne exclaimed,

"That was close!"

Eyes narrowing, I gazed out the window at the downpour. The small leaded panes were not sealed quite as well as they might be, and I heard shouts from the courtyard below as people bolted for shelter. Lightning flashed, and again the thunder answered.

It was wrong. I knew this at once, for although I did not possess the gift of weather magic myself, my father had within him the power to summon the storms, or to send the killing fogs back out to sea where they could do no harm. This, though, somehow felt different. My father always said the safest way to perform weather magic was to learn the patterns of the air currents that surrounded oneself, to know instinctively how to work with the wind and the clouds, rather than against them. But as I sat there, my face raised to the livid heavens, I felt the wrongness of the storm, of how the roiling clouds somehow fought against the air's natural currents.

Then, as soon as it had come, the cloudburst dissipated, the sky clearing with a speed anyone must know was unnatural.

The sun broke out, causing the raindrops on the window to glitter like scattered diamonds.

"Gone already, is it?"

I turned to Beranne and nodded slowly. "It would appear so."

She smiled and went back to her mending, the quick movements of her needle catching sparks from the candelabrum sitting on the table next to her. I wondered at her placid countenance, but realized of course she hadn't felt anything wrong about that sudden storm. Just another quirk of the weather, which always was a bit unpredictable at the change of the season.

Only I knew it had been much more than that. I stood and gazed down into the rain-soaked courtyard as people began to come out from beneath overhangs and doorways and went about their business once more. No harm, really, save for some dampened hems and possibly a few ruined hairstyles for those ladies of the court who hadn't managed to reach shelter in time.

Perhaps it had been only an exercise, a flexing of a muscle in need of use. Even mages required practice, after all. But I felt a chill in my bones that had nothing to do with the drafts leaking in around the window frame, and wondered what on earth was to come next.

That night at supper Kadar seemed in high spirits, and I watched him carefully. Was he so lighthearted because he knew he no longer faced any threat from my family, or did he smile and laugh because his mage had demonstrated his powers in a very real and tangible way?

I could not ask, of course, and so ate what I could, although my appetite seemed to have deserted me, and I smiled at Kadar when the occasion seemed to warrant it. I had no way of knowing whether those smiles reached my eyes, but at least he seemed not to notice anything wrong.

Some players had come in to entertain the court with their tumbling acts and a few carefully chosen scenes from the comedies that dominated the local houses. I had never been one to find amusement in pratfalls and dancing dogs, but the rest of the court did not share my tastes. Somehow I managed to laugh in the correct places, but in truth I only wished for the evening to be at an end.

At length the entertainment concluded, and Kadar led me to our suite as he did every evening. By then we were used enough to staying out of one another's way as we prepared for sleep that we almost unconsciously wove in and out of the other's steps—he washing his face as I gathered up my bedclothes, I slipping into my warm sleeping chemise as he was occupied with removing his boots and placing his doublet in the wardrobe.

It was a good thing that Northerners stood on far less ceremony than their counterparts in Sirlende. I knew that even my brother, after years in the Duke's household, would never have agreed to fold his own clothing. But Kadar, for all his faults, had very little of pretense about him. Truly, the household rubbed along with far fewer servants than I might have imagined a royal court could. The Dowager Empress of Sirlende had, it was rumored, fifty ladies-in-waiting, and my own Queen Carinne a more modest fifteen, but apparently the consort of the Mark was expected to make do with only the one maidservant. Not that I minded, as I found it exhausting enough trying to keep the truth of Kadar's and my sleeping arrangements from Beranne and the other members of the household staff who kept our apartments clean and brought up our breakfasts.

We bade each other goodnight as we always did. To his credit, Kadar never pressed me, never tried to coax me to make our marriage true in something more than merely name. It appeared he intended to keep his promise not to force me, although I wondered how long his forbearance could possibly last. This state of affairs had gone on for more than a month. I would be a fool if I thought it could continue forever.

At any rate, I was able to lie down on the divan and pull the covers up to my chin, secure that this had been an evening much like any other. Throughout the day I had found myself worrying at the problem of the mage and the spells he'd apparently cast, but there had been no repetitions of the unnatural storm, and as evening approached I allowed myself to let the matter rest.

Sleep always came easily to me, and this night was no different. I closed my eyes and let myself slip into the darkness, comforted by the welcome oblivion of slumber.

But that serene dark tide turned into the harshest of undertows. In my sleep I gasped, fighting for air, somehow knowing it had been stolen from me. Cold washed over my limbs, dragging me down, seeking to drown me forever in a black so bottomless its depths could never be measured. I screamed, and icy water filled my mouth, choking me, crushing my lungs, devouring every bit of life and warmth and—

"Lark!"

Strong arms went around me, holding me close. Awakened from my terror, I did not stop to think it was Kadar who held me thus, only that his body was warm and reassuringly real. I clung to him, felt him stroke my hair as I burrowed my face into his shoulder and laid my cheek against the rough linen of his nightshirt.

"Was it a nightmare?" His voice sounded calm, soothing, so unlike his usual ironic drawl.

I nodded.

"Do you want to tell me?"

Truly I didn't, as if the mere act of describing the dream to him might somehow give it a life of its own. I said, my tone short, the words muffled by his shoulder, "Drowning. The ocean."

"Ah, well, I can guess that would be unpleasant." He lifted a tangled curl from my brow and added, "But as we are a good three hundred miles from the sea, I believe you have little to worry about."

I almost pointed out that while we were very far from the ocean, the lake just outside our window offered ample opportunity for drowning. But I held my tongue and instead wondered at how it could feel so good to have the strength of his shoulder against my cheek, the warmth of his arms around me.

I told myself it was only because I would have welcomed any human contact at that moment, even Kadar Arkalis'. Although the lingering dregs of my nightmare had begun to fade away, I could not quite dispel that sensation of inexorable, icy death. I shivered.

"Still cold?"

"A—a little." How I wished my voice hadn't shaken. I added, trying not to sound too piteous, "Perhaps if we stirred up the fire?"

"I have a better idea than that."

And he pulled me closer as he stood, lifting me, blankets and all. He carried me into his bedchamber and pulled back the hangings on the bed before depositing me therein.

At once I sat up, spluttering a little and kicking my unneeded bedclothes aside. "A transparent ploy, my lord! Surely you do not believe I will stay here!"

"Yes, I do," he replied, his expression amused. "Dear wife, this is no attempt to ravage you. Two bodies are warmer than one, and when the hangings are closed, it is quite cozy in here. You have my word I will not touch you—at least, not intentionally. I cannot speak for what I might do in my sleep. Tanira used to complain that I kicked a good deal."

The casual mention of his former mistress only served to increase my ire. Did he honestly expect me to sleep in the bed he had shared with that woman? Without bothering to reply, I reached out and prepared to haul myself off the edge of the bed.

His hand clamped down on my wrist. "You seem quite recovered."

"Yes, I am." I jerked my arm free of his grasp. "Please do me the courtesy of not manhandling me like that. I will do very well to return to the divan."

He gave me a careful, measuring look. "What are you so afraid of, Lark?"

"Afraid?" I repeated, my blood boiling anew at the question. "I am afraid of nothing!"

"Are you? Because it seems to me your behavior would suggest otherwise. I have already given you my word that I shall not touch you. Do you believe that counts for nothing? Or is it that you do not trust yourself?"

Oh, he was impossible. To suggest I would fling myself at him, merely because we shared the same bed? "You flatter yourself, my lord."

"Perhaps I do. It is true that I have a good deal of experience with women throwing themselves at me. Perhaps I do you a disservice by expecting the same of you."

"More than a disservice," I replied. "At any rate, I'm not sure there would be room for me in this bed, as you and your vanity seem to take up a good deal of space."

He laughed then. The dim candlelight seemed to twinkle in his gold-colored eyes. "You may have a point. But look—do you not feel better? Tell me I have at least distracted you."

That was true enough. The heat of anger had done excellent work in dispelling the last shivers of my nightmare. "Perhaps."

"Then do me the service of staying. It could be that it is I who will next need comforting after a bad dream."

I fought to keep my lips from quirking. It would not do to show that he had come very close to making me laugh. "The Mark of Eredor admits to having bad dreams?"

"On occasion, and particularly if I have had cheese too close to bedtime."

I heaved an exaggerated sigh, and, without immediately replying, drew the covers on my side of the bed back and slid beneath them. "I will stay—although I did not see you eat any cheese at all tonight."

"I thank you for your solicitude." He, too, climbed beneath the sheets and blankets, then leaned over and blew out the candles on his bedside table before drawing the hangings closed.

It was very dark then, but, as Kadar had promised, I was warmer in the bed's confines than I had been on the divan, even positioned as it was in front of the hearth. I lay on my back and closed my eyes, trying to ignore the movements of the bed as he shifted his weight, or the way the heat of his body seemed to flow out from him, surrounding me in its warmth. Several hand-spans separated us, and yet he seemed so very close.

"Goodnight, Lark," he said.

"Goodnight, Kadar," I replied.

I closed my eyes and willed myself to sleep. What else could I do? Surely it was a kind of madness which had led me to think, only a second or two before he spoke, that I would have liked to reach out and twine my fingers in his, feeling the comfort of his touch as a shield against the darkness.

Kadar's touch, comforting? Perhaps my brother was right in thinking I had taken leave of my senses...

The Mark was gone when I awoke, which was strange, both because I was not normally such a heavy sleeper that I would slumber uninterrupted while someone got ready for the day in the same chamber, and also because we usually, with a few notable exceptions, shared the morning meal before he left to go about his duties.

Feeling unaccountably nettled, I clambered out of the tall, unfamiliar bed and drew on a dressing gown. My irritation grew when I emerged into the main chamber of our suite and saw the remnants of a hurried breakfast on Kadar's work table.

At least he had left me some tea. I poured its lukewarm remnants into the unused mug on the tray and sipped at the liquid, trying to tell myself it was of little concern to me what Kadar did with his time. Surely he was under no obligation to break his fast with me. After all, sleeping as chastely next to one another as a brother and sister might did not exactly signal a sea change in our relationship.

Why, then, did I feel betrayed?

Luckily, Beranne appeared soon afterward with my bath, and the preparations for the day helped take my mind away from that curious sense of desolation, as if I had lost something I only realized I possessed after it was already gone.

It was a day of audiences in the Hall of Grievances. No matter where Kadar had taken himself to, he must surely appear for that. I wore a gown of dark crimson he had once commented particularly upon, and garnets glinted from my neck and ears. Usually I did not worry overmuch as to what I wore; Beranne took very good care of my wardrobe, and of course my feminine vanity was pleased to have such lovely things at my disposal, but one gown seemed to me good as another. Today, however, I found I wanted to make a particularly good impression, as if by thus arraying myself I could force Kadar to take notice of me.

Foolish, of course. A few weeks ago I would have given anything to avoid the Mark's notice, and now I sought to draw it to me?

I did not have the time to ponder the imponderable, for he appeared just as I approached the Hall. As was his habit for these audiences, he had taken some care with his own appearance, and was impeccable in a dark green doublet with the familiar silver circlet holding his hair back from his forehead.

But even as we seated ourselves I saw a certain restlessness in his manner, a distance most unlike him. Hitherto he had always treated these audiences with the utmost gravity and attention, and I had followed his example. Today, though, his judgments seemed peremptory, as if his thoughts were very far away. Luckily he made no ruling that I disagreed with, or I would have felt compelled to speak, but still, it was most unlike him. And afterward he dismissed himself almost at once, leaving me to make the ritual closing comments.

If we had been more intimate, perhaps when I saw him later at dinner I would have commented on his behavior, or at least attempted to divine why he acted in such a way. We were man and wife in name only, though, and I occupied a precarious enough position as it was. I said nothing during the meal save the commonplaces all people exchange during such occasions.

I had sensed no workings of magic that day, which told me little enough. Kadar's preoccupation could have everything to do with the mage hidden somewhere in the castle—or it could be due to something completely different. I certainly did not confide in him; I could not expect him to share his secrets with me.

When we retired for the night, I halfway expected him to make some protest as I gathered up my bedclothes and proceeded to arrange them on the divan as usual. But he said nothing, although I thought I glimpsed a quick twist of his mouth before he turned his attention back to removing his boots.

Some weak part of me wanted to return to the green-hung bed, to its confining warmth and the dubious comfort of Kadar's presence. Logically, I knew that was more than a little dangerous. I did not wish to give him any encouragement.

...or did I?

I took care to make sure the fire was well stoked before I lay down and drew the covers up to my chin. While my nightmare could have been caused by something else entirely, I thought it wise to ensure I would not take a chill this evening. Through the open door to the bedchamber, I heard Kadar moving about for a few more moments before the ropes supporting the mattress creaked slightly as he climbed into bed. The candlelight that gleamed through the doorway disappeared a few seconds later.

It was not full dark where I lay; the fire kept the worst of the shadows at bay. Curiously, I did not feel weary at all, though the day had been full enough. I did not close my eyes, but instead stared up at the ceiling, at the way the flickering firelight caught in the carvings there and made them seem to dance and move.

Then I felt it once more, that enormous magical tide, sweeping over me in one long, rushing wave. This time, however, it seemed to seek not to drown me, but to lift me up and bear me away on its swell.

I realized I stood, though I had no recollection of rising from the divan. My dressing gown lay, as always, draped over the back of a chair near the fire. I gathered up the garment and drew it on, following the insistent flood of magic. At the door I hesitated—after all, I knew four guards waited outside—but the power filled me suddenly, and I knew they were no threat.

The words were the same, the syllables and the shape of the spell. The power, though, was very different, rising from someplace outside me. Indeed, it seemed almost as though I had little agency in working the charm, but served only as a channel for a power that emanated from someplace far away. Perhaps later I would realize this more clearly and learn fear, but at the time I only reveled in my unexpected strength as I opened the door and walked calmly past the guards, whose blank stares told me they would remember nothing of my passing.

Dreamlike, the castle's corridors slid past me, dim and candlelit. I saw no one, although even at that late hour there should have still been guards and the occasional servant about. Somehow I knew to take the west branch of the main corridor, to a little-used hallway ending in a flight of stairs that led downward.

Below me was utter blackness; apparently the servants did not expect anyone to pass this way, for none of the sconces had been lit. I spoke the words under my breath, and a ball of blue light danced off the tip of my finger and positioned itself about a foot above my head. With my way thus illuminated, I began the descent.

The graceful ornamentation I had seen in other parts of the castle was nowhere to be found here; the passageway I traversed was of plain, rough-hewn rock. After walking for five or six yards, I discovered yet another stairway leading down and took it as well. All this time I could feel the magic pulling me, drawing me inexorably to it the way metal filings are pulled to a lodestone.

It was very cold. My feet, bare against the stone pavings, told me I was quite mad for undertaking such a venture. I ignored their complaints but pulled my dressing gown more closely about me, even as I followed the will o' the wisp down a long, narrow hallway, a hallway that ended unexpectedly in a prison cell.

I saw no guards, nor any other sign of life. At first I thought those thick iron bars guarded only empty space. But then there was a stirring in the darkness. Black against black, a shape moved within the recesses of the cell. I caught a glint of pale hair, followed by an odd rustling sound.

The prisoner stood. In the soft blue magic light, I saw him quite clearly—the proud-boned face, the fall of white hair. The enormous wings, pale as his hair, that swept the ground behind him.

His eyes were grey, the same cloudy shade both my father and I shared. Those eyes fastened on me, and the prisoner smiled. Magic was thick in the air between us.

"Welcome, Lark Sedassa," he said. "I've been waiting for you."

~ CHAPTER NINE ~

My heart beat once, twice, thrice. I stood very still. "You know my name."

"How could I not?"

His voice was warm, mellow as a Sirlendian horn. He spoke the common language of the continent perfectly, and yet I somehow knew it was not his native tongue.

I met those cool grey eyes, so unexpectedly familiar. "Then you have me at a disadvantage, sir."

"You may call me Ulias."

Curiously, despite his odd form, and despite the weight of power I sensed filling the cramped underground chamber, I felt no alarm, no sense of danger. The chancy light of the will o' the wisp revealed an expression of friendly curiosity, but no more.

I asked, "How do you know who I am?"

"I have known of you for some time, Lark Sedassa. There are so few left with power, so few..." His words trailed off as he shut his eyes briefly, as if against some remembered pain.

Then he shook his head, and continued. "When I was brought to this keep, I felt your presence at once. You may imagine my surprise."

His rueful smile almost brought an answering one to my lips. Stepping forward, I looked up into his face. "Why have you been brought here? And why are you imprisoned thus?"

"Ah, that." He turned away and gave a negligent flick of one finger. At once the room blazed with a light that put my poor little will o' the wisp to shame, although I could see no source for the illumination. It seemed to come from everywhere, as if the very stones themselves pulsed with radiance.

Yes, he was a prisoner, but his cell was quite a luxurious one. I saw a folding wooden camp bed heaped with blankets and sleeping furs; the metal goblet and plate that had most likely held his evening meal were as fine as those used on Kadar's table itself. A small wooden table bore a stack of books and a few pieces of paper.

"You see how they try to appease me," Ulias said, with an offhand wave toward the contents of his prison. "I wish I could send my compliments to the cook, as the roast joint this evening was particularly fine."

His manner confused me, as did his situation. I knew I had not imagined the power flowing out from him; indeed, I still felt it as a warm pressure against every inch of my body. "But surely—surely you could easily escape? Your powers—"

"—cannot help me here," he broke in. He turned his hands palm up, and I saw dreadful red welts crisscrossing them. "The bars, you see."

"The bars?" I repeated stupidly.

"Cold iron, dear girl. Anathema to my kind."

"Your kind?" Of course I knew he could not be a mortal man, not with those wings, but I had never heard tell of any being matching his description.

Another of those shadows crossed his features. "A tale for another time. Suffice it to say your husband has utilized the only method that could keep me imprisoned. That is, his pet mage has."

Again I could only repeat his words. "Pet mage?" Did Ulias mean there was someone else with magical abilities working for Kadar? But I knew I had sensed only Ulias' presence, felt only his power.

"A man named Maldis. Unpleasant fellow."

I had never heard of such a person, but of course that meant nothing. Kadar kept his own counsel...as did I. "I do not know this Maldis."

"I didn't expect you would. The Mark has taken efforts to conceal his presence, for obvious reasons."

His mild demeanor lent me a little courage. It required only a few more paces for me to close the distance between us. I reached out to touch the bars.

"I wouldn't," Ulias warned, but I paid him no heed. How could iron hold any terrors for me? I had handled my mother's cast-iron cook pots back home, and the fireplace tools in my suite were composed of iron as well.

But as soon as I laid my fingers on the bars, a flash of white-hot pain lanced its way up my arm, and I jerked my hand back. Biting my lip, I looked down and saw faint reddish stripes painting the pale flesh on the inside of my hand. They throbbed, each pulse seeming to mock my folly.

"You see."

I glanced up to find his cool grey eyes watching me with a sort of resigned concern. "That's not ordinary iron."

"No."

"Then what is it? And how did Kadar come by it?" For all his talents, dubious or otherwise, I couldn't quite see the Mark concocting an alloy that would harm only those with magical abilities.

"This Maldis. A dangerous man, one who has discovered a way to pervert magic."

A shiver worked its way up my spine. I tried to tell myself it was only the chill from the flagstones underfoot, but I knew that was a lie. "I don't understand."

"I didn't expect you to, child."

If anyone else had called me a child, I would have bridled at his words. But although I knew next to nothing of this Ulias, somehow I sensed he was far older than he looked. At the very least, his powers so far outstripped mine that he had every right to address me thus.

He added, before I could speak, "I cannot answer all your questions tonight. You stole past the guards and came here unremarked, but your husband may note your absence if you stay away too long."

Somehow I could not bring myself to admit to this mild-voiced creature that Kadar and I did not share a bed. At any rate, that counted for little. If the Mark were roused in the middle of the night and went out into the main chamber of our suite, he would see at once that I was not asleep on the divan as I should be...unless Ulias had cast some sort of illusion to make him believe I was still there.

But I found I must ask one question. "Why did Kadar bring you here?"

Ulias smiled, but somehow in his eyes I saw the sorrow of uncounted ages. "He is ambitious, your husband."

"That is not an answer."

"Oh, but it is. Go now, Lark, and know this is not our last meeting. I will summon you again when I believe it is safe. I called you here tonight because Maldis left the castle earlier today, but I cannot say when such an opportunity will present itself once more."

His tone told me he would countenance no further conversation. For myself, it seemed every answer he had given me spawned yet more questions, like the many-headed serpent of legend who grew three more heads for every one cut off. But I knew I had little choice in the matter. Ulias' will had summoned me here, and it seemed it was now his will that I should go.

Still, I felt as if I should make some protest. "You must let me help you. If Maldis is gone, there must be something I can do. Perhaps if I wrapped my hands in a blanket to protect them, or stole the key from the guards—"

Another smile. "Your courage does you credit, but it is not yet time for me to make such an attempt. As curious as your husband is about me, I must confess to wishing to know more about him. He is clever, and quite gifted at finding hitherto under-utilized resources. No, I am comfortable enough here for now. Do not trouble yourself with me, Lark. I merely wished to take your measure, and learn something of you."

"And what have you learned?" I inquired. His unruffled patience mystified me. I knew I certainly would not have been so resigned, had I been in a similar situation.

"That I have an ally, and one it seems I can trust. You will not speak of this, will you?"

"Of course not."

"I thought as much. I could make you forget, if I thought you would not hold your tongue. But I am glad to find that is not necessary."

"So you can still cast spells, despite that—" And I pointed toward the bars, the pain in my fingers a reminder of their unnatural properties. Then I realized it was rather a foolish comment, since I had seen him bring the light from within the rocks only a few minutes earlier.

"Of course. They only prevent my escape. If I could not practice my magic, I would be of little use to your husband."

I shook my head. "But if that's the case, then surely you could do something else...force one of the guards to release you, or turn yourself invisible and sneak past when they bring you your supper."

He laughed then. "You have an inventive mind, Lark Sedassa. I appreciate that. But now is not the time for such gambits. As much as the Mark wishes to learn of me, I wish to study him in return."

"But—"

"Ah, the impatience of youth. Rest assured I am quite comfortable here, and have little wish at present to make any alteration in my circumstances. Go now. I will call you again when the time is right."

And I felt a gentle push, one that could only have come from him. I raised my eyebrows, and he nodded. And while under normal circumstances I might have been more than a little annoyed at being summoned and then dismissed in so summary a fashion, I thought I understood something of Ulias' motivations. Despite his powers, he must be discreet, and yet he could not miss out on the chance to meet with another mage-born soul. And while I had many more questions, I knew that for now they must wait.

Holding back a sigh, I turned, then made my way down the corridor and up the stairs, and on through the quiet corridors of the castle. Once again I saw no living soul, and no one marked my passage, save perhaps a mouse or spider lurking in a corner.

The guards had remained in their places, still blank-faced and glassy-eyed, and I slipped past them into my apartments before closing the door behind me. I wondered then if Ulias had cast the same spell to keep Kadar quiescent, and tiptoed to the bedchamber door.

The Mark was asleep, or at least gave a very good imitation of it. The faint reflected firelight from the main room gave only enough illumination for me to see his tall form huddled beneath the covers; he had not drawn the bed hangings closed. A spill of dark hair covered the pillowcase, while a faint snore drifted out to my ears.

For some reason I had the urge to laugh, but I quelled my amusement and slipped back to my own makeshift bed. As I slid beneath the blankets, I reflected on my meeting with Ulias. Yes, I had learned who the mysterious mage was—or at least, the one I had known must be in the castle—but that discovery had only spawned more questions than I could count.

What I found I wished to know most, however, were Kadar's reasons for bringing Ulias here in the first place. Yes, my makeshift husband was an ambitious sort, or he would not have attempted the gambit that resulted in my becoming his wife. But what did he hope to accomplish with a mage of such powers as his prisoner? For all his mild manner, I doubted Ulias was the sort to be easily coerced or threatened.

And this Maldis—what did he stand to gain from all this? According to Ulias, he had somehow discovered a way to twist magic to his own ends, but how he had managed to do so, and what the scope of his own abilities might be, I had no idea. Likewise, I did not know for certain why Kadar thought it necessary to keep his presence a secret, although I guessed even he would not be too eager to admit he had stooped to taking someone with forbidden powers into his employ.

Again I chafed at the realities of my situation, that Kadar and I were husband and wife in name only, with no sharing of confidences between us. With a pang I thought of my mother and father, and how, despite their apparent differences, they lived side by side in harmony—how he could make her laugh no matter how difficult her day might have been, or the way she lit up whenever he entered the room, even though they had been husband and wife for more than a quarter of a century.

No such ease existed between Kadar and myself, and so I knew I could never ask him the questions whose answers I so desperately desired.

Instead I burrowed into my makeshift bed and drew the sheets and blankets close to me. Whether it was from my own weariness or a last subtle push from Ulias, I fell into the blackness of sleep almost at once, leaving the night and its mysteries behind.

"You are the sleepy one this morning."

I opened my eyes and blinked against the pale light flooding the chamber. Kadar stood between me and the hearth, his expression amused. The heavy curtains had been drawn back to reveal a morning white with mist, so thick I could not see the lake beyond the windows. More of Ulias' handiwork, or a simple phenomenon of the lake and the autumn weather?

"I suppose I am," I replied, and pushed myself up to a sitting position. Despite my nocturnal wanderings, I was not weary at all, but something had certainly kept me abed, when normally I would have roused at the first sound from within Kadar's bedchamber.

He said, almost too swiftly, "No need to trouble yourself, my Lark. I must ride out within the hour, and I will break my fast down in the hall with my men."

"Ride out? In this?" I gestured toward the swirling mists outside. Back home in Marestal, no sailor who valued his skin would have set forth in such a fog. To do so was testing God's patience for fools. Even my father would have had difficulty dispelling such a heavy fog bank.

"It will clear soon, I misdoubt. These mists never last long. In time you will become more acquainted with this land's moods, its shifts and changes. We would none of us get much done if we allowed such things to rule our actions."

That might very well be, but something in the ghostly landscape outside the room's many-paned windows made me want to shiver. I said nothing, though, but only clutched my blankets a little closer.

Kadar paused, watching me keenly from beneath his heavy lashes. "Can it be that you might miss me?"

It was on my lips to retort that I would do nothing of the sort. However, something seemed to tie my tongue, and I only replied, "We have not spent much time together of late."

Something in his mouth softened, and I hurried along, thinking perhaps I could win some confidences from him while he thought me weakening, "That is, it seems you have been preoccupied these past few days. Is there something you would like to speak of? Have I done something to offend you?"

At once he reached down and took my hand in both of his. I thought I would flinch at his touch, but somehow his fingers were warm and comforting, even callused as they were from riding and sword practice. "Nothing, my sweet Lark. Matters of state."

I looked up at him in what I hoped was a sweetly beseeching manner. "But surely you told me the Mark's consort was supposed to live her life in service to the kingdom. How can I be a worthy companion to you if you do not confide in me?"

He hesitated then. Very slowly he pulled his hands from mine. Some of the light in his eyes seemed to die. "It is nothing you should concern yourself with—that is, I will discuss these things with you, and soon, but now is not the time. May I beg your patience, just as you have asked for mine all these weeks?"

His point could not have been more clear. Whatever his easy pleasantries, whatever the spurious camaraderie that might have arisen between us over the short course of our marriage, he still did not regard me as a true wife, and, as such, I was not deserving of his secrets.

I saw no point in arguing. Indeed, I knew if I pressed the matter, I only risked arousing his suspicions. So I bowed my head with uncharacteristic meekness and said, "Of course, my lord."

He nodded, as if satisfied, then took his leave of me and went out the door. I sat on the divan for a long while, staring into the fire.

Would it be worth it, to give myself to him in exchange for his confidences?

I feared I did not want to know the answer.

He was gone all that day. I appeared to be the only member of the castle's household who seemed overly concerned by his absence, as he had ridden out with six of his stoutest men. Despite Kadar's careless words, the fog did not lift. If anything, it grew thicker, wrapping the stone building in a layer of seemingly impenetrable dankness. More and more wood was piled on the fires, and yet nothing seemed able to pierce the damp chill that permeated the castle. Child of the warm South that I was, I found myself shivering uncontrollably, even after Beranne produced a shawl of warm, thick wool woven in intricate patterns and laid it around my shoulders.

"Stay by the hearth," she told me as she bustled about, adding more logs and stirring the coals so the fire blazed up anew. "Poor child, you're not used to this sort of thing, are you?"

Teeth chattering, I could only shake my head. I had my fingers wrapped around a mug of hot spiced cider, and while that helped a little, still I could not imagine what a winter here would be like, if it should be so cold in the first days of Novedre. "A-and the M-mark is out in it," I managed.

"You worry for him, as any wife should. But there's no need—his lordship was born and bred in the North. A little fog would never get into *his* bones. You can count on that."

Perhaps she was right. After all, I was the newcomer here. But somehow I could not quell the rising dread in my heart, as if something had gone terribly wrong, that somewhere he was lost in the fog...lost to me. If only I could have gone down to the cellars to see Ulias, perhaps I could have set my mind at rest. I'd found something oddly comforting in his presence, alien though he should have been to me. He would tell me the truth of things, whether my worries were simply dark fancies born of the fog.

That escape was not afforded me, however. The mage had been quite explicit in saying he would only call for me again when it was safe for him to do so, and since I had received no such summons, I assumed that meant such a visit would be ill-advised at present. I recalled how Ulias told me he had brought me to him because Maldis was out of the castle. Since Ulias did not call me now, while my lord was away, did that mean the dark mage lingered somewhere still in the keep?

At that thought a fresh bout of shivering wracked my frame, and Beranne made a sound of dismay. "Should I bring some heating bricks for your feet? Is the cider not hot enough?"

"No, Beranne," I said at once. "It is just me being weak. I need to work my way through this, or I shall have an even more difficult time this winter."

She shook her head. "No, my lady, you are not weak at all. Why, to have come here all alone, with no servants of your own, and having to make do in a strange land with no one you know and a husband who—" She stopped herself, red staining her round cheeks. "I mean no impertinence, my lady. But you should not call yourself weak."

Her words warmed me the way the shawl and the fire had not. "I thank you for that, Beranne." She smiled down at me, and I pressed on, asking, "But what did you mean when you began to say 'a husband who—'?"

If possible, she flushed even more deeply. "I spoke out of turn, my lady. I should not make free of my liege lord."

"Is it making free when you're speaking to his wife?"

"I—"

"Please, Beranne. I am worried about him, and somehow it makes feel better to speak of him when I cannot have him here with me. Do you understand?"

Still she hesitated, her hands knotting in the rough linen of the apron she wore over her simple brown dress. "I spoke out of turn, my lady."

"*Beranne!*"

Whether it was the ring of command in my tone—so very unlike me—or simply that she no longer wished to stay her tongue, she said quickly, "Everyone knows why you were brought here, my lady."

"And why is that?" I inquired. Once again cold inched its way down my spine, although this time I knew it had very little to do with the temperature in the room.

"Why, to ally the North with one of the great houses of Sirlende," she said simply. "Is that not the truth?"

"Yes," I replied. "But that should have been obvious enough to anyone. I certainly would not call that speaking out of turn. And do sit down. You're making me nervous, standing there and wringing your hands."

Her eyes widened, and she plopped herself down in the large chair to the right of the divan.

"There is more, isn't there?" I asked.

"It was clear enough that you had no wish to be the consort of the Mark. The whispering the morning after your wedding!"

So much for what I had thought was a neutral and correct expression during the wedding ceremony. Good thing I had never planned to be a professional gambler...or an actor. I sighed and said, "That is also true. Most young ladies of my acquaintance do not regard being kidnapped out of one's bed as an acceptable form of courtship."

"Kidnapped!" she exclaimed.

I realized then that Kadar's court hadn't been privy to quite all my secrets. Oh, well, the tarnishing of the Mark's reputation could be laid squarely at his own feet; I rather thought it high time that some of his subjects had a truer measure of his person.

"But if that's what happened, then why—" She broke off, then continued, "That is to say, why then did you stay, when your ladyship's brother and the Duke himself came to fetch you? Especially since you hadn't—" And this time she stopped herself in earnest, even going so far as to press her lips tightly together as if to prevent any betraying words from escaping.

"Since I hadn't what?"

If she had flushed any brighter, her cheeks would have glowed more hotly than the coals in the hearth. "Hadn't—that is, that your marriage is not a true one."

She might as well have slapped me across the face. I stared at her, the cup of cider growing cold between my clenched fingers, then asked quietly, "Everyone knows?"

"Oh, no, my lady," she said immediately. "That is, only I. Perhaps Narenna has her doubts, but she is a good and meek girl. She would never say anything to anyone."

Well, that was something, I supposed. I thought then of how my mother had once said it was impossible to keep anything from your servants for any length of time, and that was why she used only day help. We never had any of the scrub maids or cooks live with us, even though there was ample space to accommodate them at the comfortable house she had inherited. Most likely it was to shield my father and me, to prevent anyone outside the family from learning the truth about our magical abilities. At any rate, it seemed she had been right. And here I had thought I had done so well to trick Beranne and everyone else into thinking my marriage was not a sham.

"I suppose I must be thankful for that."

"But why, lady?"

"Why haven't I slept with Kadar Arkalis?" I asked bluntly.

"Oh, Inyanna hear her! My lady, that is between you and his Highness. No, why you stayed. And—forgive me—why you should be so worried about the Mark now, if there is nothing between you."

Most highborn ladies would have told her to mind her own business and ordered her out of the room for such impertinence. But I was not highborn—well, not by upbringing, at any rate—and I was weary of keeping secrets. Some, of course, I must hold close to my heart, but I found as I looked into her puzzled, earnest face I missed very much being able to talk to my mother, or my friend Daris, who never seemed to take anything too seriously. I wondered then what Daris would have thought of the Mark of North Eredor.

"I stayed because I saw no point in giving myself to another man as chattel, just because he was the Duke of Gahm." Her eyes widened at that remark; apparently the Duke's offer was not public knowledge. "And also because—" I hesitated, as the truth of my heart slowly revealed itself to me, "—because perhaps I have grown to be somewhat fond of your Kadar Arkalis. Don't tell him that, though. He would only hold it over my head."

"As if I would, my lady!"

"No, I suppose you wouldn't." I gave her a weary little smile and lifted my now-lukewarm cup of cider to my lips. "So you see why I worry. I know I am being foolish, and he will return late this evening with a boar or a few bucks, and would laugh to know of my concern. But that is how it is."

Looking a little startled, as if surprised by her own boldness, she leaned forward and patted my hand. "It will be all right. You'll see." But then she stopped, and pursed her lips, as if she had begun to say something and thought better of it.

I did not press her. I had revealed enough already—far too much, some would say. So I turned from her and stared into the fire, and wondered when my lord would come home.

Very late, as it turned out, so late that I had been asleep for some hours. But of course he had to walk past the divan where I lay, and for once I slept lightly. My eyes snapped open almost the second he opened the door. I sat up, straining my eyes against the darkness. The fire had burned quite low, and Beranne had snuffed the candles before she left me for the night.

"Kadar?" I asked, and wished my voice didn't sound quite so thin.

I heard his boots heavy against the wooden floor, and then he paused next to the divan. "I had hoped not to wake you."

Apparently not. What had he been up to, that kept him out during the hours when all decent folk were in their beds? "I did not sleep very well."

"No wonder," he replied, his tone light. "You've let the fire quite die down. It's cold as death in here." And he moved around to the hearth and began prodding at the coals with the poker.

"Quite a night to be out in," I said. "I thought you'd been lost in this fog."

"That?" He chuckled. "It would take more than a mere mist to keep me from finding my way home." After setting the poker aside, he turned from the fire and stared down at me. "You cannot be saying that you were worried."

I would not meet his eyes. "And what if I were?"

"How can I task you for that?" To my surprise, he knelt on the floor in front of the divan and reached out to lay one hand on mine, where it rested on top of the blankets. Usually his hands were warm, no matter what the temperature, but the dank night chill seemed to have invaded his flesh, for his icy fingers sent renewed shivers through me. At least, I assumed my shivers were from the cold. "Truly, your concern does you credit, but nothing has gone amiss, save that we brought back only four bucks when I had hoped for five."

"Only four?" I repeated, with a shaky laugh. "How will we get through the winter?"

I did not bother to mention that on all of his previous hunting expeditions, he had been back well in time for supper. Secrets, always secrets between us. I did not like it, but neither would I poke and pry like a jealous fishwife.

"Ah, now you tease me. I see you must be recovered." He gave my fingers another squeeze and then rose to his feet. "But it is, as you say, very late, and I am wearied from a long ride. We will speak again tomorrow."

"Of course," I said. What had he been up to, all those long hours?

I somehow guessed it would be a long time before I ever did know.

Despite the lateness of his arrival the night before, Kadar was gone when I awoke the next morning. Again that sensation of disappointment swept over me, although I tried to tell myself it was foolish to pin my hopes on so elusive a target as the Mark of Eredor. As for my confessions to Beranne of the previous evening, those truths seemed far less steady in the light of day. It would not do to admit what—if anything—my spurious husband had come to mean to me. It seemed quite obvious I did not mean as much to him as I thought I did.

My bad humor clung to me as Beranne came to prepare me for my day and onward as the morning hours increased, with no sign of Kadar. I tried to tell myself that I was only on edge because of my need to speak to the mage Ulias, and because I had no means of doing so. But somehow I knew that constraint had very little to do with the discontent which clung to me as surely as the mist persisted in sticking to the keep's many-paned windows.

As I could think of nothing else to do, I sought refuge in my tower room, even though I could see very little through the swirling fog. Sounds were muffled and distant, as if they somehow came to me from very far away, rather than only yards beneath my feet. I did not even bother with the dulcimer, but lingered in my chair by the window, staring at nothing as the wisps of mist dragged their ghostly tendrils past the mullioned glass.

And it was there that Kadar found me, although he did not come alone. A wriggling ball of greyish fur detached itself from his arms and scampered across the floor toward me, only to lay its head on my knee and let out a little whine.

"I thought you could use the company," he told me.

At once I knelt to stroke the little dog's head. Black eyes circled in kohl to rival a Keshiaari princess stared up at me. "She's beautiful," I breathed, and then glanced up at my husband. "That is, if she's a she."

"She is," he said. "Grishonds, we call them. Don't let the small size fool you. They are fierce hunters, and protectors."

Truly, the dog, although not much higher than my knee, did resemble nothing more than a miniature wolf. She stared up at me, mouth parted in what could only be called a smile— although it did reveal a set of quite fierce-looking teeth. "Does she have a name?"

"That is for you to decide."

Tasked with such an important decision, I stared down at the dog for a long moment. How could Kadar have known? When I was younger I had wished for a dog, but their fur quite made my mother sneeze. I'd tried to content myself with the trio of cats who hung about the house, although, truth be told, they were far more interested in chasing mice and rats than making friends with me. And now Kadar had given me the one thing I had almost forgotten I wanted.

"Tresi," I said, after considering my options. "Her name is Tresi."

"And has that name a meaning?"

I paused. It did, of course. I only worried that he might not care for its source. "Tresi was the name of Seresa of Gathmir's dog. I thought it fitting."

"Ah."

He did not ask me who Seresa of Gathmir was. I guessed he knew the story well enough, even if he had not recalled the name of the faithful dog who stayed by her mistress' side even as the Duke of Gathmir went forth to wage his wars.

I stroked the little grishond's head and gave her a reassuring pat, then stood. "Thank you, Kadar," I said. "This was a very thoughtful gift."

The golden eyes warmed a little, and somewhere inside a rush of answering heat told me I appreciated that appraising gaze far more than I should. But then he looked past me, and the smile on his lips seemed to be there because he thought it should, and not because he had intended it particularly for me. "I know you have been feeling somewhat neglected. My time, I fear, is not always my own. I though little Tresi here could help to ease your lonely hours."

Courteous words, but they did not please me. Whatever connection we had had, I sensed it beginning to slip away. The dog was a surrogate, a substitute for the man who had once seemed so ardently interested in being my husband. But now? I could not say.

None of this was Tresi's fault, so I knelt and scratched behind her ears, and couldn't help feeling a rush of affection as she leaned into my fingers, her eyes half-closed in ecstasy. An affectionate little creature, to be sure—far more affection-ate than the man who had given her to me. Was this all Maldis' doing? Had that unknown mage usurped my husband's attention to such an extent that he no longer found any need to pursue me?

Perhaps I should have been glad. I had not chosen to be part of Kadar's life; he had forced me here. And now, just as my feelings had begun to soften toward him, he had decided to direct his attentions elsewhere. I tried to tell myself it didn't matter, that I cared very little for him and had chosen to remain here only to discover the secret behind the magic surging through the castle, but while my mind thought one thing, my heart told me something very different. It is often only when we risk losing something that we begin to realize how valuable it is after all.

I found myself wanting to weep, and inwardly scolded myself for my foolishness. I had told Beranne that I had become fond of Kadar. Fond? Would that it were so simple.

Somehow I found the strength to stand up straight and meet his gaze, with a countenance I schooled to politeness and nothing else. If he wanted to keep me at arm's length, to fob me off with gifts to distract me from what he was really up to, so be it. I would not let him know how much he had upset me. "She's a lovely dog," I said. "We will get along quite well, I think. Thank you for taking the time to bring her to me."

The words were simple politeness, phrases I would have given to anyone in similar circumstances. Their impersonal nature did not escape Kadar; his mouth tightened slightly, and he replied, "I am glad. But now I must leave you—pressing business, I fear."

I did not bother to ask what the business was. I knew he would not tell me the truth. So I only nodded, and put a false smile on my face as he bowed and left the room. It was only after he had gone that I sank back down into my chair and let my fingers comb their way through the ruff at Tresi's neck, forcing myself to find some comfort in her presence, even if I could find none in my husband's.

The next day was the Hall of Grievances, and I halfway wondered whether Kadar would bother to invite me at all. He had been so distracted lately that it seemed he had no need of a wife, even a counterfeit one such as myself. But he murmured a reminder to me over breakfast before he disappeared once more, so I did my best to prepare myself, donning a gown of deep blue wool with red embroidery that the seamstresses had just finished for me and which Kadar had not yet seen. Tresi whined when she learned she was to be left alone for some time, but Beranne promised she would look after her in my absence.

Usually Kadar came to fetch me in our chambers so we could enter the Hall together. However, as the hour drew near, and I saw no sign of him, I realized I would have to go down to meet him alone. At least by this point I knew my way around the castle well enough that I could do so without his help, but still it rankled that I should have to go there without him by my side—or even without Beranne, as she had already said she would stay behind in my chambers so Tresi would not get into any mischief.

I thought it best to go somewhat early, so I would not be traversing the length of the chamber after the audience and petitioners had already been seated. However, when I arrived in the Hall of Grievances, I saw that Kadar was already there... and he was not alone. A man of middle height, with russet-blond hair, stood next to him. From his coloring, I guessed he was not a Northerner, but otherwise he was so nondescript in appearance I would have passed him by in a crowd without a second thought.

However, as the stranger turned toward me, something in his light blue eyes sent a shiver of apprehension down my back. I told myself not to be a fool, that it was silly to have such a visceral reaction to someone I had only laid eyes on for a moment.

Kadar smiled as I approached. "Ah, Lark. I am glad you came early. I would like you to meet my new advisor."

"New advisor?" I ventured. This was the first I had heard of any such a thing. Although I had not been part of the court at Tarenmar for very long, I hadn't seen much evidence of the Mark requiring an councilor, unless one counted the household advice Althan was wont to dispense.

The stranger smiled as well, but I found no comfort in his expression. No warmth touched his eyes, and the way he looked at me made me feel unclothed, although I was dressed warmly and modestly, and my new gown did not display much at the neckline.

"Yes, I thought it time I had some assistance." Kadar's smile did not wane, but something in the taut look of his mouth told me he was less than sure of my reaction. "My dear, meet Maldis of Purth."

~ Chapter Ten ~

It took every ounce of strength I possessed not to recoil, not to gasp aloud at the man's name. Somehow in my mind, when Ulias had spoken of the dark mage Maldis, I had envisioned some black-robed sorcerer, a dark-visaged conjurer straight out of legend. I had not expected such a commonplace evil as that which confronted me now.

I do not think I will much like the advice you give my husband, I thought then, even as I forced my mouth to curl into what I hoped was a natural-appearing smile. And though I wanted nothing more than to turn and run, to remove myself from the sickening gaze of those light blue eyes, I managed to extend a hand, to keep myself from gagging as he murmured something wordlessly polite and touched his fingers to mine.

In that moment I felt it, as if something cold and dank had crawled up from the sewers and wrapped itself around my flesh. Again my throat tightened in disgust, even as my mouth somehow managed to keep smiling.

And I realized something then, once I dropped my hand after the requisite number of seconds had passed. His own expression did not alter, although I wished I could tell him to stop looking at me, to direct that pale, loathsome stare elsewhere.

I had felt his power.

But he had not felt mine.

How this was so, I could not say. My father had once mentioned my sensitivity to magic, how I always knew when he cast a spell, and what kind of spell it was, and he wondered if that had something to do with my particular gift, although he had never heard tell of such a thing. So much knowledge had been lost, though, so many details as to how magic worked in general and how it worked on us in particular, that we had no way of knowing if my talent was once widespread, or whether it was something peculiar to me and me alone.

Luckily Kadar spoke then, apparently noticing nothing. "I think you will find observing the Hall of Grievances valuable, Maldis. It is one of the best ways to see what is happening in my kingdom, to see what is of importance to my subjects. I have had a chair brought for you."

He indicated a large carved seat that had been placed to the left and slightly behind his own. Not a throne, no—it appeared my own position had not been usurped. Not completely, anyway.

Not yet.

I let Kadar take me by the hand and lead me to my own throne-like chair so I could sit down. He settled himself next to me in his own seat. It was only after he did so that Maldis sat as well. So careful, so obsequious, so correct. But I knew this, as with anything else he did, was only an empty gesture. He knew the time was not right to make his move. For now he would play the courtier, the humble advisor. What his precise credentials were for such a position, I had no idea. Not that it really mattered. I guessed that he would have manufactured whatever references, whatever background he required to insinuate himself into my husband's confidences.

The chill of the night before seemed to find its way up my spine once more, spreading through me until I could barely feel my own fingers as they rested on the carved arms of my chair. I tried to tell myself that was foolish, that nothing could go awry here in the heart of the castle, with my husband next to me and the steady, gracious Althan standing only a few yards away, not as the onlookers and petitioners began to file into the room. But somehow I knew the cold flooding my body had little to do with what I saw here and now, and a great deal more with what was to come when I least expected it.

The cowardly part of me wished then that I had accepted Lord Senric's offer, had let him take me away from this place. At least if I had done so, I would not have had to face the cold malice that seemed to radiate outward from this Maldis of Purth. How Kadar could not feel it, could not see the casual evil in the man's face, I had no idea.

But he was not the only one oblivious to the malignant presence in the chamber; the common folk seated on the benches cast a few curious glances in Maldis' direction, but then almost seemed to shrug, as if to say, *Well, it is by our lord's desire that the man is here, so surely he must serve some purpose.*

That he did, but a purpose of his own, I guessed, and none of Kadar's...although he most likely had made sure that Kadar thought it was his purpose as well.

Then I had no time for further speculation, for Althan stepped forward and said the simple ritual words: "The Hall of Grievances is free to its petitioners."

The first complainant approached the dais and bowed. His objection seemed simple enough—he owned an inn near the heart of Tarenmar, and the property was located on the site that had been chosen for Kadar's pet project, the central exchange where goods and commodities could be traded.

"It is not that I can complain about losing my inn," the man said. He was probably in his fifties, but still broad and strongly built, looking more like a man who worked the land than one who spent his days behind a bar. "I was offered compensation, and, truth be told, the building needed repairs. When I was first told of this, I thought it no great thing to start over again elsewhere. But now the representative from your lordship's treasury has come to me and said that he can give me but half of what was promised, for times are lean and the money not there." He hesitated for a second or two, and added, "I told him I did not believe this was so, that an Arkalis would not seek to cheat his subjects in such a way. I thought if I came here and presented my case, you would understand that I cannot rebuild with the sum I am now offered."

Throughout this speech Kadar had listened with eyes narrowed, chin on one hand. I had seen him assume that position before, usually when thinking over some difficult conundrum. He straightened, and appeared about to speak, but then Maldis leaned forward and whispered something in his ear—what, I could not tell, for the words were hurried and muted.

Their effect on the Mark was clear enough, however; he gave a grim little nod, then addressed the petitioner. "We understand your concerns, but we must all make sacrifices during times such as these. Perhaps you will not be able to build a larger, better inn, but you will still have something to show for your efforts."

I could not believe what I was hearing. Impetuous Kadar might be—and ruthless, and uncaring at times—but I did know that he cared greatly for his subjects, took very seriously the role of the Mark as protector and champion. The careless remark had its origins in Maldis' prompting, I had no doubt. I was not so naïve that I couldn't see why the man might want Kadar to keep a tighter hold on his purse strings than he had in the past.

Without stopping to consider the repercussions of interference, I cleared my throat and said quickly, "My lord, a word—"

Kadar shifted in his seat, dark brows lowering over the golden eyes. I rarely spoke during the Hall of Grievances, as his and my opinions generally ran along the same lines. Behind him, Maldis straightened, staring over Kadar's shoulder at me. His expression was mild, but again a ripple of cold passed over me as that pale stare met mine.

Do not think of him, I told myself. *Look only at Kadar.*

And so I did, holding his gaze even as I lowered my voice and asked, "Do you think it wise to hand down such a decision when all it will do is tell your subjects that the word of their Mark is not to be trusted?"

His mouth tightened. "The treasury—"

"The treasury should be able to bear this expense, or the original sum would never have been promised. I think it more likely that the official in question thought of this as a way to line his own pockets, by keeping the difference between the original sum and what he planned to hand over to the innkeeper."

A silence, as Kadar appeared to think over what I had just said. I knew I might be over-reaching, accusing someone who could very well be innocent of what I had suggested, but I somehow doubted it. Over the years I had seen my mother and father have to manage the petty avarice of local officials, and I did not think the character of such men would be so very different here in the North than it was in my homeland.

After a heavy pause, Kadar turned from me and back to the innkeep, who had stood there waiting in obvious trepidation during our exchange. The Mark forced a smile and said, a little too heartily, "It seems my lady is willing to forgo a gown or two in order to ensure that you receive what has been promised you. Althan will make sure you do not leave here today without those funds."

"Thank you, my lord." The man bowed to Kadar, but I noticed his gaze was fixed on me, his dark eyes shining with gratitude. "I knew it must be some sort of misunderstanding."

And he was led off by Althan, who wrote down something on the sheaf of paper he always carried with him at these times, and gave it to the man. No doubt it was a direction to the treasurer's office.

The next complainant stepped forward, and luckily the case was simple enough—only a dispute as to who had first right to a prime spot in the marketplace. This time Maldis said nothing, but only looked on with heavy-lidded eyes. Kadar decided the case as I would have, giving precedence to the farmer who had the longest claim to the location, and I let out a little sigh of relief. At least not every grievance would involve a battle of wills between the Mark and myself.

So the rest of the afternoon proved, although every time a new petitioner stepped forward I found myself stiffening, worried that this time Maldis would again proffer some unpalatable advice and that I would once again have to take up arms for the downtrodden. But he remained quiescent, watching only, until at last the hall was emptied and Kadar rose from his seat. I stood as well, glad to be out of the uncomfortable chair, whose carving was quite grand but whose upholstery should have been replaced years ago.

And then Maldis got to his feet as well, saying, "Very educational, your Highness. I did learn a great deal this afternoon." For the briefest of seconds his gaze moved past the Mark to fasten on me before shifting back to Kadar once again. "If I may take my leave?"

Kadar grinned and clapped the man on the shoulder. "Of course, my dear Maldis. There's just enough time to rest up a bit before supper."

"Excellent, your Highness." Maldis bowed, and moved past us to descend from the dais—but not before I caught one last baleful glare from those blue eyes. His manner might have been obsequious, but I knew then that I had made an enemy that afternoon.

I ignored the icy tendrils of dread creeping down my back, and smiled sweetly and said, "Thank you for your service this afternoon, Maldis."

He could do nothing save bow again before hurrying away. I held my breath, but he did not look back, and was soon gone.

Kadar touched my arm. "I would speak with you, Lark."

"This does not surprise me," I replied lightly. "But would you not rather have such a discussion in our apartments?"

To that he offered no argument, only nodding before taking me by the arm and leading me from the chamber. Truly, it was not that far from the Hall of Grievances to our tower rooms, but the journey seemed to take a good deal longer than it usually did.

Once we were inside the suite, he had to hold his tongue for a while longer, as Beranne was there, since she had been watching Tresi during my absence. And even once Beranne had departed, the dog decided to show her displeasure at our being gone so long by running in circles around Kadar's feet and pausing to paw at his tall boots from time to time, looking so silly that the grim set of his mouth relaxed and he laughed, bending down to scratch her behind the ears while she joyfully panted during these ministrations.

"I should be angry with you, Kadar Arkalis," I commented, "for you said the dog was to be mine, but it seems she loves you far more."

"Ah, well, she is only making up to the pack leader," he replied, still smiling. "I have no doubt that if she were to hear something that frightened her, it is to your arms she would go running."

"I thought you said grishonds were great fighters."

"Some, it is true. But I am beginning to think that Tresi here has more in common with those silly long-haired lapdogs the court ladies in Sirlende love to carry about."

I couldn't argue with that; the dog was sweet-tempered and always looking for affection, and thought nothing of her dignity when it came to rolling on her back and exposing her belly for a good rubbing.

But then the grin faded as Kadar straightened and stared down at me. "I have never seen you contradict me in the Hall of Grievances before."

"That is because you gave me no reason to contradict you." I did not flinch away from the sharp, speculative look in his eyes as I added, surprised at my own daring, "I cannot say I care overmuch for the counsel your new advisor gives."

"Is that so?"

"It is."

He did not reply at once, but went over to his desk, where a decanter of wine sat. After pouring a measure into a pair of goblets, he held one out to me.

I could think of no way to refuse, so I crossed the room and took the heavy glass from him. He seemed to be expecting me to continue, and I said, "It is only that you never seemed to require anyone's advice before now. So what has changed?"

Something shifted in his expression then, a shuttering of the eyes. I did not pretend to know him well, although I thought I had gained a few insights into his mind over the past month. Once again I experienced that sensation of being shut out, of him concealing things from me.

What would he do, I wondered, if I were to go to him now, to press my cheek against his chest and put my arms around him? Would such a demonstration allow him to open up to me?

Foolish questions, for I knew I did not have the courage to do that...even if some traitor part of me very much wished to.

This all would have been much easier if I could have hated him.

He said then, "The world is changing, Lark, and we must perforce change with it. I thought it wise to enlist the services of someone who had experience of these things, who comes from a land more wealthy, more powerful than ours."

Ours. Such a small word, but it told me something that heartened me a little. Despite the distance he had put between us, Kadar apparently counted me as his fellow Northerner, even though I had lived here little more than a month. True, a wife took on the country and connections of her husband, but even so, it meant that somewhere in his mind and heart he thought of me as kin, not a simple pawn.

"I see nothing wrong in that," I said carefully. "But who is this Maldis? What are his recommendations?"

Again I got that sense of Kadar closing away from me. His eyes did not quite meet mine as he replied, "He was lately in service to the king of Purth, but several of the king's other advisors grew jealous of his influence, and saw that he was removed from his position. Not being of high birth, he had little recourse but to try to offer his talents to someone else— and North Eredor is far enough removed from Purth that there is no chance of the king worrying about him revealing any state secrets to me."

And what precisely are those talents? I wondered. *Magic, yes, but of what sort? What has he promised?*

I knew I could never ask these things, of course. To do so would be to reveal my own abilities, and sadly, I did not trust Kadar enough for that. "It is unfortunate that he was put in such a position. However, I do not think he understands North Eredor."

A short, humorless laugh met this comment. "And you do? Forgive me, my lady, but I hardly think a month here allows you to assume the mantle of an expert."

"I did not say I was an expert," I replied, refusing to let the anger show in my voice. "All I said was that neither is Maldis."

Kadar shrugged, and took a sip of wine. "True, he does not have much experience yet with our ways, but he does understand the management of a kingdom, the demands required for its protection, the burdens that a ruler must carry. I know you have quite the education, for a young woman, but I somehow doubt you were raised to counsel a king."

To that remark I had no ready answer, for he was correct, of course. Perhaps I could have argued that my study of history allowed me some perspective on such matters. Even so, it was one thing to remember the names and dates of a succession of kings, or even to know what treaties they made and which laws they passed, and quite another to live with these concerns from day to day, to know when to make peace or make war, to judge correctly when the population might support an extra tax, or when to let such things relax in times of flood or drought or famine.

"This may be true," I said slowly. "But I have come to like your people, Kadar, like them very much. I only want what is best for them."

At these words a certain light I had missed lately shone once again in his eyes, and he smiled as he answered, "It is to your credit that you feel this way. And glad I am to hear it, for I know now that you spoke this afternoon only out of a desire to help that innkeeper, and not from some wayward desire to contradict me."

I smiled back, glad that he could recognize that much in me. And though I wished I had the courage to step forward, to move closer to him, something seemed to hold me in place. He appeared similarly thwarted, his gaze holding me for a second before he returned his attention to his wine goblet, and then made some offhand comment about supper, and the moment was lost.

If only I knew whether to be disappointed or relieved.

The next day I awoke feeling oddly light of heart, considering what had transpired the day before. The reason for that unexpected joy soon revealed itself—it appeared that Maldis had left the castle on business of his own, and though Kadar's brow knotted as he read over the note his advisor had left behind, it smoothed itself soon enough as he decided to spend his day going over plans for the exchange with his architects and artisans.

This should have left me at loose ends, but almost as soon as Kadar departed the castle, I felt the half-expected tug of Ulias' magic. I rose from my seat, and saw that Beranne now slept, her needlework neglected in her lap. Even Tresi had curled herself into a small ball in her basket and didn't so much as twitch when I walked past her and out the door.

The guards seemed to be busy elsewhere, and as I moved through the corridors, I saw how Ulias' magic wrapped around me and protected me even now, at a time of day when there were many more people about to note my passage. This did not surprise me quite as much as it once might have, for I knew now who wove this spell, and why.

Maldis had left the keep, and therefore it was safe for me to visit the mage he'd locked up in the cellars.

Ulias did not seem to have moved or changed at all since the last time I had been in his dungeon, although I noted the stacks of books in his cell were piled even higher, and a half-eaten loaf remained on its pewter plate. He stood as I approached, and smiled.

"So am I to come now when you call, like my little dog Tresi?" I inquired in arch tones, but I smiled as well, and I could see that he took no offense at my words.

"I would prefer to think of it as you accepting an important invitation." Ulias gestured toward a rough stool that sat a few feet away from the iron bars of his cell. "I wish I could offer you something finer, but alas, that is the only accommodation they have left here."

"It will serve well enough." I grasped the stool and moved it a little closer to the cell, although I made sure to note its position before I did so. No point in trying to keep our meetings secret, only to give ourselves away with something so silly as a misplaced stool. I sat, glad that today the summons had come at a time when I was warmly dressed, my feet covered in cozy fur-lined boots. "And I think we shall have rather more time today, since Kadar seemed to indicate that Maldis will be away for several days."

Instead of looking pleased, Ulias' expression darkened, as if he had guessed something of why Maldis had left the castle and was troubled by it. But then the mage's brow cleared, and he said, "I have been thinking about you a good deal since last we met. And I thought perhaps we should speak more of your magic."

"What little of it there is," I replied, and tried not to sigh. After all, it was quite inconvenient to have the burden of magical abilities which must be concealed at all times, and yet have the sensation that they were not really worth concealing in the first place.

"Ah, that." The clear grey eyes watched me carefully, and I tried not to shift on my uncomfortable stool like a schoolgirl caught in a transgression. "You say that about your magic, and yet I sense in you great power."

"Indeed?" I did not want to allow myself to believe him, and yet something in me ached for him to be right.

"Indeed." He sat down on his bed—the only seat allowed him in his prison cell—and placed his hands on his knees. I noted that he wore a dark wool doublet and breeches, typical garb for a man of the North, and wondered how on earth it had been tailored to fit around those enormous wings of his. At the moment they were folded to either side of him, allowing him to sit comfortably enough. "Tell me of your father's magic."

"My father?" For a second or two I could only stare at Ulias blankly, but then I gathered myself and replied, "He is a master of weather magic—it is by his will that he can keep the fogs away, so the ships do not founder on the rocks, and he brings the rain when it is needed. Southern Eredor has not suffered a drought for the last quarter-century."

"And you wished to have this same skill, did you not?"

I lifted my shoulders. "It is a very useful one. But although my father tried to teach me the spells, they never seemed to work. I can perform the smaller magics—the sleep spells, the locking charms, the cantrips that ensure I never lose a ring or a book or a hair ribbon. Anything else, though..." And I trailed off and lifted my shoulders in an eloquent shrug.

"But can you sense when your father is working his magic?"

"Always."

"And you can tell when I work mine as well, can you not?"

"Yes."

Ulias looked pleased, for some reason. "I can understand why you would think your gift is of little import, as you have had no exposure to the working of magic save that which your father performs. The power is a chancy thing, skipping genera-tions, manifesting in different ways when it does surface. It is rare enough that it should appear as it has in your family, show-ing in both the father and the daughter. It is unheard-of that you should possess exactly the same abilities."

"But it does run in families."

"Yes. If magic has never appeared in a bloodline, then it will never manifest itself." His pleasant expression faded somewhat, and I saw that he would not meet my eyes for some reason. "Just as it will always appear eventually, even if several scores of years should pass before it returns. At any rate, you are what used to be called a Protector, one who instinctively feels magic as it is being worked."

Puzzled, I stared over at him, at the downcast eyes with their sweep of pale lashes, the white wings that might have been carved from marble, so still were they. "How does that make someone a Protector?"

At once the shadow was gone from his face, although he did not smile. "Because one who feels magic, who senses it in all its forms, is one who understands it, someone who knows how to block it, or tear it down, if necessary. Back in the days of power, rare was the king who did not have a Protector in his service, someone to act as a safeguard against the ill-intentioned spells of his rivals. Protectors were raised near as high as royalty, and were courted for their abilities as soon as those powers began to manifest. It is no small thing to be a Protector, Lark Sedassa."

Pride stirred in my breast, that I should possess such a gift. Then again, while it might have been of very great use back in the days when every noble house had its mage, and terrible could be the consequences of the magic-fought feuds and squabbles between courtiers, here and now, I saw little utility in it.

Despite my ability, I did not yet have any reasonable measure of Ulias' powers; I certainly did not know if he could read my thoughts, but I wondered then if he did, for he said,

"It is not I, or your father, or even Khaspar the Nimble, who dwells in secret in the slums of Iselfex, or Lorenne the Fair, wife of a minor baron in Farendon, against whom you should be guarding. I think you know all too well who your enemy is."

I swallowed, seeing in my mind the commonplace features and glacially cold eyes of Maldis of Purth. Maldis the magician. Maldis, who radiated such malice I wondered that everyone else in the keep could not feel it.

"I know," I said, and was glad that my voice sounded steady enough, even though my fingers shook somewhat...and not from the cold in that bleak cellar.

"Well, then," Ulias said simply. "I think it is time that we got to work."

❧ Chapter Eleven ❧

By the time I climbed the steps back up to my tower rooms, my legs were shaking. Only two hours had passed—even Ulias said he could not keep my absence hidden any longer than that—and yet I felt as if I had spent at least a day, if not more than that, pushing boulders uphill.

None of the work with my father had prepared me for this. I would say that was partly because we had not delved into any great wielding of my power, since we hadn't even known what it actually was, and partly because my father, being my father, had perhaps not pushed me quite as much as he should.

Ulias, however, had no such scruples.

He had me cast spells over and over, simple things such as making the stones on one wall glow as if imbued with the sun's radiance, or making objects materialize in the cellar and then disappear to whence they came. And once I had done this to the point where my whole body shook with weariness, he would cast spells of his own, and demand that I tell him what they were. I had to sit, eyes shut, letting only that odd sense of mine tell me what he had done, so that I might relay this information to him.

Such an exercise sounds simple in theory, but in reality I had to strain to distinguish one spell from another, to make myself understand that it was not enough to merely feel the working of magic, but to know what kind of magic was being worked. It was not unlike an inexperienced youth working his way through the forms of the swordsman, and beginning to realize there was far more to the activity than merely swinging a blade about.

God knows my muscles ached as if I had spent the afternoon in sword practice rather than sitting on a stool, eyes screwed shut, while I forced my mind down pathways it had never trodden before. I collapsed on the divan, and barely had time to compose myself before Beranne's eyelids fluttered open and she said,

"My goodness! Have I slept?"

"A little," I admitted. I could not pretend that she hadn't been asleep for the greater part of two hours; Ulias was a great magician, but even he could not stop the passage of time. "It is the weather, I suppose. I must confess that I'm feeling rather tired myself."

She nodded, and cast a concerned glance at my face, as if she could read the weariness there. Truly, I wanted nothing else but to lie down on the divan and sleep for at least a day, but I knew that was not possible. No, the best I could hope for was a quiet evening and an early bed.

Luck seemed to be with me, for Kadar stayed out for most of the day, and dinner that night was subdued enough, only the usual gathering of courtiers, with soft music in the background, and no other entertainment. He seemed to be in a pleasant enough mood, and if he noted my own weariness, he did not mention it.

But once we were alone in our chambers, he turned to me and said, "It seems I owe you some thanks."

I had been removing the earrings I'd worn to dinner, and went ahead and placed them in the box reserved for my jewelry before I replied, "Thanks? For what?"

"For the advice you gave me yesterday in the Hall of Grievances."

Startled, I shut the box and gazed over at him. He stood a few feet away, near the fire; the dancing flames caught the edges of his dark hair and seemed to shimmer there, copper and dull gold. "Indeed?"

Although my tone had not been all that encouraging, he still smiled and said, "Your intuition was correct. I made inquiries, and it seems the man whose duty it was to disburse the funds to the innkeeper and those others whose properties we are acquiring has rather a taste for gambling, and is sorely in debt. As you said, he thought to line his pockets by telling the innkeeper that the treasury could not afford to pay him the sum originally promised and then pocketing the difference himself. We are lucky that the innkeeper is a man of mettle, and spoke up for himself, or the embezzler might never have been discovered."

"I am glad of that," I said, and indeed I was. Encouraged by his smile, I stepped away from the cabinet that contained my jewel box and went toward him. It felt good, to stand thus by the fire…or perhaps I was only glad of a reason to be closer to him. "I have seen it more than once, when my parents had dealings with the man whose job it was to inspect our wine casks, or the one who walked our acres to determine our taxes. Our king is a good man, but those who serve under him are somewhat less…admirable."

"It saddens me to hear it, but it is the way of the world, unfortunately. At least in this case the man's perfidy was discovered. He has been relieved of his post, but not before Althan also relieved him of the money he had taken from some of the other property owners. The funds have been restored to them, and all is well."

"Good." I paused then, weighing my next words. It would not do for me to seem too importunate, but I thought I should press my advantage now, while Maldis was still out of the castle. "Then perhaps I might ask a boon?"

Kadar raised an eyebrow, but only nodded. "What is this boon?"

"Only that you might reconsider your appointment of Maldis as your advisor. I cannot say that his counsel has been so very sound, and I think you did very well on your own before he ever came here."

At these words the Mark frowned, the golden eyes fixed on my face. "I would very much like to know what you find so objectionable about my councilor."

If only I could tell you. But of course the truth, however per-suasive it might have been, was not a tool I could use at the moment. Not that I knew the whole of that truth, of course; I sensed Maldis' evil without knowing yet its actual source.

"'Objectionable' is a harsh word," I replied, taking care to keep my tone mild. Standing like this, with only a foot or so between us, I could almost feel the heat of his body. Foolish. It was only the warmth of the fire, radiating outward. And yet somehow I thought his arms would warm me far more than the fire ever could. I cleared my throat, pushing those treacherous thoughts away. "All I am saying is that I do not see his value to you. By your own admission, my counsel has done you more good. Or is the advice of a wife of less worth to you than the advice of paid advisor?"

"I think you know how much I value you." The words were soft, but there was an edge to them that told me he, too, had sensed the tension between us, and did not know what to do about it.

Do I? I wanted to ask, but of course I did not. "Then can you not grant me this smallest of wishes?"

His hands knotted where they hung at his sides. That small gesture told me all I needed to know. He would not change his mind on this, no matter what he might feel for me, no matter what it might do to the fragile trust that had begun to grow between us. "I fear I cannot dismiss him simply because of one small error in judgment. He has too much to offer."

Again I wished I could ask what promises Maldis had made, what he had offered Kadar to make his services so valu-able. And I wished that I could cry out how I had felt his evil, knew he would bring nothing but misfortune upon North Eredor and its ruler. But somehow I knew the time for that was not now. I did not know enough...yet.

I looked away from Kadar then. It was easier to harden my words, my heart, when I did not have to look at his face, at those features that had become perilously dear to me. "I see where I stand, then. Very well. I suppose there is nothing for us to say to one another save 'goodnight.'"

A silence, as he stood there a moment longer. I could feel the weight of his gaze upon me, even though I would not meet his eyes.

Then, "Goodnight, Lark," and he brushed past me to his own sleeping chamber, leaving me to the spurious warmth of the fire, and the realization that, although I had done what I knew was right, I could take little joy in it.

At least Maldis was still gone the next day, and although it pained me to see Kadar quiet and guarded, speaking only of commonplaces before he could excuse himself and go about his business, I would be lying if I said I was not relieved that at least his advisor did not appear eager to return to the keep.

This time the summons came when I was blessedly alone, Beranne having been called to the house of her sister, who was taken with a fever. "But if you cannot do without me, my lady, I can send word that I must stay here."

"Of course not," I told her. "I managed well enough for the first twenty or so years of my life, so I think I can spare you this day. And I hope your sister is well again soon—make sure you take what stores and supplies you need from the castle. Do not worry about the expense of summoning a physician, if that should become necessary, for you can tell him that the Mark's household will cover the cost."

Grand words, and I hoped I had not overstepped my boundaries. But they seemed to hearten her, and she stammered her thanks before rushing off, promising that she would be back by nightfall. Then I was mercifully alone, quiet in my tower room with only Tresi for company. Not a quarter-hour later I felt the tug of Ulias' magic, and saw my little dog asleep once more, curled up on the rug she'd appropriated as hers.

I bent down to stroke her behind her soft little ears, and she twitched but did not awaken. Smiling, I descended the stairs, moved like a ghost through the throngs in the main corridor, and headed on down to the cellars. My heart pounded somewhat, for I had a far better idea of what awaited me than I had the previous day. Exhilarating as it was for me to feel magic stir to life within me, its use was also far more tiring than I had ever imagined. And I had not slept well the night before, turning and tossing on the divan, even though it had given me plenty of restful slumbers before then.

Ulias was standing, watching me as I approached. "You do not look quite so eager as you did yesterday."

"That is because I now know what to expect."

I had thought he might smile at my remark, but his expression remained sober. "We have much lost time to make up."

"So all the training with my father was for naught?"

"Not precisely. At least you have learned something of discipline. But you have a long way to go yet."

Of course I did. Only a fool would think she had acquired any sort of mastery after only a day's practice. I pulled out the stool and sat down, then asked, "Who is Maldis, really? And why did he leave so abruptly, when he had barely begun to assume his duties here?"

The pale features went very still then. Ulias said nothing for a long moment, but only gazed at me as if attempting to take some measure of my mettle. Finally he said, "I think it would be better if you discovered that for yourself. Think of it as another exercise."

Which was Ulias' way of saying that he would not give me a straight answer. Very well. I hadn't really expected him to, but, as my father was wont to remark, one cannot get an answer if one is not willing to ask the question in the first place.

I said only, "In which case, I suppose we must begin at once."

And Ulias smiled and nodded, and once again we were off.

Maldis returned the evening of the third day. By then I was so weary that I could barely keep my eyes open at dinner. Kadar could tell something was wrong, but we had not yet mended the rift between us, and so he only watched me narrowly, wondering what was amiss but too proud to ask. And I knew my pallor and weariness was the subject of some gossip among the household servants, according to Beranne, who had returned to report that her sister was doing much better, thank you.

"And now they're saying you're doing poorly, and wondering if himself has an heir on the way."

I let out a brief, bitter laugh at that. "Too well you know how wrong that speculation is, Beranne."

"Yes, my lady," she said, suddenly formal. "But of course I would never tell them that, my lady."

"Of course not."

And a little pang went through me as I wondered what it would be like to actually be carrying the Mark's child...and I thought I probably would never know.

But these worries were cast aside when the dark mage returned at supper that evening. To all outward appearances, he did not appear to have changed at all, but I almost gagged when he came into the dining hall. Something oily and black and loathsome seemed to swirl around him, and for a second or two it was almost as if I could smell the stink of spilled blood, hot and metallic.

Somehow I managed to maintain my composure, to nod at him and smile, although I wanted nothing more than to run from the hall, to find a bowl so I could relieve myself of my half-eaten dinner. But that would only lead to more speculation. Besides, I could not let him know how he affected me. My wizard senses had sharpened enough for me to tell that he could discern nothing of my reaction to him...as long as I did not betray myself with a chance grimace or scowl.

Kadar, of course, welcomed him, and bade him take a seat at the high table. In the process he dislodged an elderly nobleman who looked none too pleased at being bumped so unceremoniously but who also seemed to realize that protests would do him no good. Luckily, the seat in question was on Kadar's other side, and so at least I had him as a buffer between me and the man who felt like no true man to me at all, but rather some sort of animate sink of foetor and despair.

Although a good deal of food remained on my plate, I could no longer touch any of it. Instead I reached for my goblet and drank, staring out into the hall, watching as servants came and went and the guests laughed and talked and ate of their venison stew as if nothing had changed, as if all the darkness in the world had not coalesced and come among us. For a second or two it was as if all those laughing faces were turned to skulls, their chatter the skittering swirl of dead leaves in a graveyard.

And after that I recalled nothing, because the room spun and broke apart around me, and I fell into blackness, cold.

Nothing.

"Lark."

I opened my eyes, saw green hangings directly overhead. At first I could not think where I was, then realized I must be lying in Kadar's bed. And as that understanding dawned, I saw his face above me, pale and grim, and behind his wine-clad shoulder Beranne hovered, her own features equally pinched and white.

My head pounded, although I knew I had drunk barely one glass of wine. "What happened?"

"You fainted," Kadar told me. "One minute you were sitting beside me, and the next—" He broke off, and shook his head.

Yes, I remembered now, remembered how I had swirled down into darkness, overwhelmed by the sensation of Maldis' evil, as if it had grown somehow during his absence, strengthened in a way I could not begin to comprehend.

This did not bode well for any future confrontations I might have with him.

Somehow I managed a smile and said, "My own foolishness, I fear. I did not eat much today, and I suppose the lack caught up with me."

Kadar did not appear altogether convinced, although I thought he seemed to relax somewhat. "You should take more care, my lady wife." He cast a sharp look over his shoulder at Beranne. "And why did you not keep better watch over her ladyship, Beranne?"

She began to fumble for a response, even as I pushed myself up against the pillows and broke in, "It is none of her fault, Kadar. I am not a small child who needs to be cajoled into eating all of her vegetables. I was caught up in some reading. That is all. If my parents were here, they could tell you that it would not be the first time I missed a meal because my nose was firmly stuck in a book. The first time I have fainted, true, but you know well that I have had a difficult time accustoming myself to the cold here. Just an unfortunate combination of circumstances."

It all sounded reasonable enough. I halfway believed it myself.

A pause, and Kadar said, "Well, Lark, if this is how you take care of yourself, then perhaps I shall have to keep a closer eye on you as well."

"I assure you, it won't happen again."

He stood there for a long moment, staring down at me, while I returned his gaze as guilelessly as I could and prayed that he saw nothing untoward in my features. Then, to my surprise, he reached down and cupped the side of my face with his fingers, a brief touch, but still one that seemed to linger long after he removed his hand. "Don't frighten me like that again."

And then he was gone, giving a curt nod to Beranne as he went—no doubt an unspoken order for her to quell the whispers that must have arisen after my collapse. I could only pray that Maldis saw nothing in it save the sort of affliction that often strikes a young wife. No doubt the whispers would increase tenfold after this.

What they would say, as the weeks wore on and I showed no thickening of the waist, I didn't want to think. No time to worry about that now. I had, as they liked to say back in my seaport town, bigger kettles of fish to fry.

Beranne approached me. "My lady—"

"I'm fine, Beranne. It was a momentary dizziness, nothing more. In fact," I added, summoning a smile that probably didn't convince her but which I deemed necessary, "I am quite hungry. Could you bring me up a tray? No venison, but I would like some bread and cheese, and soup, if there is any left."

"Of course, my lady," she replied automatically, even though her eyes were alive with questions. "I'll see to that right away. You rest now."

I nodded, and let out a little sigh of relief as she turned from me and left the bedchamber.

As I lay back against the pillows—and tried not to think of what I should do if Kadar insisted that I stay in bed for the night, instead of returning to my divan—I heard Ulias' voice in my head, clear as my own thoughts.

I would stay there, for the nonce. You have had more of a shock than you realize.

Dumbfounded, I felt my eyes widen, and even looked from side to side, as if I half-expected the winged mage to have somehow materialized in Kadar's bedchamber.

No, I am still in my cellar. I thought it time to try this form of communication...we have had enough contact now that I guessed I would be able to establish a connection.

I took in a breath, and told myself not to be so astonished. After all, I had read that in ages past the great mages had been able to speak to one another with their minds, treating time and space as if they were nothing. But I had never been able to speak thus with my father, and had thought it either a fairytale or yet another skill lost along with so many others.

So you can hear me? I thought then.

Yes.

What happened to me?

A hesitation. In the back of my mind I sense an odd pulsing, as if Ulias were thinking but somehow shielding those thoughts from me. Then, *He grew strong, this last time. You were doing as I taught you, sensing his power, but the source of it was too raw, too new, and you were unprepared for it. Your mind stepped in to shield you before it could touch any more of that... negative energy.*

How was it that our minds were touching, and yet I somehow knew there was much he still concealed from me? And what is the source of his power, Ulias?

Yet another pause, one that dragged out so long I began to think he would not reply at all. At length his response came to me, slow, as if he knew he must tell me the truth but was loath to do so.

You have sensed the evil in Maldis. I told you when we first met that he has discovered a way to pervert magic, to bend it to his own will. You see, magic is in the blood—it is as much a part of you as the color of your eyes, the sound of your voice. And so it is for all the mage-born who yet live. So few of you—of us—in these latter days, and yet the magic has not been completely denied, still comes forth in odd places and in odd generations, the blood bringing with it the power. It is that which Maldis has learned to harness. The mental voice took on a harsher tone. *He was not born with any powers of his own, but being possessed of a hungry soul, a need to make more of himself than his mean birth and meager talents could provide him, he delved into dark knowledge, found at last a way to give himself a power he does not deserve.*

How? I asked, although part of me did not wish to know the answer, wished to remain in happy ignorance.

By taking it from those who do possess it. This time the victim was a farmer named Rogin, a man who had made peace with his odd abilities, and lived a quiet life. If he never lost a flock to hoof disease, and if his hens always laid, well, you could say it was simple luck. But Maldis knows to look for these patterns, to see what is hidden beneath the surface, and to seek those at the source of these disruptions, to take them for his own purposes.

He—he killed this Rogin?

A mental sigh then, cold and hollow as the rustle of dead leaves in a graveyard. *If only it were that simple. Yes, this man*

Rogin will die, but only after Maldis has sucked the lifeblood from him slowly, using it up as it suits his purposes. For it is by perverting the powers within the living blood that Maldis can claim them for his own, and so he must try to make his victims live as long as he can. For when one is used up, then Maldis has only his own cunning to support him, and he must needs seek another mage-born soul to revive his evil powers. That is why he left this last time—to find a new victim. And once Rogin can give no more, and is an empty husk, then Maldis must venture forth again.

I was glad then that I had not eaten much, for my stomach heaved and waves of nausea passed over me. Closing my eyes, I took in a deep breath, and then another. As horrifying as what Ulias had just revealed might be, I knew I must be strong. I must face this, even though nothing I had ever been taught could have prepared me for such a foe.

Something in what Ulias had said pricked at my mind, prompting me to ask, *Are there so many of us? Those born with magical powers, that is.*

More than you might think. All in hiding, all doing what they can to conceal what they are. Most of them do not have your powers, or your father's powers, of course, but even so, they all have enough to make them potential victims of Maldis' evil intentions.

I shifted on the unfamiliar bed. *You say "of course" as if our powers are so very great. How is this so? What is it about my father, or me, that makes us stronger than Rogin, or that Lorenne the Fair you mentioned?*

Only silence in my mind, a sense that Ulias had withdrawn for some reason. Then, the unspoken words heavy, he replied, *This is something I know I must speak of to you…but not now. Not like this.*

When, then?

When I can see you again in person.

When Maldis is off hunting another victim.

Yes, then. It is a sad necessity that drives me, but I can do nothing else. But now, I must go. I hear your husband and his "advisor" approaching. Take care, my Lark, and do what you must to keep yourself safe.

The contact was broken then, and I almost gasped aloud, the sensation not unlike being dashed in the face with a bucket of cold water. I sat up in bed, blinking, just as Beranne came in with a tray of food, Tresi at her heels, tail wagging frantically. The dog knew better than to expect anything of Beranne, but I was far more soft-hearted when it came to giving away table scraps.

"You look better, my lady," Beranne said as she settled the tray in my lap and looked me over with a critical eye. "Color back in your cheeks, if I may say so."

"I feel better," I replied, and it was the truth. Although Ulias' revelations had been horrifying, in an odd way I felt better now that I knew who—*what*—I faced. And since I was no longer in Maldis' loathsome presence, strength had begun to return.

However, I knew that if I attempted to get out of bed, Beranne would tell me I certainly should not be getting up, not so soon after I had fainted, and so I broke off a piece of bread and ate it with a piece of soft yellow cheese, and interspersed bites with sips of the small beer she'd brought to supplement the meal. After a minute or so of this, however, I paused and said, "Do sit down, Beranne. It makes me nervous to see you hovering there like that."

Looking somewhat startled, she nevertheless sank down into the nearest chair, the one at the small table where our breakfast tray was often brought. Since she did not have her ubiquitous mending with her, she could do little but sit there with her hands in her lap, brushing Tresi away from time to time whenever the dog wearied of watching me eat.

Seeing this, I tried not to smile. Beranne wanted to be stern with Tresi, but that was easier said than done. My smile faded, though, as I wondered what Maldis and Kadar were up to, down in that chilly cellar several floors below where I now lay. I wondered, too, how much Kadar knew of his counselor's true nature. Very little, I guessed, for although the Mark might be ambitious and somewhat lacking in scruples, I thought even he might draw the line at sacrificing any number of innocent victims to feed Maldis' unholy appetites.

Then I pushed the tray away and looked over at Beranne. "How well do you know the Mark?"

"*Know* him? He is my lord and master. What else is there to know?"

I suppose I should have expected no less, but still I pressed on. "Yes, but how long have you served here in the castle? Did you know him as a boy? What of his parents?"

The expression of puzzlement on her features only deepened. "I have been here since before he was born, my lady. I was but a girl then, younger than you, but I remember well enough when his mother, the Mark of her time, wed the *corraghar* leader. Such a thing was quite beyond the pale, as you might imagine." Even now, when the event in question had occurred more than a quarter-century earlier, her lips compressed in disapproval.

"It was not a popular match, then?"

"Popular? Hardly, my lady. It was only the great love the people had for Corliss that kept them from rising in the streets. Everyone thought her consort—Marak—would bring the wolf-people with him, and chaos would soon follow. This did not happen, although one sees more of the *corraghar* about now than they did back then."

"So why did she do it?" I asked, genuinely curious. "Was she in love with him?"

A snort, although Beranne cut it short and tried to make it seem as if the unbecoming sound had actually been an abortive sneeze. "No, my lady. That is, not that any of us could tell. I believe she thought being allied with the *corraghar* in such a way would strengthen North Eredor, make us more fit to compete with larger, stronger lands. But none of that came to pass, of course. The *corraghar* fight under no one's banner but their own, just as they always have."

"And is this why Kadar has no brothers or sisters?" I certainly had never heard anyone mention them, so I assumed they must not exist.

Beranne's face grew shadowed then, and she looked away from me, out the doorway into the main chamber of the suite. "Two were born before him, and died before they lived a month. When he came, it was thought his mother would not survive the birth, so difficult it was. And after that she was never the same. She survived, but there was no more talk of any other children. Lord Marak was killed in a hunting accident when Kadar was just learning to walk. And you can imagine how carefully he was watched over as he grew up, being the only heir. Poor lad lost his mother when he was barely sixteen, and no time to mourn, for he had a country to rule."

"That's terrible," I murmured, heart wrung as I thought of what it must have been like to be orphaned at such an age, and to have to take up the reins of rule while still grieving the only parent he probably knew. "No wonder..." And I broke off, thinking I should not utter such a thing in front of Beranne, that no wonder Kadar sought to strengthen his country by any means necessary, when that was probably something which had been instilled in him from his earliest youth.

But somehow Beranne seemed to understand something of what I had meant to say, for she nodded solemnly. "Perhaps it is not possible for you to agree with everything he does, but—"

"—but I can begin to understand. Yes, Beranne."

She smiled at me then, and stood and took the empty tray from my lap. "You should try to sleep, my lady. You must keep up your strength."

True words, although she perhaps did not know how true. There was no way I could begin to explain, so I only nodded and slid down the pillows, making myself as comfortable as

I could. The last thing I saw before I shut my eyes was Tresi dancing after Beranne, hoping for a scrap of bread or a rind of cheese.

And, despite all I had seen, all I had learned that day, I smiled.

~ Chapter Twelve ~

It was blackest night when I felt Kadar settle into bed next to me. At first I startled, forgetting where I lay, but then I realized I was the interloper here, in this bed not my own.

I must have made some sound, for I heard his voice in the darkness. "Forgive me. I did not mean to wake you."

"It is all right." I turned on my pillow, facing toward him, although I could see nothing of him save a darker shape against the gloom in the chamber. "Is it very late?"

"Late enough. And how are you feeling?"

"Much improved. I hope I did not give everyone too much of a fright."

"Not at all." A grim chuckle. "You may imagine what most of the court thinks of it."

I already had imagined it. But I could think of no way to phrase such a thing without only increasing the awkwardness between us. Instead, I replied lightly, "Well, if I have supplied some new gossip, then I suppose I have done my work for the night."

"Ah."

He shifted as well, and for the first time I sensed the heat of his body, his warmth taking some of the chill from the heavy linen sheets. And somehow that heat seemed to touch me, made me want to move closer to him, to...what? Press my body against his, put my arms around him?

Insanity.

I was so woefully unprepared for this. I had no experience of men, unless you could count a stolen and entirely unwelcome kiss from my friend Daris' twin brother Rillan. Unfortunately for her twin, Daris had gotten all of the charm and the looks of that pair, and I would have sooner kissed the man who came to clean out our wine barrels than the awkward Rillan. At any rate, that boy had not made my blood seem to run hot and then cold, nor made me want to experience in real life the things my mother had described in a bluntly roundabout way that nevertheless got the point across.

This was all a dreadful mistake. I should have slipped away to the divan once Beranne had gone, and not fallen asleep in Kadar's bed. But I had been so very tired, and the bed was so very comfortable—far more comfortable than the divan, truth be told—and now I was fairly trapped. If I attempted to leave now, Kadar would be sure to comment, and I had no ready replies to give him...save the truth, which was the one thing to be avoided at all costs.

Somehow I forced myself to roll over on my back, to stare up at the hangings above, which in the darkness only seemed to be more darkness, and not the rich green they were in daylight. Was it my imagination, or did I hear the faintest of sighs come from the lips of my husband, as if he regretted my turning away from him?

It had to be my imagination. I could not allow it to be anything else.

I closed my eyes then, and willed sleep to come take me.

Although he moved with care, I had slept more lightly than usual, and so I felt it at once when Kadar shifted in bed next to me, swung his legs over the side, and stood. I rolled over, pushing a few tangled curls from my face and blinking. The chamber was still dark enough, although a few chinks in the heavy draperies seemed to indicate that the day outside was sunnier than it had been in some time.

"Good morning," I said.

He looked over at me, surprise evident in his features. Apparently he thought I yet slept. "That it is, with the sun out for once."

"Mmm, that is good. I think I would like some fresh air." Feeling strangely bold, I added, "Perhaps we could go for a ride, if your schedule allows it?"

This suggestion seemed to astonish him even more. After all, I had made no secret of my dislike of horseback riding. "Truly? That is...perhaps. I think perhaps we could take our luncheon that way, if you like."

"I would like it, very much." Even with the sun out, I did not know how comfortable such a picnic would be, given our location and the time of year, but I would make do. The prospect of being out of the castle and away from Maldis over-rode any other concerns I might have.

He smiled. "Then I will make haste this morning, so we have ample time for our ride. Be ready in the great hall a quarter-hour before noon."

"I will," I promised.

Our compact made, he went about the business of washing his face and getting dressed, barely pausing when Narenna came in with the breakfast tray. He grabbed some bread and bacon and left, leaving me still in bed and reaching for my morning cup of tea. I would not allow myself to be discomfited by this behavior, because at least today I had secured a promise from him that we would spend some time together.

I had halfway expected him to break off our luncheon plans, to manufacture some crisis or council that could not be avoided. But my fears proved to be groundless, for he met me in the great audience hall as promised and even gallantly offered an arm to guide me out to our waiting horses. This time I did not hang back, but laid my hand lightly on his, feeling the strength of his arm beneath mine. And he helped me up onto Raven himself, instead of allowing a groom to perform the task.

Whether this chivalrous behavior was solely for the benefit of the watching nobles, or whether he had realized he'd been neglectful of me lately, I did not know. What I did know was that I felt the pressure of his arm on mine for some time after he had released it, and when he lifted me onto my mount, I wished that his hands had lingered just a bit longer around my waist.

Perhaps at some point this foolishness would cease. If not, perhaps Ulias knew of a spell to knock me back into my right mind. I could not afford to be so scattered, so torn by this unwelcome attraction. I thought suddenly of the girls back in Marestal, and how they had sighed over Thani every time we went into town to visit the bazaar or purchase supplies. True, he was very handsome—even a younger sister might admit that—but at the time I had thought that insufficient reason to act quite so foolish. And yet here I was, just as stupidly besotted as those empty-headed girls had been.

Mouth thinning, I followed Kadar out of the courtyard as six of his guards fell in around us and we moved through the gates and on into the streets. The people there watched us with curious eyes, and I wondered what they might be thinking. Certainly I had not been out and about very much, although the weather was mainly to blame for that. Perhaps Kadar had only agreed to this expedition because he saw in it a means to show the people that all was well between us.

What humbled me was the realization that I did not much care, as long as we could spend this time together.

Truly, though, it was a beautiful day. The sky overhead was a clear, hard blue, with only a few clouds off to the east, hanging from the peaks of the Opal Mountains, to break up that sapphire expanse. And while the air was colder than what I would consider comfortable, with my warm cloak and woolen riding suit, and with the sun shining down on me, I found I could tolerate the chill well enough, and indeed hardly noticed it after a few minutes.

We took the same route we'd followed a little more than a month earlier, when Kadar had brought me out to the woods and lectured me on the duties of the Mark's consort. Then, however, the trees had blazed in their autumn panoply of russet and orange and gold, while now they were mostly bare, save the sentinel pines and firs which stood dark and solemn among the pale branches of their deciduous cousins.

And as last time, a blanket was laid upon the cold earth so we might take our luncheon there. Actually, this time several blankets were set out for us, to better ward off the chill seeping from the ground. I had heard that when the Emperor of Sirlende ventured forth for these sorts of outdoor excursions, he did so with pavilions and banners and furniture as fine as that which graced the rooms of his palace. But there was not nearly so much ceremony here in North Eredor, and I found I was glad of it.

The guards moved out to take up their positions, leaving Kadar and me alone in a glade ringed by the graceful naked forms of birch and ash. He poured wine for us, this time mulled and still warm from the great cauldrons in the castle's kitchens. I wrapped my hands around the earthenware goblet, glad of that warmth, which I could feel through my gloved fingers.

The food—a loaf of bread, roasted chicken, cunning little individual pies with berries I didn't recognize, dark and sweet and lush—was still warm as well, although I doubted it would remain that way for very long. However, I found I did not mind all that much, as we ate in companionable silence and felt the sun on our faces and the chill wind in our hair.

At length, though, after Kadar had poured me another goblet of wine, he said, "You seem to be at home here now."

Sipping my wine, I considered his words. Truly, I hadn't thought of my situation in such terms—especially not now, with the specter of Maldis hovering always in the background—but I supposed Kadar's comment had some merit. Despite everything, I had grown accustomed to my new life in the castle, to gossiping with Beranne and learning the dulcimer and sitting with Kadar in the Hall of Grievances. A pattern had begun to form, a quiet order which appealed to me. At least, it had been appealing enough...until Maldis came on the scene.

I looked at Kadar then, at the dark-lashed golden eyes, the fine expressive brows, the mouth...well, best not to linger on the mouth. Hastily I said, "Well, Beranne and Althan have made me feel very welcome, and I find life in the castle to be quite fascinating. It is so very different from South Eredor."

"I suppose it would be." He ran a finger over the edge of his goblet and met my gaze squarely. I had to force myself not to look away, to hope that he would see nothing in my face save mild interest. "Tell me of the South. We have not spoken much of your family."

"I thought you said you had traveled to South Eredor," I replied, perhaps too hastily.

If he noticed, he gave no indication. "Once, when I was newly come to my title. It is a custom, for the new Mark to meet the King of South Eredor, and to renew the vows of peace between our two lands. But such a visit, couched in ceremony and custom, hardly compares to your own experiences."

What to say to that? To cover my hesitation, I drank some more wine, which by then was barely lukewarm. After all, up until this moment, Kadar had only seemed interested in my Sirlendian relations, the ones with titles and power. My Southern family, those prosperous but oh-so-plebeian merchants and vintners, could not be all that interesting. Still, he waited, watching me, and so I said,

"My mother inherited her father's vineyards, and I grew up there. The house stands on a hill, and from its windows you can see the vines stretching away, all around you. When the wind is right, you can smell the sea, but oftentimes it's warm, dry grass and flowers in the air. My mother still walks the vineyards, to see how the grapes grow, to feel the earth and make sure it is properly drained. My grandfather taught her to do this, and she will have no one else do it for her."

To my surprise, Kadar appeared fascinated. "And so were you taught this? To cultivate the vines?"

I shrugged. "A little. I was more interested—" I stopped myself before I could say *in magic*. "That is, I was a more bookish type, like Father, and of course we all knew Thani would be going to Marric's Rest one day, so one of my cousins is being trained to oversee the vineyards, to take over when the time comes."

"And your mother does not mind this?"

Of course she did, but I did not feel comfortable divulging that particular of my family's concerns. Of course she had known that Thani must inherit the lands my father had left to my Aunt Laranel's stewardship, but she had hoped that I would love the vineyards as she did, could one day find a husband to manage them alongside me. And perhaps I would have—I did enjoy learning about the winemaking process, and had a good grasp of the details, and my mother praised my palate as being fairly discerning—if not for my magic. Once the power began to rise in me, it was the one passion that consumed all my energies, and there was no more talk of perhaps finding a match for me amongst the sons of our neighbors.

Not to say that wielders of magic could not marry, or have families; my father was proof enough of that. But he had been honest with my mother from the time they declared their feelings for one another, and she had accepted his magic just as she accepted the color of his hair and his eyes. It was one thing, though, for a wife to be accepting of such qualities in a husband, and quite another for a man to overlook those things in a wife. My lack of a betrothed was, I knew, the subject of some speculation amongst our acquaintances, but most of them seemed to think it was because I had been promised to some great lord in Sirlende.

I wondered what they would think, those prosy merchants and vintners and farmers, if they ever came to discover I was the consort of the Mark of Eredor.

No time for further speculation, though, as I felt the weight of Kadar's watching eyes upon me and knew he expected a reply. Without meeting his gaze, I said, "She always knew that the chances of my staying on at Ash Hill were not good. Once Thani inherited his title and lands..." And I let the words trail off, giving another lift of my shoulders as I did so. My neighbors were not the only ones who thought I would one day make a grand marriage, though my parents always made it clear that I would not be forced into anything I did not wish for.

Kadar was no fool; he understood what my silence meant. No doubt he was thinking the marriage he had trapped me in was far more lofty than anything even the most scheming parents might have hoped for...but at least he had the good grace not to say such a thing out loud. Instead, he favored me with one of his smiles, which, I had to admit, were most disarming. "Perhaps you can offer my cellarer some instruction in wines. We do not have much luck with our local grapes, and import almost everything, as much of a blow as it is to my Northern pride to admit such a thing."

"It is probably the cold, and the soil," I said. "It is rocky here, and while that may promise good drainage, the vines need the earth to feed them as well. But perhaps in the spring I can help to point out some spots that may be more promising than others."

"I would like that very much." His eyes warmed, and I guessed he was pleased to hear me speaking of my future here, of making plans for something so many months away.

The words had come so easily that I hadn't even thought of the implicit promise in them. I had only been thinking of the problem of Maldis, and how to remove him from Kadar's circle. Only now did I begin to realize there would be a life after that, something the Mark and I could share.

If, of course, I managed to conceal my powers from the dark mage. Given his proclivities, I could not imagine I would last long if he knew magical blood ran in my veins.

I shivered, and Kadar said at once, "Does it grow too cold for you here?"

Until he mentioned it, I hadn't been paying much attention to the chilly day, warmly dressed as I was. But then it seemed I could feel the cold seeping up even through several layers of woolen blankets, finding its way through my heavy divided riding skirt and stout boots. "Perhaps it does," I admitted.

"Well, then, let me take you back. I would not want you to catch a chill."

The two of us gathered up the remnants of our meal and put them away in their baskets. Then he offered a hand to me and helped me to my feet, even as the guards returned at some unspoken signal. Two of them secured the baskets on their horses—I wondered if they'd drawn lots to see who would have to carry such an ignominious burden—and after that Kadar assisted me into the saddle once more. This time it seemed his hands lingered somewhat on my waist, and I could feel a rush of heat pass through me at his touch.

Somehow, though, I maintained my composure, although I might have given him the briefest of smiles before he let go and moved on to his own mount. I could not say whether my lack of any real response discomfited him, although surely by then he was used enough to the somewhat strained relations we shared. No doubt he thought I had begun to soften toward him, and indeed I had...but I could not let him know that for certain. Not now, while the shadow of Maldis still hung between us.

And when that would change, I had no idea.

Rogin, Maldis' latest victim, must have been quite a strong man, because it was some five days before the dark one begged his leave of Kadar once again, and departed from the castle. And I could not even be relieved to see him go, for I knew what black purpose drove him forth to seek yet another mage-born soul that he could suck dry, like a spider turning its prey to mere husks.

Even so, and though pangs of guilt assailed me, I could not help but feel a certain lightness of spirit once Kadar's "advisor" was gone from the keep. And I had the notion that I was not the only one who experienced this lessening of care, although I was the only one who knew the reason why.

At least during the past five days I had seen nothing untoward occur. Whatever advice Maldis might be giving the Mark, it seemed Kadar was either not following it, or it was nothing exceptional. I knew better than to think of this as a good sign. It merely meant that, whatever their grand plans, now was not yet the time to reveal them.

During that time I did chafe at the constraint on my time, since Maldis' presence meant I could not go to continue my training with Ulias. We shared several more of those strange mentally voiced conversations, but I had nothing new to reveal, and he informed me that Maldis and Kadar had merely continue to question him about his gifts, rather than asking him to provide a demonstration.

I lied, of course, he told me. *This is one advantage I have over them, for Maldis cannot coerce me, although he rather wishes he could. But even his stolen power is no match for mine.*

I had wanted to ask then how Ulias had even allowed himself to be captured, if the dark mage's powers were not great enough to openly confront him, but I kept that thought to myself. By then I had begun to get the knack of it, to have one part of my mind active in this nonvocal speech while at the same time I could keep other thoughts buried deeply enough so Ulias could not hear them.

And so you know nothing of what they want, then?

Nothing they have said in so many words. But Maldis questions me on weather-magic, and Kadar on my powers of illusion, whether I can make a certain number of men appear to be many more, and it does not take a Keshiaari calculatician to put two and two together. Or even ten and ten, as is more appropriate in this case.

This revelation, of course, put me even more ill at ease, for it seemed clear enough that Maldis was feeding the flame of Kadar's ambitions, making him believe that perhaps in magic there would be a way to strengthen the North, to make it a force that might one day challenge the strength of Farendon, or even Sirlende. To an outside observer, this might have seemed patently foolish, but I had felt Ulias' strength and somehow knew there was very little he couldn't do, if pushed to it. That push had not yet come, but that did not mean it never would.

And then that night, the pull of his magic touched me again, and I rose from my makeshift bed on the divan and glided down to the cellars, silent as a ghost through the sleeping castle.

It was bitterly cold; the first snow had fallen that day, blanketing the world in white. I had never seen snow fall before, and entrancing as it might be to watch from a high tower window, it also brought home to me how trapped I was here now. Even in the South I had heard tales of the winters in North Eredor, the blizzards that closed the mountain passes and the roads so that days and even weeks sometimes went by before they were opened again. True, I was here in the heart of Tarenmar, and not in some remote keep on the northern marches of Kadar's kingdom, but even so my options now were far more limited than they had been a few days earlier.

But those worries slipped away from me as I made my way to see the mage again—although I wasn't so far detached from this world that I hadn't stopped to slip on my fur-lined boots, or throw a heavy cloak over my nightdress and dressing gown. That made the chill around me a little more bearable, although I guessed I wouldn't be able to stay overlong, unless Ulias cast some sort of spell to make his prison cell somehow warmer.

It actually did feel almost comfortable in his cellar, although whether that was because of a spell, or the brazier that had been left burning outside the cell, I couldn't say. Even so, I clasped my hands together under my cloak and wished that I had hunted up my gloves at the same time I had fetched my boots.

"First snowfall, and already I miss summer in Marestal," I said, as I once more took up the stool and moved it a little closer to the bespelled iron bars that separated us.

"Ah, so it did snow. I thought I felt it, even down here." Ulias rose from his seat on the bed and moved toward me, although I noted that he took care to keep a few inches away from the bars.

"Could you—could you not keep it away?"

"I could, but to what end? Winter is upon us, and in the North, that means snow. It does not do to circumvent nature and push and pull the storms to do our bidding."

"But...isn't that what my father has done, all these years?"

The faint smile that had touched Ulias' somewhat thin lips disappeared then. "Yes, and no. He has always been careful when working with the weather. It is more a matter of coaxing the clouds to come a bit closer, so a parched field might get the rain it so desperately needs, rather than trying to send the clouds away entirely so everyone might enjoy week upon week of sunny days."

I thought about that for a bit, trying to absorb what Ulias had said. "Bending the rules, but not breaking them?"

"Precisely. Too many mages met bad ends simply because they didn't stop to consider the consequences of what they were doing. No power comes without its cost."

"And what is the cost to Maldis of this dark magic he is working?"

Those grey eyes, cloudy as the skies above the keep, grew even cloudier. "His soul." The words were spoken simply, with no hint of drama for its own sake.

"I don't understand."

"As I said, power has its cost. When you work with your power, and not against it, the costs can be managed—you may be wearied, may need to consume a great deal of food to replace the energy you have used. But when you use power in a way that runs counter to the laws of nature, it begins to eat away at you, to destroy your very mind in the end, if it is not checked. And because Maldis has no innate power of his own, but is stealing that of others to fuel his unnatural needs, well, the damage is twice as deep."

"Would that it might carry him away now, while he is on the road, so he might trouble us now more."

"Ah, now, Lark, you know it is never that easy."

I did not reply, but merely twisted my hands beneath the heavy wool of my cloak. "But perhaps—perhaps Kadar will begin to see the true spirit of the man, and will send him away."

Ulias shook his head, even as his mouth twisted in a mirthless smile. "You are very young, but I do not think you are so young as to believe a man such as Maldis would leave willingly. And the Mark, while a man of some talents and intelligence, certainly does not have the ability to drive his so-called advisor forth."

"Damn him," I remarked, my voice heavy with bitterness. "If it were not for Kadar's foolish ambitions, then Maldis would not be here at all."

"And neither would you," Ulias returned dryly. "Do you wish you had never met the Mark of North Eredor?"

I bowed my head then, for I knew I would be lying if I told him that I wished it so. True, I would have much preferred a more innocuous meeting—at some ball in the Imperial palace, or one of the great tournaments held in Sirlende where the nobles from many lands would gather to take their chance at great prizes. But to not have him in my life at all?

I realized I could not bear the thought. "No," I whispered.

"So, then." Ulias hesitated. "Be not ashamed of the truth of your heart, my child. It is no disgrace to have a loving soul. Love is the greatest power of all."

"It is?" Looking up, I saw that he had sat down, long pale hands clasped in his lap. Something about his posture spoke of remembered pain, and I found myself driven to ask, "So—you loved someone once?"

"Yes." He raised his head and met my curious gaze. "I promised you almost a week ago that I would tell you more of the source of your powers, once we had the opportunity to speak in person. Well, you are here now, and I have no way of knowing when such an opportunity will come again."

"You don't?" I asked, surprised despite myself. "I thought the great mages could see the future."

"Ah, no. That is the one thing denied us, being the province of the gods, I suppose. We can make better guesses than most, as we have access to information that many others do not, but in the end we have no more of that ability than some granny-witch telling fortunes from the lines on your palm."

He spoke of such things with a hint of irony in his voice, but I did recall that one time when I had gone into Marestal with my mother, my friend Daris had tagged along, claiming she wanted to purchase more embroidery silks at the bazaar. We had gone off alone together while Mother conducted her business, but the silks only took up a small part of our time in the bazaar. After Daris had made her purchase, she dragged me to a shabby little stall at the end of the row of spice merchants, where one of those same granny-witches told fortunes. The old woman had looked at my palm and said that I would marry a tall, dark-haired stranger and go to live in a foreign land, which had turned out to be no more than the simple truth. So perhaps the granny-witches knew something that great mages such as Ulias did not.

However, I did not think that he would much appreciate it if I related this story to him, so I merely nodded and said, "What is it you wished to tell me?"

For a long moment he said nothing, but stared past me, as if seeing some long-lost vision in the damp rock of the cellar walls. "You asked how it is that your powers are so much greater than those who are yet mage-born in these latter days. It is because of your bloodlines. It is because of where the power originated in the first place."

He seemed to gather himself then, and the grey eyes, pale as morning mist, fastened on mine.

"It is because it comes from me."

~ Chapter Thirteen ~

Stunned, I could only stare at him, at the ageless face, the fine, proud features that, if I were forced to admit it, were not that dissimilar from my father's.

I suppose I might be forgiven for being somewhat inarticulate, when faced with such a pronouncement. "I—*what*?"

"I know it must sound mad. But I am your great-great—well, with so many generations lying between us, it is of little use to pronounce all those 'greats.' Many, many years ago, so many years that even I have stopped counting them, there was a woman who loved me, if only for a short time, and bore me a child." He closed his eyes, and I saw the lines around them deepen for a few seconds before he continued, "And the child lived, and went on to have her own children in time."

Somehow I found my voice. "But how—that is you're—you're not—" And I stopped in my floundering, for I could not voice what I had been thinking. *You're not even human...*

"I am not as other men, if that is what you meant to say." An incongruous smile touched his mouth. "And neither were my compatriots. But we tried to make a life here, once we knew this place must be our home forever."

"'This place'?" I echoed. "North Eredor?"

He shook his head. "No, I meant your world." A pause, as he seemed to consider his next words."I have been here a very long time...but even as long as I have dwelt here, I still cannot call this world my own."

That statement didn't make any sense to me. This world was not his? How could there be any world but this one? I stared at him blankly. "I don't understand."

"And it will probably be difficult to make you understand, when these concepts are so foreign to you." He hesitated again. "It is enough for you to know that there are many worlds besides this one, and many universes, so close to one another it is as if the thinnest pane of glass separates them. My people were experimenting with psi powers—"

"What kind of powers?"

"Magic, for all intents and purposes. We used these powers to try to move ourselves between universes. Such explorations of course were not without their inherent perils, but this did not keep us from trying. All scientific advances have their risks, after all." He fell silent then, and I prompted,

"So you came here—"

"Yes, we came here, so long ago that there is no record of it. So long ago that Iselfex, the wonder of the world, was only a collection of mud huts, and men warred with bronze instead of steel." Ulias lifted his head, once again gazing past my shoulder.

I had the impression he was not looking at the grey stone walls, however, but something which now existed only in his memory. "There were seven of us, working together, minds linked, to bring us across the void between universes. As the strongest, I guided us through that void. At the time, we had no idea there would be no return journey."

My heart ached for the undercurrent of pain I heard in his voice. So he was an exile, only one so unimaginably far from his homeland that I could not begin to comprehend the distance. "What happened?" I asked softly.

"The same thing that has plagued many pioneers. That first successful trial could not be duplicated. Whatever combination of power had managed to bring us here somehow did not work when we attempted to reverse the process." Ulias made a restless movement with one hand, as if even now the hopelessness of the situation aroused his anger. "After some time—a decade or so, as your people reckon the passing of years—we gave up, and attempted to find some way to exist here."

So many questions crowded into my mind I didn't quite know which to ask first. If his little group of explorers had numbered seven, and they were all but immortal, what had happened to the rest of them?

It seemed I did not need to voice these questions, for Ulias said, his voice hardening, "We kept to ourselves for many years, trying again and again to return to our home. It is not in our nature to cast blame, but toward the end even we began to quarrel, to try to find some culprit for our terrible exile.

"And that was not the worst of it, for when we were finally discovered by the local population, they thought us demons, unnatural creatures, and came at us with fire and bronze. We had our powers, of course, but we were caught unawares, and we lost two of our number that day. And we gave men more cause to hate us, as we fought back with storm and lightning. Our attackers scattered, but we five survivors knew they would return. They could not match us in magical strength, of course, since magic was unknown in your world. However, even the greatest of magics can be overcome by sheer numbers."

There seemed to be little I could say, so I only waited as Ulias paused, apparently gathering himself for the next part of his tale.

"And so it was decided that we must split up, if we were to have any chance of survival at all—that we should flee to the four points of the compass, and go from the place men now thought of as haunted by demons. For of course they had never seen beings such as us before then, and had no other explanation as to what we could possibly be.

"I went west, toward what is now Sirlende, heart-sick and footsore, traveling at night, using what glamours I deemed necessary to hide myself from the eyes of men. It was a wretched, ragged existence, one that I, who had once been a man of science, who had enjoyed comforts in his home world that you cannot even begin to imagine, had never thought I would have to suffer. And perhaps it was my wretchedness that allowed me to be caught, for after several weeks of this I was come upon by a hunting party, and barely escaped with my life."

He ran a white-fingered hand through his equally pale hair, and shook his head. "I sought shelter in a cave, bloodied by many wounds, so wearied that I could barely summon enough of my powers to slow the bleeding. It was there that she found me."

"She?" I asked, knowing somehow that this woman must be my long-ago great-great-great...well, as many "greats" as were needed to describe such a relationship...grandmother.

"She was the daughter of a local warlord, escaping her wards to run free in the forest, one of the last times she would be able to do so, as she was the intended bride of another warlord, with the wedding to take place in a fortnight's time. For whatever reason, she was more amazed by me than frightened. She tended to my wounds, brought me food. I healed under her care. And then..." He lifted his shoulders. "I do not think I need to tell you of what passes between a man and a woman. Our people are not so dissimilar that we cannot come together thus. What I did not know was that she went away bearing my child, and it was my daughter, and not her warlord husband's, whom she bore some nine months later."

"Were there more?" I asked. "That is, it seems that once upon a time there were a great many mages in the world. They could not have all come from that one child, could they?"

"As a matter of fact, they did not. I was not the only one to father a child, even though those children were spread out across the continent. After Lisara left me alone in the woods, I knew I must hide myself from the world of men. I did go to the agreed-upon meeting place, but none of the other exiles ever came there, although I waited for the greater part of a week. After that I made a home for myself far to the north, almost to the Bay of Ice, where I knew men would not come. But my brethren were not so cautious, and the others fell at the hands of frightened and superstitious men, until I was the only one left of my crew."

The only one left... I could not imagine the loneliness of being the only one of my kind remaining in the world. "Why did no one come for you? From your home, I mean."

"Because we were the only ones with the power to even attempt what we had done. Perhaps they tried—I know they must have tried—but trying to track exactly where we had gone was no easy feat. The universe is vast, Lark...far vaster than you can begin to comprehend. It would be like looking for a single grain of sand in all the beaches of the world."

I had no way of replying to that. Instead, I asked, "When did you realize that the children had powers?"

"Oh, it came to me soon enough. I looked in on Lisara, to see how she fared, and the minute I saw her child through the far-seeing I knew the girl had to be mine. No wings—thank the Powers that those were not passed on—but the child had eyes like silver, and skin paler than any seen in Sirlende. She was thought to be cursed, and her father shunned her...but not so much that he did not sell her off to someone willing to over-look those defects, once she was of an age to be wed. And so it went."

From generation to generation, children passing on the powers of fathers and grandfathers and great-grandfathers they didn't even know existed, until there were mages in every land, magic-workers who lent their talents to those with the coin to buy them. It was a time of wonder and might—but, like all else in a world governed by men, that same strength became corrupted, until those powers were used for ill, and all collapsed, bringing the Black Time, the age of cataclysm, when the last of the mage-born were hunted down and killed.

Or so the stories went. Obviously some had survived to pass along their powers, even in the great houses of Sirlende. I wondered then from whom my father had inherited them. His mother? His grandmother?

Who could say?

I ventured then, "This explains from whence my father's and my powers come, but it still does not tell me why my powers should be stronger than those of poor Rogin, or Khaspar the Nimble, or anyone else who might possess them."

"Because you come from my line. I was the leader, the one with the ability to guide my small group from one universe to the next, so that we might come to a world whose air we could breathe and whose other conditions we could stand. It was a lonely burden, one that no one else could assume. The women of my world also possessed great powers, but not the kind that could open the bridge between worlds. A pity, for perhaps we would have fared differently if some of our number had been women. At any rate, all the members of my team were required to make the crossing, but my powers were greater."

He told me this simply, with no hint of vanity. Perhaps to him possessing such power was a mere accident of birth, like the color of his hair or skin, and so nothing in which he should take pride.

"But why would you undertake such a journey," I asked, "when you knew the risks were so high?"

The silver-grey eyes, so like my own, regarded me gravely. "Did you hesitate, when your powers began to manifest in you? Did you stop to think that you should not pursue such a path, when it might end in ostracism or even death?"

"No," I said at once. It was not something I had to even ponder, for from the first time the magic stirred to life in me, I knew I could do nothing but allow it to grow and strengthen. To deny a mage-born person their magic would be like taking away the very air we breathe.

"That is how it was for us. It terrified us, and yet we knew it was something which must be attempted. We knew we risked death, and possible exile, but we did not turn away."

I could not pretend that I understood completely, for it still seemed quite a different thing for me to begin training in magic under my father's tutelage, and something yet again to set forth on a journey no one else had ever attempted, a journey from which there might be no return. Still, the quest for knowledge was familiar enough to me, and so I decided to let the matter go for the moment.

"Well, then," I began, then hesitated. "So should I call you grandfather?"

A smile, a true one, almost a grin. "I do not think that is necessary. It was a very long time ago." His gaze sharpened, and he continued, "I do, however, think it time to take up your training once again. You know enough of the 'why's. It is now time to address the 'how's."

For myself, I did not believe that I knew enough yet of Ulias' origins, or of the line of mage-born that had eventually traced its way down to me, but I could tell from his tone of voice that he wanted no more of questions. And truly, with the specter of Maldis hovering still like a black shadow at the corner of my mind, I knew it would not be prudent to dwell much longer on ancient history, however fascinating it might be to me. Just as my brother had trained in swordplay and state-craft under Lord Senric's tutelage that he might be prepared to take over the stewardship of Marric's Rest, so must I now learn everything I could from Ulias to gird myself for the eventual confrontation with Maldis.

I rested my hands on my knees and stared directly at Ulias, this strange being who, somehow, as improbable as it might seem, was my long-ago forebear. "I am ready," I said.

His grey gaze was very sharp. "Well, we will have to see about that."

In truth, though I had begun these exercises with Ulias the week before, this day he pushed me harder and harder, casting spells of increasing subtlety so that I had to strain with every ounce of that odd sense of mine to know what he had wrought—that a stream some three miles away had begun to flow uphill, or that a flock of hens who had only laid prosy white eggs up until that point suddenly laid a batch all in a lovely fawn-brown. Simple things, on the surface, ones I knew Ulias had chosen so they should not cause any lasting harm. In all things he was wary of the effects of his magic, although I guessed Maldis had no such scruples.

And even my small triumphs in such things were not enough for my exacting master. No, once I had discerned what he had wrought, I had to locate those fine, shining strands of magic and delicately unpick them the way one might remove unwanted embroidery from a garment. Difficult work, so much so that the sweat began to stand out on my forehead despite the chilly dampness of the cellar, and my breath began to come in short gasps.

"Enough," Ulias said finally, after I had finished undoing his spell to concentrate a patch of freezing rain out in the very middle of the lake, where at this season none of the local fishermen would dare to congregate.

I looked up with bleary eyes and blinked. "Did I not do it correctly?"

"Absolutely correctly. But we have been at this for three hours. Any more, and you will either collapse, or be discovered missing. Neither of these is to be desired. Besides, you must get at least a few good hours of sleep, or we will risk another fainting incident."

While I wished to protest, I knew he was right. Although Kadar was a heavy sleeper—and probably slept even more deeply this night, with Ulias' spell of calming peace blanketing the castle—the risk of discovery grew with every minute I was gone.

So I rose from the stool, noting absently the shakiness of my limbs, almost as if they belonged to someone else, and said, "Will we do this again tomorrow night?"

"If possible. Maldis cannot conceal what he is from me, but I am not always able to discern precisely how long he will be gone. I do not know the identities of his victims until he brings them hence."

"'Hence'?" I repeated, aghast. "You mean he keeps them here, in this very castle?"

"Oh, no," Ulias said at once. He moved closer to the bars, apparently intending to reach out to comfort me, but stopped at the last minute, as if just then remembering what would happen to him if he touched that bespelled iron. "Maldis is not bold enough for that. He speaks honeyed words in your husband's ear, promising him power, but he knows he dare not reveal to the Mark precisely whence that power comes. No, Maldis has a house on the outskirts of town, and it is there that he takes his victims. But even though that house is on the opposite side of Tarenmar from this keep, it is still close enough that I can feel the presence of these victims, sense it when Maldis begins to drain their magic."

"That's...dreadful," I said, a shiver moving over me as I contemplated what it must be like to feel someone's life force, their magic, being slowly stolen from their soul. At the same time, however, a tiny flicker of relief came into being deep within me. So Kadar did not know of Maldis' abhorrent practices. Yes, he was taking the counsel of someone with dubious origins, in the name of a foolish (to my eyes, at any rate) ambition, but he was not a murderer, or even a party to murder.

"It is," Ulias replied, and something in his expression made me even colder, although I had not thought that possible. "And it is something you will have to learn to experience, whenever it is that Maldis brings his next victim back to Tarenmar."

I crept back to my rooms, soul-sick and so weary I barely had the strength to return my cloak to the wardrobe where it usually hung, and to place my boots in their customary spot by the hearth. But I knew I must do these things, in case either Kadar or Beranne should notice anything amiss.

When I pulled the heavy pile of blankets up to my chin, however, I found that, tired as I was, I somehow could not sleep. Ulias' words haunted me.

Something you will have to experience...

Could I bear it? Could I keep myself still and calm as I felt my way along the twisted skeins of such dark magic, feel it robbing someone of their own innate power? At the moment I thought such a thing most unlikely, but perhaps when the time came I would be strong enough to do what I must, even if it tore me to my very core.

Over the low crackle of the fire I fancied I could hear Kadar's breathing from the other room, deep and regular. Again I wondered if I should simply rise from my makeshift bed and go to him, shake him awake and tell him everything, that he harbored a magic-worker of the worst sort beneath his roof, that surely he would be dragged down into darkness himself if he did not swerve from this course.

The compulsion was so strong that I sat up and began to push back my covers, and even swung my legs over the edge of the divan. But it was there that I stopped myself. The habits of a lifetime were simply too strong. I had been taught—told—over and over again that I must not reveal the truth of my magic to anyone. At best, ostracism and exile awaited me; at worst, probably death. I knew even in these latter days those proven to have mage-born powers were executed in Sirlende. No whisper of such things had come to me here in Tarenmar, but then again, I had known better than to ask. Matters were slightly more enlightened in the South, but still, if I had ever told anyone of my gifts, I would have been shunned forevermore.

No, as much as I wanted to go to Kadar, to tell him who and what Maldis really was, I knew that in doing so I would reveal myself, and in that would surely lie disaster. Perhaps I could think of some way to remove him from the dark mage's influence without betraying my own magical abilities, but at the moment no solution presented itself to me. And even though I had begun to think—to hope—that there might be the beginnings of some regard for me in this makeshift husband of mine, I could not trust such a fragile thing to survive the shock of learning that his stolen wife herself had magical blood flowing through her veins.

Choking back a sigh that was almost a half-sob, I tucked my legs back under the covers once again, and drew the blankets to my chin. The fire was warm enough. I knew the chill that overtook me then came from within, and not without.

At last I did sleep, deeply, in a black oblivion that was much welcomed after my trials that day. In fact, I slept so heavily that I did not hear Kadar rise at all, nor did he disturb me as he moved past and went out into the keep to begin his day. It was only when Beranne came in sometime in the mid-morning to bring me a pot of the herbal tisane that passed for tea in these parts that I sat up at last, blinking in a bleary fashion at the equally wan daylight pushing its way past the heavy velvet draperies.

"His lordship said not to disturb you, but I thought I shouldn't wait much longer, or it would be too close to luncheon to even bother with breakfast. Have you the appetite to eat a mite?"

I had to smother a smile at Beranne's use of the word "mite," which in her estimation appeared to be a large slice of smoked pheasant, half a loaf of bread, and a generous pile of dried fruit. "I think I could manage."

So I rose from the divan and drew my dressing gown about myself, and went over to Kadar's work table to eat. I pushed some papers and maps out of the way to do so, frowning a little. What was he doing with those, anyway? Even the beginning of winter was no time to be mounting a campaign...unless he was counting on Maldis to create a false spring with more favorable conditions for fighting.

Beranne left me alone to eat, busying herself with folding the blankets and sheets on the divan (I had long since given up trying to fool her into thinking that Kadar and I shared a bed), selecting my garments for the day, and laying them on the back of a chair. I munched away on the pheasant and the bread, interspersing bites of each with the dried berries she'd brought as well, but all the while my eyes were busy scanning the papers Kadar had left out on the table.

Of course I had studied my geography, along with all the other subjects my father deemed it advisable for me to learn, but somehow it seemed far more immediate now that I dwelt within the boundaries of North Eredor, and not safely on the outskirts of Marestal. True, South Eredor was itself not a large kingdom, and its military could not hope to match that of Sirlende. But the small kingdom was still a rich one, positioned as it was where the trading ships from both Purth and Keshiaar would put into port to restock. A natural barrier separated Purth from the South, as a southern spur of the Opal Mountains extended almost all the way to the shore, so we had little fear of invasion from that side. And as for Sirlende, well, I suppose some hundreds of years earlier its rulers had wearied of gobbling up smaller territories and decided to leave South Eredor alone. It does not hurt conquerors to appear magnanimous every once in a while.

But the North's only real protection was its poverty... and the strength of its warriors, I supposed. Looking at those maps, I saw how fragile a land it seemed, with Sirlende on the one side and Farendon on the other, both of them large enough to swallow up North Eredor many times over. And in his notes Kadar had written, *Four months until the wedding*, and underlined the word "wedding" several times, then scrawled out "Sirlende" and "Farendon," circling the names of both countries.

Wedding? I frowned, even as I buttered a bit of bread. Now that I had slept enough, I found I was ravenously hungry, as if all my exertions of the night before had finally left their mark.

I cleared my throat. "Beranne?"

She looked up from her task of blacking my boots. Apparently I had scuffed them during my wanderings in the cellars the night before. "Yes, my lady?"

"Do you know—that is, have you heard anything about a marriage taking place between someone important in Sirlende and in Farendon?"

Her brows lifted. "Keeping you sheltered down there in South Eredor, were they?"

"I beg your pardon?"

An odd twitch of her mouth seemed to indicate that Beranne would very much like to smile at my ignorance but was too well-trained to do so. "His Imperial Majesty is betrothed to the oldest daughter of the King of Farendon. As she has come of age this autumn, they are to be married in the spring. The Mark is...well, I suppose it is no great secret that he is less than pleased with the prospect."

No doubt. I stared down at the map once more, seeing the two countries almost as a pair of pinchers that could close in on tiny North Eredor with barely a second thought. No, it could not be comfortable to think of two great nations being joined in such a way.

Perhaps I should have paid more attention to what was happening in the world, but my tendency had always been to bury myself in stories of people long dead—when I was not being instructed in magic by my father, of course. Sheltered as I had been in the South, it was of no great import to me who the Emperor of Sirlende married, or how the King of Farendon disposed of his numerous (at least, that was what I had heard) daughters.

But now, as a citizen of the land which lay between these two giants, I could see why such an alliance would be of utmost concern to Kadar...and why he might go to great lengths to stop it.

A chill ran through me then, and I wondered if that was why he had enlisted the aid of someone such as Maldis. No doubt a dark mage would have no problem at all stopping the match, if given the proper resources.

The fresh bread suddenly seemed dry as crumbs in my mouth, and I almost choked, then reached for some water to keep myself from coughing.

"Are you all right, my lady?" Beranne asked, laying aside her blacking brush and getting somewhat ponderously to her feet.

I could not answer that question honestly, and so I said only, "I must see his lordship at once. Is he yet in the keep?"

"As far as I know, my lady." Used enough by now to my vagaries of mood, she lifted my chemise from where it lay across the back of the divan. "Let me help you get dressed."

Truly it was probably the fastest I had ever performed my toilette, as she helped me into my chemise and warm gown of green wool, then worked out the worst of the knots in my curly hair before I impatiently pulled away from the comb and set forth into the crowded hallways of the keep. With snow once again falling, it seemed as if yet more people had taken shelter within the castle's sturdy walls, finding what excuses they could to conduct their business inside and not out in the icy courtyard.

I could not be bothered with any of that. Pushing my way through the crowd—with the beleaguered Beranne at my heels, as she at least knew propriety did not allow me to set forth with no one in attendance—I looked this way and that, hoping that I would see Kadar somewhere in the throng.

But he was nowhere in evidence, and even though I slowed enough to inquire as to his whereabouts from the guards who always maintained a post outside the Hall of Grievances, even when it wasn't in session, no one seemed to know where he was. I forced myself to quell the rising tide of panic within me, trying to ignore the frantic voice in my head.

He must be here. He must be, for I must find him, speak with him, before Maldis returns and they embark on whatever dreadful course of action they have planned.

And then I neared the huge double doors that were the main entrance to Kadar's castle. The crowds were thicker here, if that were even possible, but the air around me was far colder, blown in every time one of those doors was opened.

At last I saw Kadar's shaggy dark head, higher than that of almost everyone around him. I pushed forward, Beranne snapping angrily, "Let her ladyship through. Let her through!"

But the crowds did not part quickly enough. Through them I saw Kadar pause, and that lightning smile of his illumine his face. And before him was a man with fair hair, rare enough in this part of the world, and I ground to a halt, Beranne almost bumping into me from behind.

The cold air touching my face was nothing to the chill that shivered its way up my spine then. For all my haste, I was too late.

Maldis had returned to Tarenmar.

CHAPTER FOURTEEN

"Let us go," I said dully, and Beranne stared at me with lifted brows.

"Whatever do you mean, my lady? His lordship is right over there—"

"His lordship is otherwise engaged," I snapped, cruel disappointment sharpening my tone.

Her expression softened then, as she looked past me to see Kadar standing there with Maldis. I had tried to hide as best I could my revulsion for the so-called "advisor," but Beranne was no fool. She bowed her head and murmured, "Of course, my lady."

We pushed our way back through the crowd. This time I was glad of the teeming mass of humanity, glad they were there to shelter me, keep me from Kadar's watchful gaze. Under the cover they provided, I was able to make my way back to my suite, where Tresi jumped up from her basket and came running joyfully toward me.

"Oh, Tresi," I murmured, bending down and scooping her up into my arms.

She wriggled a bit, for, despite her size, she did not much care for being carried about—although she would have cheerfully slept on my lap every night if I had allowed her. But then, as if somehow sensing my disquiet, she burrowed in closer to me, pushing her little wet nose up against my chin.

"My lady," Beranne said, and I turned. She watched me in some concern, arms crossed over her breasts. "Why such haste? Is it not something you could speak to his lordship about when he returns this evening? For you know he always comes back to escort you down to dinner."

Which he did, almost without fail. It was yet another of the things that had helped to endear him to me—so careful he was to show me the little courtesies, to prove to everyone that ours was a true marriage of love and respect. Now, though, it seemed as if an eternity stretched between now, when it was barely noon, and the time when we would take our evening meal, some six hours hence. So much could happen in that amount of time, and yet I knew there was nothing I could do. With Maldis returned, the two of them would be closeted together for much of the day, and of course I could not speak to Kadar if the dark mage was anywhere around.

I supposed I should count myself lucky that he had not detected my magical abilities, but I had been careful, and his dubious energies had so far been directed elsewhere. His opinion of me was, I thought, quite low, as he seemed to consider me a shallow, empty-headed chit jealous of the time he spent with Kadar. As that opinion suited me at the moment, I had done nothing to alter it. If Maldis thought me a silly young woman not worthy of his attention, then he would continue to ignore me, a situation I thought could only be for the best.

"I know, Beranne," I said, and set down Tresi, as she had begun to wriggle so much I knew she was getting fine grey dog hair all over the bodice of my green gown. I brushed ineffectually at the fabric before adding, "It is just—something of some importance occurred to me, and I wanted to speak to him in private. And now I fear it will be too late before I have the chance to see him alone again."

Beranne somehow managed to appear both sympathetic and puzzled at the same time, no small feat. She said, "Ah, well, we will have to hope that it is not as you feared, and that there will still be time. Not that I don't blame you for not wanting to speak in front of that—" And she broke off abruptly, as if suddenly realizing she should not be speaking of her betters in such a manner.

Of course I cared nothing for such niceties. Indeed, it heartened me a little to realize she had very little use for Maldis of Purth as well. "What is it, Beranne? Do not feel as if you must guard your tongue in front of me."

Her lips pursed and she glanced over her shoulder, almost as if she expected to see someone looking in on our conversation, even though the door was shut and the heavy draperies pulled closed as well, to ward off as many drafts as possible. "Well, although I know it is not proper to say such things, when the man is now right hand to the Mark, I cannot help but think he is a very poor sort of person. I've heard things..."

"What?" I asked eagerly. Had Maldis slipped up somehow? To be sure, it must be difficult to hide such foul acts as he was committing to feed his own counterfeit magical abilities. Hope grew in me as I thought perhaps I could gather some proof to give Kadar that his counselor was perpetrating vile deeds within the boundaries of his capital city.

Her mouth pursed in disapproval. "Not that I've seen anything myself, my lady, but several of the maids have whispered that he seems to consider them fair game. The pretty ones, of course, have complained the most about his roving hands. But it doesn't seem to have gone much beyond that, thank goodness. I wouldn't want to be the one to bring that to his lordship's attention!"

This intelligence took me aback. Of all the perfidy I had been expecting, groping the maids seemed a very commonplace evil. Not that this excused it, of course, but such a thing went on far too often in the great households, or so I had heard.

Still, it was something. And better I should go to Kadar with this concern, rather than wild accusations of Maldis being a worker of dark magic. "I shall speak to his lordship of it."

"Oh, no, my lady!" Beranne said at once. "I do not think that is wise."

"Whyever not?"

"Because it's the ones who complain who end up being dismissed," she said frankly. "Perhaps you have no experience of such things, but maids are easy enough to come by, and if one or even two should prove difficult, well, it's a simple thing to replace them. You would not wish to bring such a hardship upon them, with winter here and no way of knowing whether they could find another position?"

Of course I had not thought of that. Back home we had a girl come in to do the heavy scrubbing twice a week, and of course there were the seasonal workers who arrived for the harvest as regularly as the equinox itself, but we had no one who lived with us in our employ. Too chancy, with two workers of magic in the household. But because of this I did not really know how such things were ordered in the great houses. I had not thought that trying to protect those women might in fact lead to them being cast out.

"Perhaps if I speak to Althan instead?" I suggested. "Not anything too direct, but only a suggestion that the plainer girls wait on Maldis. They have had no problems, have they?"

Beranne shook her head. "Not that I have heard, my lady. Fancies himself an authority on 'the female form,' or so Narenna told me when she came to me about her problems with Maldis. Ill-favored sort that he is, I'm sure he's trying to take advantage of his position here, for surely no woman would go to him purely for his looks."

Her vehemence surprised me, for although I certainly had the lowest opinion possible of Maldis, I thought there were many men who, feature for feature, were far uglier than the dark mage. My first impression of him was that he was merely ordinary in appearance, although now of course I found it hard to be objective.

"I think you are right," I said. "All the more reason for me to speak to Althan as soon as possible. Could you let him know that I wish to talk to him, and have him come here at his earliest convenience?"

"Of course, my lady." Beranne did not try to hide the relief that swept over her face as she bobbed a curtsey and went out, moving in greater haste than was usual for her.

I wouldn't say I was exactly relieved myself, although in an odd way it felt good for me to focus on something else besides what Kadar and Maldis might or might not have planned for either of the parties involved in that upcoming state wedding. My feelings told me that it was most likely the princess who would be their target, and not Emperor Torric. Not that I doubted Maldis'—or Kadar's—ambitions, no, far from it. However, my father had informed me once that the Imperial palace in Iselfex still bore powerful wards and sigils left over from the days of magic, spells buried in the very stones themselves to provide protection for the Emperor and indeed all who dwelt within those walls. It would have to be a very powerful sorcerer indeed who could pierce those defenses.

As I waited for Althan, I thought on what Beranne had just told me. I did not know exactly why I should be surprised that Maldis would have a venial side such as this. After all, users of magic were not like the monks of far-off Damarkeen, who swore an oath at the age of ten to have no dealings with women ever after. My father had a family, of course. Even Ulias had loved once, and fathered a child...a child whose blood had come down to me all these hundreds of years later. No, Maldis had sworn no oath of celibacy in order to practice his powers, and I supposed it should be no great surprise that he would be as lacking in scruples in his dealings with women as he was in all other things.

I realized then that my hasty search for Kadar earlier had made me quite thirsty, so I crossed the room to the table where Beranne made sure a pitcher of well water always sat. No sooner had I poured a measure into an earthenware goblet, however, than a knock sounded at the door, followed by Althan's voice.

"My lady?"

"Do come in, Althan," I called out, and he entered, expression polite as always, but with a certain lift to the brows that seemed to indicate his puzzlement at being summoned in such a way.

It was true that I tried not to call on the steward any more than I absolutely had to, as I knew his day was full enough without me making further demands on his time. He had had the management of the household for many years. I was new to all of this, and so would not presume to tell him how he should run things.

He bowed slightly. "Beranne said you wished to speak with me."

"Yes, I did." I hesitated then, not knowing the best way to phrase my request. But Althan, being who he was, would know what I meant as soon as I said the words, even if I tried to couch them in innocuous terms. "Unfortunately, it has come to my attention that certain of the maids are being...approached...by Maldis of Purth in ways that make them uncomfortable. While it is true that the Mark has made Maldis a member of his staff, and therefore a part of this household as well, I do not think that gives the councilor the right to make our maids' jobs more difficult for them. It appears it is the pretty girls who are most at risk, so I believe if you set the plainer and older maids to these duties—"

"—Then they should not be molested," Althan finished for me.

In truth, I had not expected him to speak so frankly, but I was glad to hear him do so. He, too, appeared to have taken Maldis' measure, and found it wanting. So why, then, was it so difficult for Kadar to do the same?

Because Maldis is promising Kadar something he wants. We are often blind when we desire something so very badly.

Sometimes I wished that inner voice would not be so bald in its assertions, even when I knew it was right.

Clearing my throat, I told Althan, "Yes, that is my hope. Thank you for understanding."

He bowed again. "Thank *you*, my lady."

"'Thank you'?" I repeated. "For what?"

"For taking an interest in the household, for being concerned enough that you would wish to protect even a maid."

"They are all members of this household, and so they should feel safe as they go about their duties, should they not?"

"Yes, my lady, but..."

"But?"

For a second or two the mask of politeness slipped a little, and I saw something of the proud man beneath. "It is not my experience that those with a rank such as yourself would concern themselves with such things."

I couldn't help letting out a weary laugh. "Well, Althan, perhaps you are right about that, since you probably have far more knowledge of such things than I. However, since I was not raised to be a great lady, no one ever told me it was not my place to worry about matters such as this."

"But that is where you are wrong, my lady."

I lifted an eyebrow.

"All I mean to say is that you may not have been instructed in such things, but you are a great lady. I will see to this immediately."

He gave a final bow, then turned and left while I looked after him, dumbfounded. I had been called a number of things in my life, but certainly "great lady" was not one of them.

Despite everything, I couldn't help smiling a little as I turned to my neglected goblet of water and lifted it to my lips. Although of course they could do little to help me prevail against Maldis, it still cheered me to think I had allies in the household, that they counted me as one of them, and not some foreign interloper.

Out of nowhere, a wave of black power washed over me. The water I had just swallowed seemed to lodge in my throat, and I fell to my knees, choking and coughing. At once Tresi came running over to me, whining, even as she nudged me with her nose.

"I'm...all...right," I gasped, trying to pull some air into my brutally constricted throat. All around me the atmosphere felt noisome and dank, heavy as if I crouched in some fetid swamp, and not in the comfortable chambers Kadar and I shared. Wheezing, I could only remain hunched over, palms flat on the floor, as I forced myself to breathe, to recall the exercises Ulias had taught me.

For I knew this was no spell of his. The times I had felt his magic, even when it frightened me with its immense power, I had not experienced this sensation of evil, this cloying, heavy darkness that seemed to cling to me like the fumes from one of the factories in Iselfex, where I had heard the very air was poisoned by the smoke that belched from their chimneys. No, this could have only come from one person.

Maldis.

Somehow I managed to drag myself to my feet, poor Tresi still hunched in a little grey ball on the rug, her ears flat and her breathing coming shallow and fast. How she felt it, I did not know, but I supposed that animals had their own special senses when it came to danger.

Clutching the edge of the table for support, I closed my eyes and forced myself past the black cloud that surrounded me, made myself recall the exercises Ulias had taught me. I would be a poor Protector indeed if I could only manage these spells when I was calm and unmolested, and not under duress.

Unlike Ulias' spells, which always seemed to shine in my mind like pure, molten silver, Maldis' evil magic glowed dull red, like old blood. I could barely see it with that strange inward eye, only enough to sense that it somehow stretched out and away from the castle, moving almost due east.

Due east...

Toward Farendon, and, I supposed, the king's unsuspecting daughter.

My own breath coming in great gasps, I saw in my mind then a pale, pretty girl a few years younger than I, with wide dark eyes and soft, fawn-colored curls. And I saw her descending a staircase of dark green marble, polished, gleaming. And her foot slipped, and she fell, tumbling, as voices cried out around her, and she rolled, over and over, petticoats showing like white foam beneath her blue skirts, until at last she came to rest on a landing, neck at an angle that told anyone watching that it was broken. Those dark eyes stared, glassy and blank, at the ceiling, even as her poor broken body was surrounding by a crowd of wailing attendants.

Choking back tears, my breath strangling in my throat, I tried to follow the darkly gleaming trail of magic back to its black source. Almost before I began I felt cold start to wash around me, as if Maldis had thrown out his own nets to catch whoever dared to track down the person who had cast that foul spell.

And then Ulias' voice in my mind. *Stop now, Lark! Before he discovers you!*

My eyes fluttered open at once. Almost like snipping an embroidery thread, I cut off the part of my mind that had been following Maldis' magic. It hurt, as if I had ripped away a piece of my own flesh, but I knew better than to ignore Ulias' warning. Thank God he had been able to reach me.

And the black tide of magic flowed away, disappearing to whence it had come. Tresi's breathing quieted, but she looked up at me, dark kohl-circled eyes worried.

I knelt beside her, buried my ice-cold fingers in her warm, thick fur. Her presence reassured me a little, although I knew it had been a close call.

That was not the worst of it, though. I knew now what evil Maldis had just carried out.

The only thing I didn't know was whether my husband had anything to do with it.

When Kadar came to escort me down to dinner, I had more or less recovered my composure—mostly because I knew I had little choice but to maintain as calm an appearance as possible. Maldis could have guessed everything, or nothing. I would not give him any additional ammunition. And although I had tried to reach Ulias, stretching my thoughts out to where he waited in his cellar prison, he did not reply. This did not improve my mood, even though I tried to tell myself that he was only staying quiet so there would be no risk of Maldis learning of our secret communications.

The Mark looked even grimmer than I felt, his mouth tight and his jaw set. He answered my half-hearted questions about his day with short, noncommittal answers, and said only, "Let us go."

I nodded meekly, knowing better than to spar with him when he was in such a mood. As we descended to the dining hall, I could not help wondering if his current black state was because Maldis' evil spell had succeeded, and the Mark was now having second thoughts.

There was no way to ask, of course. And I was not sure what to think when I saw Maldis seated already in his customary place at the high table, although he did rise with the rest of the company as Kadar and I mounted the dais and took our regular seats.

There was also no way for me to scrutinize the dark mage for any signs of weariness, to discover if his spell-casting had taken its toll as such things usually did on me. At least there was little chance of Maldis misbehaving here, in front of the company; he was seated between Baron Trennhelm on one side and the mayor of Tarenmar on the other, and as neither of them were the sort to awake lecherous thoughts, I thought little harm would come from his presence. Indeed, better that we should sit at the same table. At least that way I could keep an eye on him.

I also noted that the prettier of the serving girls had been assigned to the other tables, and I murmured a silent thanks to Althan for implementing my recommendations so speedily. Again, not that Maldis probably would have done much in sight of everyone present, but better that they should not even come close enough to invite his interest.

We ate in silence for the most part, although Kadar did engage in a lengthy conversation with Lord Niel on his left, something about planning a hunting expedition for the next day if the weather cleared enough. I did not much care for the idea of Kadar venturing forth on such an outing, especially since I guessed Maldis probably would not accompany the group, not being much of one for exercise. However, because of the anger I sensed running just under the surface of Kadar's brittle good humor, I guessed that protesting the expedition would only serve to irritate him further.

No, I would just have to thank my stars that at least Maldis generally stayed far away from any of my haunts in the castle, so it would be easy enough to avoid him. Even so, I found myself praying that the storms would return on the morrow, and that bad weather would keep the men inside. Kadar would grumble and fuss, but I found as time went on that I didn't mind so much.

And even as I sat there, mind thrumming with the aftereffects of that hideous spell, I found myself trying to make sense of it, to come up with some way to absolve Kadar, to tell myself he must be innocent of this, that he would never stoop to the murder of an innocent. Foolish, I know, but one never wants to think the worst of those one holds dear. Despite everything, I found myself craving the sound of his voice, the brilliance of his smile. How I could want so much of him, and yet hate what he was doing with Maldis? Truly, the heart was a very unruly organ.

At last the meal was over, and Kadar stood, giving the signal for all in attendance that it was time to retire to their various chambers. This was no feast day, only a simple evening meal, and so there would be no dancing or music or players performing pantomimes. I stood as well, smiling and nodding as my position required, while the lords and ladies bowed and went on their way and the servants began clearing away the tables.

Usually Kadar would accompany me upstairs at this point in the evening, but now he touched my arm and said, "I would have conversation with Maldis before I come to our chambers. Do you mind making your way alone, just this once?"

"Not at all," I replied, although of course my thoughts began racing, wondering what he had to say to his advisor that could not wait until morning. And truly, by "alone" he meant only without him, for as always Beranne waited for us near the door. It was her duty to make sure we had everything we needed before we retired for the night, although most of the time those needs had been attended to before we even headed back upstairs. "I will see you shortly?" I asked Kadar.

Just the smallest of pauses, so small I almost wouldn't have noticed it, except that I had grown accustomed to his moods and manners over the past month or so. "Yes, of course."

And he lifted my hand to his lips to take his leave—a simple gesture of courtesy, but a shiver ran up my arm as his mouth touched my flesh, and I felt his breath warm against my skin. Of late I had begun to wish for something far more than that, but I knew that to increase our intimacy was only to invite disaster.

I smiled at him, and turned and went to Beranne, but I had no intention of meekly returning to my apartments, not when I had a chance of finally learning something of what he and Maldis were plotting. She followed along behind me as I left the dining hall, but then I turned a corner and halted, and she almost walked into me.

"My lady!" she gasped. "You did give me a turn. But why are we stopping here?"

"Because I want to do a little spying," I told her calmly, and tried not to grin at her obvious discomfiture.

"My lady—"

"Oh, do hush, Beranne. I need to listen."

Her eyes widened, but she did fall silent. Her expression, however, seemed to indicate that she thought I had taken leave of my senses.

Actually, I was doing just the opposite—or at least sharpening the one I needed at the moment. Ulias had taught me the listening spell only a few days earlier, and I was surprised at how simple it really was, no more difficult than the little cantrips I used to locate lost objects or unlock a door. In truth, I wondered why my father had not taught it to me, as he had taught me so many other of the minor magics...until I realized that perhaps a parent would not wish to have a child who could listen in on private conversations.

When I mentioned this to Ulias, he had smiled and told me, "This is why parents were advised never to teach their own children, even in instances when the power did not skip a generation or two. It is difficult to subject one's own child to the sort of rigorous effort required for the true study of magic... and it is also difficult to be objective, to teach everything, even if it might be a little inconvenient."

Inconvenient. That was one way of looking at it. At the time I was only irritated that my father had withheld information from me, but now I was simply glad that Ulias had taught me the trick.

"Tell me if anyone is coming, but otherwise do not speak," I told Beranne, and she nodded.

"Yes, my lady."

I shut my eyes then, listening to the various voices within the hall—the light, sweet tones of the maids as they cleared away the last of the dishes, Althan's deep, smooth baritone. And then the tread of two pairs of feet, one heavier, but brisk, and the other almost undetectable, but keeping pace with the first. I knew those footsteps belonged to Kadar and Maldis.

They moved off in the opposite direction from where I stood, going to a place where the corridor dead-ended in a little alcove with an arched window that afforded a fine view of the lake. I guessed, however, that was not why they went there. That corridor saw little traffic, and of course no one would be going to look at the view after sunset.

It was there that the two men stopped. Kadar spoke first, his voice tightly controlled, low, but no less furious for all that.

"I told you not to do anything this drastic."

Maldis sounded singularly unruffled. "My lord, you wanted the marriage stopped, did you not?"

"Yes, but—"

"Well, there is certainly no chance of it happening now, is there?"

A silence. I wished then that I could see them in addition to hearing them, but this spell was not the far-seeing. I could only attend their words and try to fill in the missing pieces later.

Then Kadar spoke, his tone still taut, angry. "All I requested was that she be made unsuitable for an Imperial marriage. A dalliance with her dancing master, a liaison with a penniless second son—there are so many things that could have prevented the match. Torric Deveras is a proud man, even for an emperor of Sirlende. He would not have stooped to marry a girl so sullied, even if she were a princess of Farendon."

"But there would have been a chance."

"Perhaps, but—"

"But nothing, my lord." Maldis' mild tone turned silky, the words meant to persuade, to calm. "It would have been a constant fear, would it not? And now that fear is ended."

"As is that poor girl. Eighteen, Maldis! She was only eighteen. I cannot bear to think that I have her blood on my hands."

"But you do not, my lord." A pause. "I do."

So he had not known, or commanded that vile act. Not that causing an honorable girl's reputation to be sullied was something to dismiss lightly, but of course such a deed paled beside cold-blooded murder. The relief that washed over me was almost equally touched with guilt, for I knew I should not be allowing myself to feel this happy, not when a young woman had been killed in such a foul way.

Next to me I could hear Beranne shift and make a worried noise low in her throat. Perhaps I had let out a sigh, or betrayed my roiling thoughts in some other fashion, but I could not let my concentration slip any further.

It wasn't quite a growl, but the sound Kadar made next was very close to one. "You may have secured the North's safety... for now...but the cost is far too high. The thing is done, and we must live with it. For now, though, leave me. I do not wish to look on you any more this evening."

"My lord." Maldis' reply was neutral enough, but I thought I heard underneath it a curl of amusement, as if he found it laughable that Kadar had ordered him away.

Be careful, my love, I thought. *For this creature is not your servant, and will only pretend to be one until the pretense serves him no longer.*

And then those soft footsteps made their way back down the corridor and off in the direction of the castle's main entrance. No doubt Maldis had decided to return to whatever shack or other dwelling housed his latest victim. I could not hold out any hope that that hapless mage-born soul still lived; the death-spell must have taken every ounce of power their blood possessed.

It seemed that Kadar lingered there in the alcove for a moment or two more before he strode forth, obviously heading toward our tower apartments. I broke the spell then, knowing I must return there as well, and before the Mark arrived, or he would most certainly question me as to where I had been this past quarter-hour.

"Quick, Beranne!" I gasped. "I must get to my suite immediately. Is there any way besides the main stair?"

She raised an eyebrow, but, apparently recognizing the urgency in my tone, said, "There is a second way, up the small staircase the servants use."

"Show me."

There were no questions or words of protest. She merely nodded and led me down the hallway to another narrower corridor, one that terminated in a narrow stairway barely lit by one or two mean little sconces. It did not look at all appealing, but I knew I had little choice. "You may go first," I said, figuring that it would be safer to follow her, since she most likely was far more familiar with the treacherous little staircase.

A nod, and then she began the ascent as I trailed behind her, putting a hand out to either side so I might let the cold stone help guide me upward. As we moved up the stairs, I tried not to think of time passing, made myself pray that this truly was a more direct route. And perhaps Kadar would pause on the way to our rooms to speak to a courtier, or to Althan, so that his arrival might be more delayed.

Anything that would allow me to get there first.

We emerged from the stairs in a corridor I halfway recognized.

"This way, my lady," Beranne said, moving briskly off to our right, to another, larger hallway, where we turned left and suddenly were confronted by the shallow stairway that led into my apartments.

There was no sign of Kadar, and I let out a little sigh of relief. So the shortcut had worked.

I strode past Beranne and practically ran up the stairs, ignoring the somewhat startled looks of the two men who stood guard outside the large double doors. Grasping the handle on the one to my right, I flung the door open and hastened inside.

Only to be confronted by my husband, who stood next to the hearth, arms crossed. His brows lowered, and he inquired, "And where have you been, my dear?"

~ Chapter Fifteen ~

I could do nothing but stare at him for a few seconds. Somehow I found my voice. "I was—that is, Beranne and I were—"

Bless her, she stepped forward and dropped a quick curtsey. "Beg pardon, my lord, but I thought her ladyship might be diverted by the new litter of kittens one of the kitchen cats dropped last week. They—"

She might as well not have been speaking at all. His gaze remained fixed on me. "Lark."

"Thank you, Beranne," I said clearly. "That will be all, I think."

An expression of confusion flitted over her features, but she did not question or contradict. Only another curtsey, and then she was backing away, shutting the door behind her.

Silence fell. Kadar and I stared at one another for a long moment. What had made him so suspicious, I could not say, except that he had suffered a blow this night. It would be easy to be angry with him and say it was his fault for housing a viper in his bosom, as my friend Daris might have described the situation in her somewhat dramatic way, but of course he could have had no idea of the sort of evil Maldis of Purth had brought with him. Whatever doubts I might have had about Kadar's intentions had been put to rest by that quietly vicious little exchange with his "councilor." The Mark's ambitions were great, that was was true, but even he had lines he simply would not cross.

I had no idea what the dark mage would do next, but I was fairly certain Kadar was no longer in his pocket...and perhaps even in danger from him. Despite my worry, something in that realization gave me a surge of hope. Perhaps things were not as broken between us as I had thought.

And oh, I was so weary of the secrets and subterfuges, the lies I uttered on a daily basis. Would it not be better to tell the truth for once? Now might be the perfect time, coming fresh on my husband's rift with Maldis. Now that Kadar's eyes had been opened, perhaps he would be better suited to see what was right in front of him.

A little shiver went through me, and I moved closer to the Mark. He might not read anything in my change of position save a desire to be closer to the warmth of the fire. It was a bitter night, snow falling again past the thick walls and poorly glazed windows of the keep.

I wished then for a sip or two of that bracing honey-liquor to strengthen me for what was to come next, but I knew better than to request such a thing. That would surely be a sign of weakness. Instead, I gathered my breath and said, "You asked me where I was, my lord. I was down the hallway and around the corner from the alcove where you stood and spoke with Maldis, and you berated him for murdering a princess of Farendon with some fell magic."

Silence again, as Kadar stared at me, golden eyes wide, glinting with shock...and something else. Fear?

Not that. I did not want him to fear me.

In the heavy quiet I fancied I could hear the thudding of my own heart as I gazed up at him, willing him to say something... anything.

At last he spoke. "And how is it you could hear this conversation?"

"Magic," I said simply.

A lift of the expressive brows, and then he went past me, going to the table where the squat bottle of *methlyn* sat with its accompanying glasses. He pulled the stopper from the bottle and said, "A glass, my dear?"

"Yes," I replied uncertainly. I supposed I could be forgiven for wondering if he'd suddenly acquired the gift of reading thoughts.

After pouring a sturdy measure into each glass, he handed one to me. "That must have been difficult."

"'Difficult'?" I repeated.

"Making such a confession."

Not knowing what else to do, I lifted my shoulders. "Not as difficult as continuing to lie to you." I drank then, letting the heat of the *methlyn* work its own magic in bolstering my courage.

Again he was silent, staring down into the amber liquid in his own glass, but drinking none of it. "Well, I suppose this would explain some of your antipathy toward Maldis. You knew from the very beginning, didn't you?"

"I—" I gathered myself, and went on, "I did feel the darkness of his power when I first shook his hand. But that may have only been because I was warned."

"Warned?"

I had given him one truth. It was only fair that I should give him all. "Ulias summoned me to see him, and warned me of Maldis of Purth."

The golden eyes glinted then. "Ah."

"Even then I did not know the extent of his perfidy. It was only later, when Ulias explained..."

"Explained what?"

"Explained how Maldis was getting his power."

"Is he not a mage, the same as you?"

I shivered. "No. Not in any true sense of the word. He... steals...his power, takes it from those honestly born with it."

Kadar's expression darkened. "And how does he manage this theft?"

"By slowly draining the power along with their blood. I know no more than that—Ulias did not give me any more details. I did not need to hear them."

"Gods." He passed a hand through his heavy dark hair, his face pale. At last he lifted his glass with his other hand and drained the liquid inside in one long swallow. "And to think I brought him here."

"You could not have known—"

"I should have known, or at least guessed. Whenever something sounds too easy, then usually it is." Without looking at me, he set the empty glass down on the table. At first it seemed as if he would move to refill it, but instead he turned it upside down, the dregs inside dripping, marring the polished wooden surface. At last he looked up, the golden eyes meeting mine squarely. "Tell me one thing."

"What is that?"

"Why are you still here?"

Mouth dry, I forced myself to maintain his gaze, to not look away. "My lord?"

"Do not play coy with me, Lark. If you truly are a mage, why did you not escape?"

I almost smiled. "I did try. Do you not recall how sleepy your retainers were, back at the hunting lodge the first night I was taken?"

"They did seem somewhat over-weary." His brows drew down slightly. "I was not, however."

"Some people do not feel the effects of such minor charms. You seem to be such a one...as I found out, to my dismay. And I tried again, as you should remember. But once again I was caught. And after that..." I lifted my shoulders.

"After that?"

"I found I did not have as much stomach for it as I had thought."

Kadar's gaze sharpened. "You did not?"

"I..." I moved toward the hearth, and made rather a show of setting my own empty glass down on the mantel so I could rub my chilled fingers that much closer to the fire. "That is, by then I had felt the magic in this place, knew that something very strange was going on. And then I met Ulias, and..."

"Yes, Ulias. You said he summoned you?"

"He did. He sensed my power, and wanted to take my measure. He knew at once I was not one such as Maldis. And since then, he has been training me, as much as he is able."

Kadar's tone sharpened. "Training you? Training you for what?"

"Nothing fearsome, I assure you. Magic doesn't work that way." I shifted so my back was to the hearth; somehow the warmth against my wool-clad skin was oddly strengthening, giving me the courage to go on. "My talents lie in detecting magic, knowing how it is being worked, and stopping it if possible. It is a talent that no one save another mage should fear."

"And does Maldis fear it?"

"He would, if he knew I possessed it."

The implications of that remark were not lost on Kadar. His brows drew together as he considered what I had just said. "And you trust me with this knowledge?"

"I do now," I said simply.

"Lark—" He broke off and appeared to wrestle with his next utterance. "*Why?*"

"Because I heard what you said to Maldis. I knew then that whatever outcome you might have hoped for, it was never to be at the cost of someone's life...an innocent's life. And I knew I could not let the man I loved face Maldis' wrath unaided."

The words had barely left my lips before I realized what I had just said. I might have thought such a thing to myself, but I had never expected to say it aloud, and so baldly. Surely now he would laugh, or lift a mocking eyebrow, or say something witty and cutting to dispel the tension.

But he did none of those things. For a second or two he stared at me, his expression unreadable. And then he moved so swiftly I could hardly register that he was now next to me, that those were his hands reaching up to cup my face, or that those were his lips pressing against mine, strong and tasting slightly of the sharp honey-heat of the *methlyn*.

And his arms were around me, and all I wanted then and forever was the warmth of that embrace, the taste of his mouth, the beating of his heart somehow merging with mine. This was what a kiss should be, was always meant to be. I had never thought such rightness could be found in Kadar Arkalis' arms.

We clung to one another for a moment that seemed to last forever, neither one of us wishing to be the first to pull away. The very blood in my veins seemed to pound and pulse with the rhythm of his name—*Kadar, Kadar.*

At last, though, we did pull apart, just the smallest bit, so that we might catch our breath.

He spoke first. "I had hoped..." A rueful head shake. "No, it was a foolish dream, a hope that perhaps you would come to me like this at last. A dream only, though, one I hadn't dared to think might come true."

The flush in my cheeks had very little to do with the blazing fire that burned in the hearth. So he did care for me. Of late I had begun to wonder if I had only imagined the beginnings of warmth between us, that I had flattered myself to think we might share anything save guarded courtesy. It was Maldis who had come between us, Maldis filling Kadar's head with poisoned hopes for a future that would profit no one but himself.

"A dream I shared, but one I would not admit, even to myself," I told him.

That was enough to bring him close to me once again, for our mouths to touch in wonder and desire. I felt it then—heat running through my body even as I shivered with need for him. Oh, I had never thought I might feel this way, as if I wanted to crush myself against him so that our separate bodies might become one, if only for a little while.

He pulled away slightly, his gaze questioning as he stared down at me. I nodded, not trusting myself to speak.

Oh, yes, Kadar...make me your wife in more than name only.

My eyes must have told him everything he needed to know. A swift rush of movement, and then I was in his arms, being lifted from my feet so he might bear me to the bedchamber, take me as he had not allowed himself to do all these weeks.

As we crossed the threshold to the sleeping quarters, at once my head felt as if it were being burst asunder by a mighty cry.

Maldis! NO!

I cried out as well, a great gasp of denial and despair. It was as if the space in the world that Ulias had once occupied was now empty, as if he had somehow been torn away, the thread that had tied his mind to mine now irrevocably broken.

Kadar stopped at once, staring down at me in consternation. "You do not want this?"

Somehow I managed to gather my wits enough to shake my head, even as I replied, "No, Kadar—it is not that. Something dreadful has happened."

At once he set me down on my feet, although he kept a hand on my arm, as if realizing I was none too steady. "What is it?"

I hesitated, trying to form that cry of inchoate horror into words that made some sense. "Ulias—he is—gone."

Shock roughened Kadar's tone. "Gone? What do you mean? Not...dead?"

"No. That is, I do not think so." Again I paused, trying to make sense of the wash of terror that had passed over me. "But something dreadful has happened. Maldis has taken him."

And as my husband stared down at me, still not entirely comprehending, I forced myself to give shape to the horror building within me, give it a form as hideous as it was terribly, terribly logical.

Blood Maldis must have, to give him the power he needed. And what blood was more powerful than that of Ulias, whose magic had spawned generations of mage-born?

I wrapped icy fingers around Kadar's strong, warm ones and whispered, "He plans to steal Ulias' power and take it all into himself."

Chapter Sixteen

Kadar maneuvered me back to the divan, had me sit down in front of the fire before he went to pour me some more methlyn. "Drink this," he said. "You've had quite a shock."

That was no more than the simple truth. I took the liquor from him and drank it as I had seen him do, but had never dared to do myself—by tossing the contents of the glass to the back of my throat and then swallowing. The fire of it burned through me at once, and I coughed, spluttering, while Kadar held my hand and waited for the fit to pass.

Once it had, I found myself steadier than I had any right to be. I wrapped my fingers around Kadar's and said, "We must find him. We have to stop Maldis before—before—"

I broke off then. I did not want to contemplate a world with Ulias gone from it, much less a world in which a demon in human form such as Maldis had somehow appropriated the mage's powers.

The only thing that gave me any comfort was the knowledge that such a process took time—at least, according to Ulias it did. How Maldis had managed to take him in the first place, I had no idea, but the dark mage must have sucked dry yet another hapless soul—or several—to give him the power to do so.

I breathed in, then out again. "Where are Maldis' quarters in the city?"

Kadar's brow darkened, and he shook his head. "I do not know. Maldis said he needed a place of quiet for reflection, and so did not wish to live here at court, even though he had rooms here and did in fact stay in the castle once or twice. I did not pursue the matter, for of course at the time I only thought of pleasing him, and it mattered little to me where he stayed, as long as he was available to me when I needed him."

Worse and worse. I did not know how much time we had, for Ulias had never said there was a set span required to drain the power of Maldis' mage-born victims. It did seem that the stronger they were, the longer such an abomination would take...which meant that we might have up to a week to locate Ulias.

A week in which he would be suffering unspeakable horrors.

I shut my eyes and sent out the slightest tendril of thought, questing for Ulias' presence. The few times I had done this before, his mind had answered mine right away. Now, though, there was nothing, only an emptiness that sent a shiver up my spine.

He cannot be dead, I thought fiercely. *I would know it. I would...*

"Lark."

As I opened my eyes I saw Kadar watching me carefully, his features tight with worry. "You seemed to...go away."

"I'm sorry. I did not mean to worry you." I reached out and took his hand, squeezed his fingers gently, and then let go once again. As I did so I contemplated how cruel it was of fate for us to have finally found one another, only to have our minds and souls caught up in something far more imperative than the tentative regard we had just begun to acknowledge. "It was a way Ulias and I had of speaking with one another, purely through our thoughts. But he is gone. I cannot sense him at all."

Kadar's lips thinned. "So Maldis has killed him."

"No." I hesitated, then added, "That is, I do not think so. Not yet. But there is something keeping me from reaching him, and that worries me as much as anything else. I had hoped if I could communicate with him at least, then perhaps he could have given me some guidance as to where he has been taken. Now, though..." I shook my head, and blinked back the stinging tears I began to feel gathering in my eyes. "Now I have nothing."

"That is not true." Kadar sank down on the divan next to me and pulled me to him, put his arms around me, so I could feel the fierce comfort of his embrace. "You have me, and I am not entirely without resources."

Perhaps it was weak of me, but I could have wept at those words. So many long weeks I had gone with no comfort, no one to confide in. That the person who finally gave me succor was the one from whom I had spent so much time concealing the truth was perhaps ironic, but I did not care. It only mattered that he was here for me now. I would not have to face this ordeal alone.

I did sniff, once or twice, and Kadar's arms tightened about me, as if to lend me some of his strength. It did seem to help somewhat, for I could feel the tears retreat, and my thoughts began to clear.

"We will have need of all those resources," I said, the words quiet but firm. "I think we can at least narrow down somewhat the sorts of places that would be suitable for Maldis'...purposes, but even so you will need to send as many of your men as you can spare to try to hunt him down."

"And put an end to his miserable life," Kadar added, a feral gleam in those wolf-like eyes.

I shook my head at once. "I do not think it will be that easy. You must instruct them not to approach him, but only to see if they can locate where he has gone to ground. Unfortunately, I do not know exactly which powers are his to command, but if he can reach across hundreds of miles and strike down an innocent soul such as that poor princess in Farendon, then I do not want to contemplate the damage he can do to those who are much closer to him."

A grim nod was my husband's only reply. I guessed that he did not much like my mentioning the princess, who would not be dead if it were not for his ill-directed ambitions, but I could not worry about that now. I only wanted to make sure no one else suffered her fate.

"He needs privacy, so he cannot have simply taken rooms at an inn. Likewise, he would need someplace with some open land around it—a house with some sort of grounds, I think. It would not be enough to let a space above a shop or other establishment, as there would be too many people coming and going."

"That does narrow it down," Kadar said, "for there are not so many places as what you describe here within the city's borders. The nobles whose estates are far enough away that a day's ride would not bring them home have apartments here in the castle. It is not like Iselfex, where many great houses stand empty for large parts of the year, waiting for the time when their owners come to town to pay court. Then again, North Eredor is not exactly Sirlende. It does not require a ride of many days to go from the capital to the countryside."

In his voice was still the edge of bitterness at what he saw as his homeland's lesser state. Ah, well, such things were not cured in a day. I could only hope in time he would see that he should be content with what he had. For now, we had far greater things to worry about.

"But there are still some houses such as what I've described," I remarked.

"Yes, some. Merchants and artisans of the prosperous sort have begun to move eastward, out past the old city wall. The land there on the eastern borders of the lake was never much developed until the past few decades, but now there are some fine houses, each with their own large plots of land. It is the sort of place that might suit Maldis, as new people take up residence there at a greater rate than what you might find in the older districts of the city."

"Then it is there your people should look first."

An eyebrow lifted. "And what precisely should they be looking for?"

Good question. It was not as if Maldis would be striding about the neighborhood, his hands dripping blood. No, his evil was far more subtle than that. "I would look for a house that had been recently purchased, or let. And I believe Maldis would want as few witnesses as possible, so if he has hired any servants at all, it would be at most one or two. That should raise a flag or two, I suppose, since most households of any size require at least a few maids as well as a cook and a gardener and—well, more people than what Maldis would want about."

Kadar wore an expression of some astonishment, as if he were surprised I should be able to conjure such insights. I added, with some asperity, "My mother's family is quite prosperous, you know. The only reason my household was not as large as those of some of my other relations was that we could not risk any servants discovering my magical abilities...or my father's."

"Ah," he said. "I had wondered about that. Your father's story always seemed rather odd to me. But if he was born with magical abilities..."

"...then staying in Sirlende was not much of an option for him. We are not quite so close-minded in the South, even though magic there also is looked upon with some suspicion." I did not add, *As it is everywhere*, for that truth was self-evident enough.

"Some are more suspicious than others," Kadar remarked, with a rueful curl of his lip.

"True," I replied, and smiled. "You do not seem to be too disturbed by my own possession of those abilities."

He returned my gaze candidly enough. "Ah, well, if I was willing to enlist Maldis' aid to my own ends, I would be a hypocrite if I spurned you simply because you are a user of magic as well. At least you seem inclined to put it to good use, while I cannot say the same for my erstwhile councilor."

That was stating the matter mildly. Even with all the tales of cataclysm and horror that had survived the fall of the mages, I had never read an account that described a perversion of magic such as Maldis now practiced. No, his seemed to be a depravity peculiar to him. I supposed I should be thankful for that; one dark mage with his dubious "gifts" was quite enough.

"Let us hope so," I said briskly. "For I do not know how much time we have, and we must set your people to their task at once."

"Consider it already done."

Well, that was a slight exaggeration. Since by then it was already quite late at night, nothing much could be done until the following morning. Suspicions would have only been aroused if there was a wholesale knocking on doors in the middle of the night. And what an awkward night it was, for while Kadar and I had admitted our feelings for one another, I was far too on edge to continue what we had started. Sensing my unease, he did not press the matter, but allowed me to retire to my divan as I had always done. And though I ached for him, I knew that spending the night in Kadar's arms would be a pretense, a diversion to keep me from thinking of Ulias and what he might be suffering at that very moment. It would not be fair to either one of us. All I could do was hope that this ordeal would be over soon, and we might finally have the consummation we both desired.

Of course the truth could not be given to those enlisted in the search—instead, Kadar had Althan put it forth that Maldis had stolen several valuable items, including pieces of jewelry that had once belonged to Kadar's late mother, and absconded with them. However, the former advisor was not to be approached if located, for the Mark wished to apprehend the villain himself, given the personal nature of the thefts. And because we did not wish to attract any undue attention, those tasked with the search were not merely the most trustworthy of the men-at-arms, but also several of the maids, the under-cook, the hawk-nosed master of the stable...all of whom had relations who worked at one or other of the houses in question, or at least knew someone who did.

If anyone in that motley group found the fabricated tale of Maldis' petty theft at all questionable, they kept their reservations to themselves and set forth at Althan's command, fanning out through the city. I wished I could have been among them, but Maldis knew me on sight, and I could not risk being seen. Perhaps I could have attempted to put a glamour on myself, to hide my identity, but I had received no training in such spells and worried that I would not be able to maintain the spell in the presence of Maldis' dark powers. At any rate, his measure was clear enough to me now. I doubted he would recognize any of the servants now searching for him, since they were beneath his notice.

Waiting for them to return was almost unbearable, but there was very little else we could do. Beranne was, thank goodness, not one of those sent forth to hunt down Maldis' lair, and so I did not have to worry about her safety. However, her presence was still somewhat intrusive, as I wished I could be alone with Kadar to discuss our situation further. But since we did not want to deviate too much from our normal routines, he left our apartments in the mid-morning to attend to his usual tasks, and I was left with nothing much to do than play half-heartedly with Tresi, and do an even more lackluster job of attending to my much-neglected embroidery. My thoughts darted here and there, worrying at the problem, and I wished I could be doing anything but sitting there and acting as if nothing terrible had happened.

"I always knew he was no good," Beranne remarked at one point during that hideously long day, attacking her own darning with far more enthusiasm. "Not that I'm one to criticize the Mark, as he does know what's best for his people, but even so, if he was wanting an advisor, he should have chosen one from his own subjects, and not brought in some stranger from the gods know where. Shifty eyes, that one has, and I for one am not surprised to hear he had light fingers to go along with those eyes of his."

Oh, if only that lie were the truth. But the reality of Maldis' perfidy was so much worse, and I knew I could say nothing of it to Beranne. No, once again I must speak fabrications and falsehoods, although at least this time Kadar and I were allies instead of enemies.

And if only...

No, I could not allow my thoughts to stray that way. There would be time enough for Kadar and me when all this was over and done, once Maldis had been disposed of.

If he were disposed of.

How precisely I was supposed to accomplish that particular task, I did not know. What I did know was that I could do nothing until we discovered his whereabouts, and so I fought with my continually knotting embroidery thread as Beranne rattled away about this and that. Her chatter did help somewhat to keep my thoughts from moving down ever-darker pathways, although I couldn't help brooding over what might be happening to Ulias as I sat here safely in my little tower room. Somehow it seemed wrong for me to be doing nothing. But for the moment there simply was nothing to be done.

Midday gave way to afternoon, and then to the sudden dusk of early winter. It was time to return to my apartments, and, I hoped, to some news of Maldis' whereabouts.

When I entered the suite, however, Tresi trotting along at my heels, it was to see Kadar staring into the hearth, mouth twisted. He looked up as Beranne shut the door behind me, allowing me to be alone with my husband.

I went to him at once, hands outstretched. He wrapped his fingers around mine, drawing me close.

Oh, the divine oblivion of the touch of his lips, the heady sense that he was the only thing of any importance in my world.

How I wished I could stay there in his arms forever, forgetting all else, but I knew that was not to be my fate.

We parted, and I was glad to see some light had returned to his eyes, although his mouth was still very grim.

"Althan has just reported to me," he said. "The news is not good."

I had already sensed that, but still, hearing the words seemed to awaken a chill at the core of my being. "What is the news?"

"Little enough, I fear." He let go of my hands and made rather a show of poking at the logs in the hearth. "There is no sign of Maldis anywhere—not in any of the likely places, nor the less likely ones. It is as if he has vanished from the face of the earth."

Which might not be a complete impossibility; I had heard that mages in the distant past had the ability to make themselves disappear, although it was commonly agreed that they had to vanish to somewhere. Perhaps I had been overconfident in my belief that he had remained somewhere within Tarenmar's environs. After all, he did disappear for days when on one of his "hunting" expeditions. It could be that part of that time was occupied with him simply traveling from his lair back to the capital city, or vice versa.

And while I would have liked to attribute his current vanishing to more dark magic, the truth of it was that I had felt none of his twisted spells being worked since he had stolen Ulias, which seemed to indicate that he had simply done too good a job of finding a hiding place for himself. Even a city the size of Tarenmar possessed many places where Maldis could have gone to ground.

"That leaves me little choice, then," I said, sounding a good deal steadier than I felt.

Kadar's brows drew together. "I do not like the sound of that."

"I didn't think you would. But I must try to reach out to Ulias with my mind, see if I can make some contact in that fashion."

"I thought you said before you could not reach him that way."

That was true. At least, I could not reach him in the way I normally had. This was more akin to the way he had trained me to reach out to touch magic, to recognize it, find its source. Surely if he were still alive, I would be able to sense his powers. Knowing there was no way to explain this to Kadar, I said merely, "I am going to try a different approach."

"But if he is in Maldis' power, won't that put you in danger?"

"Most likely."

"I cannot allow it."

Perhaps even a few days earlier such a statement would have raised my hackles at once. I knew, however, that he spoke out of worry for me, and so my tone was gentler than I had first intended as I replied, "It is not a question of allowing anything, Kadar. A conventional search has turned up nothing, and while I do not expect you to abandon that completely, I would be remiss if I did not utilize my own resources in trying to locate Maldis. We do not know how much time Ulias has left."

Faced with these explanations, Kadar lifted his shoulders, seeming to come to a reluctant understanding. "If you must. But do make sure that you are ready to pull away if anything seems wrong."

"I will. In fact, I want you to sit here with me and hold my hand while I reach out to Ulias. If anything seems amiss to you, then do what you must to bring my mind back here."

In truth, I did not even know if this would work. But somehow the prospect of casting my mind into the void to find Ulias did not seem quite so frightening if I could perform the task while Kadar held my hand. Surely his touch could only help to bolster my courage.

If he had any arguments left, he kept them to himself. Instead, he sat down next to me on the divan and took my hand in his. His fingers were warm and just slightly roughened with calluses, reassuring, real.

He murmured, "Be careful, my love."

My love. Surely I could do anything, now that I knew Kadar Arkalis loved me.

I closed my eyes and reached outward, seeing my thoughts as white-winged birds, beating against the darkness. Here and there I glimpsed flickers of light, as if from the minds of those also mage-born, and far off in the distance a shimmering white light that I somehow knew was my father, leagues and leagues away to the south.

In that moment I could only thank God that Maldis was not true mage-born, and so could not see these shimmers in the darkness. He'd had to rely on cunning alone to find his victims.

Not that it would do to underestimate such cunning. It had served him well enough so far.

And then I saw it, nearer to hand than I would have guessed, a wan flicker that somehow gave the impression of a much greater fire, but banked down.

Ulias!

A weak pulse of thought. *Lark—you must not—* And the unvoiced words broke off, as if he'd not the strength to finish the sentence.

Ulias, where are you?

A long pause. Then, heavily, *I do not know. Dark...stone...*

Stone? A house? A cave?

No.

Damn. I had already guessed that my theory would not be borne out, but even so I wanted to curse. However, giving in to my anger and my despair would help neither of us. *Can you tell me anything else? Please, Ulias. We will come to save you, but we cannot do so if we don't know where you are.*

Must stop him, Lark. Must not let him...

I know. But please...are you still in the city somewhere?

No. That is, it seems too still and quiet here to be in the city. But perhaps that is only another of his spells, blanking out everything around me. Difficult to say...so tired.

It was not like Ulias to complain of weariness—or much of anything else, for that matter. Although I did not wish to think of it, I very much feared that his current lethargic state must be be due to the slow draining of his blood and power. And if he already sounded so spent, I knew we probably had less time than we had even thought.

Heart wrung with worry, I replied, *No, it is good for me to know that. At least we can try to narrow down where you are. But Ulias—how did he even take you in the first place?*

Treachery, of course. Foul magic...cursed iron. He fed on two at once to give himself the power. A pause, then, *And you know what he means to do with me.*

Yes.

You must stop him, any way you can. Even if it means killing me before he can go any further.

Ulias, no—

Yes, my child. Another one of those hesitations, but this time when his mental voice came to me, it sounded somewhat stronger, and perhaps a bit amused. *You spoke of "we." So the Mark aids you in this endeavor, realizing now that his councilor is not what he represented himself to be.*

He does. He's— And I hesitated, not knowing how much I should divulge. *—he's been very helpful.*

I am glad you have come to one another at last. Perhaps something good can still come of this evil.

It will. We will find you, and—

But then a pulse of pain, so bright and shocking I could not be certain whether I had felt it myself, or whether it came from Ulias and somehow passed through me, like being hit by a bolt of lightning.

I let out a gasp, and his mind was torn from mine, even as I felt, as if from another world, Kadar's hand tightening on my fingers. The link was lost for good then, and my eyes snapped open, bringing me back to here and now, to the pressure of Kadar's fingers against my flesh, the scent of wood smoke, the questioning little whine from Tresi, who had apparently crept from her basket to curl up near my feet.

My husband's voice, rough with worry, deep and almost grating against my ears after that extended conversation of no true sound but only the shape of the words in my mind. "Lark!"

"It's all right, Kadar," I said, and to my surprise my own voice struck me as rough and raw as well, as if I had not spoken for days instead of only a few moments.

"You cried out."

"Did I?" I shook my head. "Maldis, coming for Ulias again. At least, that is what it felt like. He does not know where he is, but he thinks it is not in the city because it is too quiet, and it is made of stone, and dark."

"Is that all?" Kadar said, his tone wry. "Considering that almost every building of any consequence in North Eredor is made of stone, that does not narrow it down very much."

I would not let him discourage me. "It is better than nothing. And besides," I added, recalling how that pale flicker of Ulias' presence had not felt all that far away, "I had the sensation that he was actually quite close. So it would be someplace fitting that description but not too far away from the city."

"I will have to think on it somewhat. In the meantime, though, it is nearly time for supper, and so we must go down."

As much as I wanted to protest, I knew that we should do as he said. It was important to keep up the appearance of normality, even if the situation was as far from normal as a situation could be. And, as my mother used to point out to me when I lingered over my books rather than come down for a meal, I would do no one any good dropping dead of hunger.

So I let him take my arm and lead me down to dinner. At least I could take comfort in his presence, and the feel of his hand on mine, even if we were still no closer to a solution at the end of this day than we were at the beginning.

Sometimes we must take heart in the small things, if the larger ones are denied us.

~ Chapter Seventeen ~

The awkward moment had come again, only this time Kadar gave voice to the tension between us.

"Will you not come to bed, my love?"

I looked past him to the great green-hung bed, and a shiver ran through me. Could I go to him now, even with the specter of Ulias' captivity still hanging over me? All through supper I had worried at the problem in my mind, chewing at it the way Tresi might gnaw at a bone, and I did not know if I could sufficiently divorce my thoughts from that constant concern to give myself to Kadar in the way I thought he deserved.

"Kadar, I—"

In answer he moved from the doorway where he had stood and came to me by the divan. He had already changed for bed, and so wore only a heavy linen sleep shirt. I could not look away from the lean, taut muscles of his exposed throat and upper chest where the shirt exposed them, and a wash of heat that had nothing to do with the fire moved through me.

What difference would it truly make, after all? Kadar could think of no place that fit the meager description Ulias had given me, and neither could Althan, although he had murmured to both of us that he would ponder the matter further. It was not as if I would do any good by staying up all night and wracking my brains for a solution when none existed.

And I wanted my husband, wanted to be his wife at last in more than name only. What had Ulias said?

The one good to come from all this evil.

"Yes, Kadar," I said clearly. "Yes, I will come to bed."

The shadows of worry seemed to lift from his face as he smiled then, golden eyes lighting with sudden joy. And he bent and kissed me, mouth hot on mine, his fingers finding the cord which held my dressing gown shut and undoing it so I suddenly stood there in only my nightdress, just as I had that one night when he had first taken me. Only then I had feared and hated him, wanted nothing more than to be free of him, and now—

Now I could not imagine a world without him, could think of nothing but how I wanted to lie in his arms, feel his body against mine, be with him in the way a wife truly should be.

And then I was in his arms, lifted up and away, leaving the divan to be what it was meant to be, and not a makeshift bed. We were falling, dropping to the heavy feather mattress in the bedchamber, hearing the ropes creak beneath our weight, his hands undoing the ribbon at the neckline of my nightdress, pulling it loose, his mouth hot against my flesh.

Not that I simply lay there, passively waiting for him to take me. I pulled the nightshirt over his head, flung it away, where it fell somewhere to the floor. Perhaps he felt the cool sting of the air in the chamber, perhaps not. It hardly mattered as we clung to one another, bare skin heating with the strength of our need.

I understood then why he had not wished to wait any longer. In that moment, I thought myself a fool for trying to stop what was inevitable between us. He had known, long before I was willing to admit the truth to myself. And I took him into me, crying out with the realization that I truly was not alone, that no matter what happened, we would face it together.

At length we slept, naked flesh still pressed to naked flesh, our shared heat enough to get us through the long, cold night.

A cool wintry sun peeked through the draperies the next morning, catching the side of my face as I turned over in bed. I blinked, and saw Kadar gazing down at me, wearing an expression so foreign to his features that at first I could not recognize it. Then I realized he watched me with tenderness—that, and a certain wonder.

"You'll make me fall in love with you all over again, staring at me like that," I said, fighting the blush that stole to my cheeks as I recalled what had passed between us the night before.

"And would that be so terrible?"

"Not at all."

He bent and kissed me, his heavy hair brushing against my cheek. A fierce wave of desire passed over me then, and I reached for him, pulling him down to me. I could feel his arousal, and somehow that only increased the hungry heat in my body. How delicious, to make love in the morning, with the sun lighting my way so I could see the muscles in his arms as he reached for me, see the flush steal over his face. And then—

"Breakfast, my lord, my lady!" came Narenna's voice from the outer chamber, and at once Kadar and I broke apart, starting guiltily as if caught at some wrongdoing.

A quick tug on the bedcovers, and at least we were both more or less decently covered, although it would be clear to anyone what it was that we had been up to. And, judging by the quick downward glance Narenna made when she entered the room, she knew all too well.

"You may set the tray on the table, Narenna," Kadar said, his voice bubbling with suppressed laughter.

"Very good, my lord. Yes, my lord." She put down the tray and stood there, still, her gaze directed steadfastly toward the floor. "Anything else, my lord?"

"No, I think that will be all for now. You may go."

The quickest curtsey ever dropped, and then she was gone, fleeing the scene like a startled doe.

"Hungry, my love?" Kadar asked, after a brief pause.

"Oh, yes," I said, reaching for him again. "Very."

It would have been easy, perhaps, to try to ignore the situation by spending hour after hour in one another's arms. But although the desire was still there—sated for the moment, but definitely not gone—we knew that was no solution. After we had finally eaten our now-cold breakfast, and more or less gotten cleaned up and ready for the day, Kadar turned to me, expression thoughtful.

"I have an idea."

"You do?" I put down the comb. Normally Beranne would have come up to help me dress and do my hair by that hour of the morning, but it seemed Narenna had gone to her bearing tales, and my faithful maidservant had decided to do me the courtesy of allowing me to be alone with my husband for a while. While I appreciated this, it did mean I had to fight my wayward curls on my own. She had a much defter hand with them than I, and I had to laugh at myself a little for becoming so dependent on her in such a short amount of time.

Kadar nodded in reply to my question, and finished his own toilette by buckling on his sword belt, although at the moment he wore only a long dagger at his side. "There were several warehouses along the shore that burned down last year. They were made of wood, of course, but their foundations and cellars were of stone. They are the sort of abandoned place where Maldis might very well have gone to ground."

I could have kissed him. In fact, I did, rising to my feet and crossing to him so I could reward this notion with a healthy smack on the lips. He kissed me back, with increasing ardor, until I had to pull away.

"My lord, are you going to have me undo all this hard work I just put into my hair?"

A grin, and he replied, "I like it best spread out on the pillow beside me, but I will desist if I must." That warm golden gaze lingered on my mouth as he added, "I will simply have to wait and dream of better things."

I answered his smile, but I felt my expression grow sober almost at once. "So you will send someone out to inspect the warehouses?"

"As soon as I leave this chamber, my impatient dear." His own grin faded. "I know the stakes are very high here, Lark, but somehow I sense that you have a somewhat personal interest in Ulias' safety. Is there something you are not telling me?"

For a second or two I stared at him blankly, not quite sure what he meant by that, and then I shook my head. "Oh, no, my love. Nothing like that. He is my mentor, and a great and noble soul. I cannot bear to think of him in the clutches of one such as Maldis. And there is—there is something else."

Kadar did not reply, but watched me carefully, one eyebrow cocked slightly.

No time to stop for a carefully considered explanation. I said, the words coming in a rush, "He is—well, he is my great-great-great...oh, I cannot even count the greats, as he said to me once. Many, many years ago, he and others of his kind came here, and loved, and had children. This is where the magic comes from, Kadar. From him, and from others like him."

A bit of silence, as he apparently digested that information. Then a look of wonder passed over his features, and he said, "I had guessed he was long-lived, but I had not thought he was that old. So it his blood that flows in your veins?"

"His blood, and his magic."

"Well, then, all the more reason that we must find him. And when we do, I will make sure he has far better accommodation than he did previously. That was Maldis' idea, to keep him in the cellars. He said there was too much danger of discovery if he was housed anywhere else in the castle." Kadar's expression darkened. "I am sorry to have caused him any discomfort."

"To be honest, I do not think he was that uncomfortable. I saw the furniture and the furs and the books, and besides, I offered to help him escape, and he declined."

"He what?"

"Yes. He said he wanted to take your measure, and that he was quite comfortable for the time being. I can tell you were trying to make sure he did not suffer in his captivity." I hesitated, still not entirely certain of this new intimacy Kadar and I shared. But I also had to know. "What was your motivation, Kadar? What on earth did you think Ulias could do for you— or Maldis of Purth, for that matter?"

Kadar ran a hand through his hair, even as he frowned and shook his head. "I was a fool, Lark. I dreamed of greater things for North Eredor, for myself. Always this land has been in the shadow of those far greater than it could ever hope to be. You yourself are here because of one of those foolish schemes— although that mistake turned out to be the greatest gift I could have ever received. Then Maldis came to me, whispering of ways in which the North might be strengthened, saying he had powers that could be brought to bear. And I thought only of my ambition, and put aside my prejudices, and allowed him to sway me. When he discovered Ulias, and made him captive, I still thought only of what he could do for me, for this land. It was wrong, Lark, and I can only hope that no one else suffers because of my misguided plans."

It must have cost him much to make such bald admissions to me, and so I tempered my tone somewhat as I replied, "I cannot excuse your capture of Ulias, of course, but you also had no idea what manner of man Maldis was." Because I wanted to ease his burden somewhat, I stood on my tiptoes and kissed Kadar's cheek, adding, "And I do forgive your kidnapping of me, for it brought me to you. Indeed, if I had only known what manner of man awaited me, I would have gone much more willingly!"

He laughed then and kissed me again before saying, "You are balm for my heart, dearest. But now I will see about getting several men out to those warehouses, to see if anything is amiss."

"Yes, of course." The glow from the kiss faded somewhat as I thought of what might be waiting for them at the end of their search. "Do tell them to be careful. I still have no clear idea of exactly what powers Maldis commands—it seems as if they ebb and flow, depending on the strength of his latest victim, and since he now holds Ulias..."

"I understand. I will tell them to keep a safe distance, and only to look for signs that someone has passed that way recently."

I still did not like it, but I also knew that Kadar would never allow me to accompany the search party. All I could do was wait to see what they discovered and hope for the best.

Earlier that morning, as I had risen from bed and put on my dressing gown, I had sent my thoughts forth to see if I could reach Ulias, but I felt nothing. If he were dead, I believed I would have sensed it, but somehow he was blocked. And still there were all those other little flickers in the darkness, the firefly sparks of other mage-born minds, although I did not think any of them were strong enough to reach out and help me, even if I had been able to communicate with them.

My expression must have still been worried, for he bent down and kissed me again, not passionately this time, but a soft brush of mouth against mouth, clearly meant for reassurance. "All will be well. We must trust that we are meant to find him."

To that I could only nod, and watch him go, and hope that he was right.

Beranne arrived some time after that, full of excuses about her sick sister but with a gleam in her eyes that told me she knew all about the alteration in my relationship with the Mark. Luckily, though, she was well-trained enough not to indulge her inclination for gossip, and instead suggested that we go for a turn outdoors, since the sun had reappeared after several days of snow.

Fresh air sounded appealing enough, and so I allowed her to lead me downstairs and out the smaller rear east doors to the castle, the ones that opened on the castle's gardens. To be sure, these were somewhat meager affairs, nothing like the grand formal gardens I had heard were the fashion in Sirlende, or even the great botanical constructs back home in South Eredor, where specimens from all over the continent were nurtured. No, this patch consisted mainly of a bare vegetable plot, now of course all plowed under during the winter, and several narrow walks that at least had been shoveled but which otherwise had little to recommend them. There was a rather fine stand of aspens at one end that I assumed served as a windbreak during the warmer months, and several rows of naked rosebushes.

All in all, it was rather a bleak scene, even with a bright sun overhead, but perhaps I could ascribe the impression to my mood more than anything else. And it did feel good to breathe in air that didn't smell of human bodies and wet wool and wood smoke, although I could still almost taste the scent of smoke as it rose from the keep's numerous chimneys.

Even with the sun out, it was bitterly cold, a chill I felt rising through my boots almost as soon as I stepped on the damp ground. How I longed then for the mild winters of the South, when the rains came but we never saw snow, and the hills turned green rather than dead and brown.

But this was my home now. This was Kadar's land, and so it was mine as well. It had its own beauty, one I knew I would come to appreciate as the months and then years passed.

If, of course, Maldis allowed us such a peaceful future. I still did not want to think of what he had planned for Ulias, planned for all of us.

"You are very quiet, my lady," Beranne said.

"Am I?" I lifted my shoulders beneath my heavy cloak. Since I knew I could not tell her what truly troubled me, I added, "I suppose I was thinking of winter here. It is so very bleak."

Her gaze was curious. "Is it true that it never snows in the South? That the grass grows all winter?"

"I had never seen snow before I came here. It is beautiful, I suppose, but I had never dreamed there could be cold like this. Ah, well, I suppose I shall get used to it sooner or later."

Her lips parted as she began to reply, but then the door to the castle opened, and I saw Althan peering outside, shielding his eyes with one hand.

"Ah, my lady, there you are. One of the maids said she saw you passing this way. His lordship would speak with you."

At once my heart began to beat faster in my breast. Such a summons could only mean that the men had returned from the scouting party. "Of course, Althan. I will come at once."

Whether my haste to follow him was purely born of a desire to hear what Kadar had to say, or whether I was simply glad of reason to be out of the cold, I did not know for sure. But I hurried after him, Beranne puffing along in my wake, as he led me through the castle's corridors and on into a small chamber to one side of the Hall of Grievances where I knew Kadar sometimes had private counsel with some of his nobles.

Today, though, he stood there alone, frowning as he watched me enter. That frown deepened as his gaze rested on Beranne.

"Althan, please see that my wife's companion returns to our chambers to await her."

"Of course, my lord." Althan bowed, and Beranne took her cue as well, curtseying before she turned and left. Another bow, and then Althan shut the door behind him.

I had already guessed from Kadar's expression that things had not gone well, but I still asked, "And what news from the search party?"

"No news." He came toward me and took my hands in his. I still wore my gloves, but even through the thin leather I could feel the chill of his fingers. "That is, they saw nothing at first, no footprints in the snow, no evidence that anyone had been near either of the warehouses recently. This emboldened them enough to inspect the premises more closely, even though I had told them not to go in too close. But it appears our caution was unwarranted, for while they found some remains of what looked like a vagrants' camp, left there from the summer, there was no sign of anyone having been there any time since then."

"Perhaps," I said, considering. "Or perhaps Maldis only wanted them to think that. I have read that in days past some mages were masters of illusion, and could trick a person into thinking something was there when it was not."

"Or vice versa?"

"Possibly." Once again I fought frustration as I thought of all the knowledge that had been lost, all the thousand and one ways magic could be used and which now were only vague tales and legends passed down in secret through the years. "The problem is that I have no way of knowing whether Maldis is capable of creating such illusions."

"Is Ulias?"

Kadar's question chilled me. The thought of that gentle user of magic being forced to cast spells for the foul Maldis struck cold through my heart. When I spoke, it was slowly, as I dragged forth words I really did not want to say aloud. "Perhaps. Again, I cannot say for sure. That is, he is capable of great workings of magic, and a simple illusion should be well within his abilities. What I do not know yet is whether he is so far gone that he would allow himself to be used in such a way."

His fingers tightened around mine. "Let us hope it has not come to that."

"I can only hope that as well. However, that does not address the core of our problem, which is that we still have no idea where Ulias is. The warehouses could be hidden by some kind of illusion, or they could simply be exactly what they appear to be: two burned-out, empty buildings. And if that is the case, then we are back at the beginning, with no idea of where to look next."

"It would seem that we must check the warehouses again, guarding against illusion this time."

"To what point?" I asked wearily. "If Maldis is really protecting them in such a way, then he already knows we have guessed where he might be, and will either have moved his base once again, or at least will be waiting for us. Any element of surprise would be gone."

A moment of silence then, as Kadar appeared to consider my words. "It would seem that you are determined to be defeated."

"No," I replied. "But I am trying to be practical. False hope will only wear me down that much more."

No answer, but he took me in his arms and held me a long while, the warmth of his body finally helping to dispel some of the chill that seemed to have settled in my bones. His voice came at my ear. "Do not despair, my love. For I know that if we have managed to come together like this, then anything is possible."

I wanted to believe him. For his sake, I would try.

Of course we could not stay together that afternoon. He had matters to attend to— he wished to take advantage of the clear day to walk the properties intended for the new exchange, and to meet with his stonemasons and carpenters—and I had my own minor domestic tasks to attend to as well. Midwinter was approaching, with its attendant feasts, and I guessed Althan had put a word in the ear of the head cook, who wished to meet with me to discuss the menu.

Trivial concerns, compared to what confronted us, but we had to put on our public faces while we wrestled with our private problems. There was no one else in the kingdom who could assist us in tracking down Maldis. Well, unless I somehow managed to summon the other mage-born in the land, although I wasn't sure what good that would do. I guessed that none of them were trained for this sort of thing.

Come to think of it, neither was I. Not really.

But Ulias had said I was a Protector, and so I must carry within me somehow the seeds of Maldis' doom. I would only have to discover what they were, and hope it wasn't too late.

I had never met Lander, the cook, before and had somehow envisaged a round, comfortable sort, a male counterpart to Beranne, as it were. In direct contradiction to my imaginings, he was tall and thin, and appeared to have indulged very little in the toothsome offerings of his kitchen.

But his blue eyes were kind, and he even went so far as to inquire whether there were any particular dishes served in my homeland that he might also prepare for the feast here, if the ingredients could be brought to hand. A savory fish stew was a favorite of mine, but that would not work, as the main components were saltwater fish and a particular crab found only in the waters off South Eredor. However, I also enjoyed a certain type of iced cake, and after I described it to Lander, he nodded and said he thought he could make something similar.

I had just thanked him and risen from my seat when a wave of blackness, of crushing agony, passed over me. An incoherent cry wrenched itself from my throat, and I fell to my knees, shuddering as I attempted to draw breath, to force my lungs to keep from collapsing as that weight pressed down on me, heavy as if a mountain had just collapsed upon me. From somewhere within that cocoon of black soul-seizing pain I heard a clamor of voices, felt arms reach out to catch me just as I collapsed, the world spinning, everything around me turning to darkness, blacker than the space between the stars, deeper than the deepest ocean.

And then it was gone, and I was left with blessed nothingness.

"My lady. *My lady!*"

My eyelids opened against what seemed to be blazing brightness, although I saw after I blinked a few times that it was only the last wan daylight coming in through the chamber's one window. Lander knelt over me, and Beranne had appeared from somewhere as well, hovering nervously behind the cook's lean shoulder, her own face robbed of its customary apple-cheeked flush. It was she who had spoken.

Lander asked, "Can you sit up, my lady?"

A question I would have to ponder for a bit. I lay there, staring up at the dark-beamed ceiling, feeling as if every bone and muscle in my body had been pounded with cudgels. What on earth…?

And where the pain had been, a vast gaping emptiness. I realized then what that wave of agony was. Ulias, having the last of his lifeblood stolen from him. Ulias, being torn from this earth, and with that tearing, the connection between our minds torn away as well.

God...

Somehow I pushed myself upright. The room spun around me, and I gritted my teeth. This was no time for weakness. For if Ulias had met such an end, it could mean only one thing.

Maldis had finally stolen the last of his powers. For what fell purpose, I did not know, but I did know that I could not lie there like some weak-kneed female, not when that foul sorcerer had just given himself powers beyond those of any living user of magic.

"A hand, if you would, Lander," I said, in tones falsely firm.

He shot Beranne a dubious glance, and she gave the barest of nods. Apparently that reassured him enough for him to extend his hand to me, so that I might use it to pull myself to my feet. My limbs did feel far shakier than I would have wished, and I wondered how long the aftereffects of that blast of psychic anguish would remain with me.

Oh, how I wished it were Kadar who was with me now, who offered a solicitous arm to lead me back to my chambers. He could not have felt the torment of Ulias' passing, and for that I envied my husband. At least he would have an hour or so more of blissful ignorance before he learned of this latest disastrous development.

The walk back to my apartments felt longer than it ever had, but eventually I reached those familiar, welcoming rooms, thanked Lander for his assistance even as Beranne bustled about, stirring up the fire, fetching a fur lap robe for me. The cook left then, looking both worried and mystified, but of course I could not have offered him an explanation remotely resembling the truth. What he must think—and the rest of the castle's denizens, for I was sure word would spread soon enough—after yet another fainting spell on my part, I didn't want to know.

Beranne fussed a bit more, then said, "My lady, what should I fetch for you? Some broth, or some mulled wine?"

"Wine," I replied at once. Perhaps it was not the best idea in the world to be blurring my thoughts with alcohol, but at the moment I guessed I could do with having the edges worn down a bit. Anything to blunt the echoes of pain still shivering through my mind.

She murmured her assent and departed, and I leaned over then, burying my face in my hands as I wept. Dreadful enough to lose Ulias when I had just barely found him, when we had so much more to learn about one another, but to know he had lost his life in such a terrible way only made the pain that much worse.

I felt a cold little nose push itself against my hand as it lay limply on the edge of the chair. Tresi sat there at my knee, her dark eyes staring up at me imploringly. Reaching down, I let my fingers run through her long, soft fur, taking some comfort from her presence, from her instinctive understanding that I needed reassurance just then.

"Good dog," I whispered, my voice cracking with tears.

A little push of her head against my hand, as if she wanted to make sure I knew she was still there, that I wasn't alone. I sat there, stroking her, willing myself to breathe, until Beranne returned with a goblet of mulled wine.

I took it from her gratefully as Tresi settled down near my feet. As I sipped the wine, the warm liquid seemed to dispel some of the iciness at the core of my body, but it did little to rid me of the overwhelming sense of loss...or to quell my growing fear as to what Maldis planned to do with the power he had just acquired.

"Any news of the Mark?" I asked.

Beranne shot me a surprised glance. "Why, no, my lady. That is, Althan said he had gone to the site of the new exchange with two of his engineers, and should be back in time for supper. And as it grows dark, I am guessing he will be returning soon enough."

It grows dark, indeed, I thought, but of course I did not say such a thing out loud. Attempting to explain the reason for my fainting spell would no doubt frighten her far more than the original swoon ever had. I was glad of her presence, but what I really wanted was for Kadar to be there so he could put his arms around me, so I could take some comfort from his strength, even though I knew that strength counted for very little when measured against the power Maldis now possessed.

And though Beranne's eyes burned with questions, I told her nothing, only made a brief comment about being overtired. At that her mouth twitched, and I guessed again that Narenna had been telling tales.

How I wished it were simply a night of vigorous love-making that had me weary enough to faint.

I finished my wine in silence, then handed the goblet to Beranne and told her I wished to be alone for a while. Truly, it was more that I had grown weary of not meeting her eyes, of avoiding the questions I knew she wished to ask. Besides, Tresi would keep me company well enough until Kadar returned.

So my maid took the goblet and left, although not without a reproachful backward glance. The ensuing silence did seem rather overwhelming, but I reached down and patted Tresi on the head again, then settled myself on the divan and tried not to stare overlong at the darkness gathering outside the windows. Surely Kadar should be back by now.

Perhaps it was the wine, or simply the soul-weariness that had come upon me with the realization of Ulias' passing, but I actually fell into a light doze, my cheek resting on one arm of the divan. I skirted only the edges of true sleep, but my mind was fogged enough that it took me a second or two to realize the door had opened, and Kadar had entered the room.

I pushed myself upright and began to smile. But then I realized the odd sound at the edge of my hearing was Tresi growling. Puzzled, I glanced down to where she had been resting near my feet, and saw that she looked toward Kadar, small white wolfish teeth bared as her snout wrinkled.

What on earth? Tresi had always loved Kadar—I had joked on several occasions that she seemed to be more his dog than mine, since she was always making up to him.

Blinking, I pushed myself to my feet so I faced him. As I did so, another wash of cold passed over me.

That face was his, of course, the straight nose and wide, friendly mouth, the high cheekbones and whimsical eyebrows.

But something unfamiliar looked back at me through those golden eyes, and it was not Kadar's inflection as he said, "Good evening, my dear."

The cold in my midsection congealed into a single lump of ice. I knew then what Maldis had done with that final burst of power.

By some foul magic—I knew not how—he had invaded my husband's body.

~ CHAPTER EIGHTEEN ~

I took a step backward, although I knew there was nowhere I could run, nothing I could do to save myself.

"Shut up that vile little beast," Maldis said through Kadar's lips, "before I break her neck."

Shaking, I bent down and stroked Tresi along her back, murmuring, "Shh, dear. Everything is fine. Be calm." Eventually she did subside, although her small body trembled and her ears were laid back against her head. Not taking her eyes off Kadar—*Maldis*—she slunk along the wall until she reached her basket and crept into it.

Slowly I stood and faced him, staring at that visage which once was so dear and now already seemed strangely altered, the lips thinner, the eyes cold, without the hidden laughter that usually danced within them. "What have you done to him?"

At least he did not bother to pretend. "Very insightful of you, Lark. I am surprised you could tell the difference so quickly."

"I would think a woman would know her husband," I retorted, amazed a little at my own boldness. "And since that husband has been consorting with a black magician, it does not take much effort to realize what might have happened to change him so."

"Indeed." He moved toward me, and although I wished more than anything to retreat, to run away, I knew there was no place for me to go. Instead, I stood my ground, tried not to flinch as he came within a hand's-breadth of me. "One would think that you should know him well, save that he is no true husband to you, nor you a true wife to him." His breath was hot on my cheek as he leaned closer. "A situation I plan to remedy."

My stomach curled in disgust as I realized what those words meant, and yet at the same time I felt the smallest sliver of hope. He did not know that Kadar and I had been intimate, which meant, although Maldis had stolen my husband's body, he did not know anything of what was in his mind.

Which also meant he still most likely had no idea I possessed powers of my own, that I was anything but some foolish young woman the Mark had decided to make his wife.

I did decide to disabuse Maldis of one notion. "I fear your information is not entirely correct, however. Kadar and I do have a true marriage, so if you thought to amuse yourself by deflowering me, you are too late."

A scowl pulled down the dark brows, and I thought again of how much of a person's face was determined by the soul that inhabited it, and not the simple physiognomy of nose and mouth and chin. His eyes narrowed, and he said, "No matter. I misdoubt his clumsy efforts did much to please you. I shall teach you differently."

"As you attempted to do with the scullery maids?" I inquired in tones of icy scorn, then couldn't help wincing as he raised a hand.

The blow never fell, however. Instead, his fingers dropped to my cheek, where they traced a line down to my jaw, and then to my mouth. A shudder worked its way through my frame, and he smiled. "Good. You do right to fear me, Lark. But if you are a good little bird and do as you are told, then you can remain my consort, and watch as I bring this land the greatness it deserves."

So that was his plan—to steal the Mark's body, and then his kingdom, to do...what? I had no idea which powers he still had to command, how much of Ulias' stolen energy he had used up to transact this unholy possession of my poor husband's body.

And I saw how Maldis watched me with greedy lust in his eyes, and wondered how I could avoid his vile appetites. Luckily, my wits had not completely deserted me, and the idea came to me soon enough. A simple subterfuge, and most likely one used by women in far less dire straits than I.

"Your timing is poor, my lord," I told him. "For my moon courses have just come upon me this morning, and you know it is ill luck to take a woman in that way."

A fearsome frown greeted this revelation, but I noticed he made no more moves to touch me. "An unwelcome delay. But a delay only. Do not think this changes anything."

I allowed an expression of worry to cross my features before replying, "I understand that. As you have taken poor Kadar, so you will take me...some five days hence."

"And not a moment longer."

"Understood, my lord."

He stood there, watching me, his narrowed eyes causing a chill to work its way down my spine. How terrible it was to gaze at that face and know that the man I loved was not what stared back at me. I told myself that Kadar still had to be in there, buried beneath Maldis' dominating will.

I had to learn how to break that will, to set my husband's soul free. I would do it, even if it killed me.

A terrible evening followed. Of course we must go down to supper as if nothing had changed, and although his touch on my arm made my very flesh crawl, I had to allow him to take my hand, to lead me into the dining hall in the same way Kadar had done dozens of times before. And although he laughed at the appropriate intervals and said nothing terribly untoward, from time to time I saw Althan shoot a puzzled glance in his master's direction, as if he had sensed something was amiss, even though he could not put his finger on what it was.

For myself, I assumed what I hoped was an air of uncon-cern, smiling at Maldis' jokes, even offering him some of the choicer morsels from my plate, and yet the entire time my stomach was a mass of knots, my brain churning as I tried to determine what I should do next. Yes, I had stolen myself some breathing room, but in five days—or sooner, if the dark mage discovered my subterfuge—he would claim me as his, and all would be lost.

When we ascended the stairs to our chambers after that dreadful meal, we did so in silence. It was only after he shut the door that I said, "I shall sleep on the divan."

"You will not."

My spirit quailed at those words, but I replied firmly, "I am quite restless...during. You would not want me to disturb your sleep."

Another one of those narrow-edged frowns, and then he gave me a very thin smile. "Ah, well, if it pleases you. It will change nothing, in the end."

And I pray to God that you are wrong. I only nodded, however, and went to fetch my nightdress from the wardrobe in the bedchamber. It was an awkward business to undress, for unlike Kadar, who at least those first nights had shown me the courtesy of being otherwise occupied while I changed into my night things, Maldis loitered at the doorway to the sitting room, clearly amused by my discomfort as I turned my back and attempted to pull off one chemise at the same time I slipped on the other. I do not know if I was entirely successful at concealing everything during this procedure, but at least since my back was to him, I was spared the ignominy of witnessing his lecherous gaze.

Finally I was more or less covered, and in silence I retrieved the sheets and blankets I required to sleep once more on the divan. At that point he appeared to give up the game and, after smirking at me one last time, retired to his bed. The door, unfortunately, he left open, no doubt not trusting me enough to leave me entirely to my own devices.

Not that it really mattered. What I planned to do next would not be apparent to the watching eye, and I had to hope that Maldis was so occupied in maintaining his hold on Kadar's body that he would not be watching for other forms of magic.

I settled myself down on the divan and pulled the covers up to my chin. What an odd echo of my first night here, all those weeks ago, and yet I had never feared Kadar the way I feared Maldis. I knew there was quite literally nothing the dark mage would not do in pursuit of his ambitions...or his desires. Thank God he at least shared the same foolish superstition most men seemed to possess, that women experiencing their moon blood were somehow unclean, unlucky. I had never before thought I could use such a thing to my advantage.

What I meant to attempt next was risky, and I had no confidence in its success. But it seemed that Maldis, while he could steal the power of others, had no intrinsic power of his own, and so could not necessarily sense when I worked magic, or cast my mind out into the void to touch others of my kind. True, Ulias had feared detection when he and I were communicating, but that, I thought, was because Ulias and I had shared a connection, and Maldis even then was draining Ulias' power and therefore could detect my presence through that stolen power.

We shared nothing now. And that was what spurred my hope.

I shut my eyes and breathed deeply, knowing I could not force the relaxed state I required, and yet at the same time resenting every extra second it took to push away the tension within my body, the fear clouding the edges of my mind. All those things would prevent me from casting my consciousness forth so I might seek the only assistance left to me.

The darkness behind my eyelids began to flicker with light, and once again I saw all those errant sparks spreading out in every direction, those delicate pulsing points that indicated another mage-born soul. There it was again, that gleaming beacon far away, the one that glowed almost as brightly as the lighthouse on Ralistare Point did back in South Eredor.

I reached out to the light, feeling in its radiance something warm and welcoming, reminding me of home, of warm summer afternoons and a delicious breeze from the sea. *Father.*

A long silence, and then, the silent-sounding word sharp with surprise. *Lark?*

Yes, Father, it is I.

But how—how are you doing this?

It is something I was taught by a very wise wizard. Despite my best attempts at remaining calm, my breath caught, and the thickness of tears unshed choked my throat. But I had no time for that now. *Father, I need your help.*

Are you in trouble? Is it that Kadar Arkalis? Thani wrote and said you insisted all was well, that you wanted to stay, but I still could not believe—

I am in trouble, Father, but it is none of Kadar's doing. As quickly as I could, I explained the situation with Maldis, and how he had stolen the Mark's body, intending to rule in his stead. And I asked, *Have you ever read anything of such a spell, of how it might be broken? For Ulias told me I was a Protector, but I have no experience of such things, and it is a spell unlike anything else I have ever encountered.*

A pause, heavy with thoughts I knew my father wanted to conceal from me. Then he said, *My dear Lark, would it not be better if you simply fled? These people are none of yours, and it seems this doom was brought upon them by the Mark's own ambition.*

Anger flashed, hot and bright, across the darkness in my mind, and I had to force it down, maintain the concentration I required to maintain this most difficult type of conversation. *I cannot do that. This is my home now, and these are my people. I cannot simply abandon them—abandon Kadar—to their fates.*

Ah. It seemed as if my father's mental voice sharpened. *You care for him, then, this Mark of North Eredor?*

More than I ever thought possible.

Well, then. My father was silent for a second or two. *You cannot fault me for wanting to see you safe.*

No, I suppose not, but running away is not something I can or will do. There must be some way to reverse this spell, to send Maldis' black soul back to his body.

Ah, that is the trick.

So you do know something?

Only bits and pieces, scraps of lore preserved and handed down through the years.

Lore you never bothered to teach me.

He gave the mental equivalent of a weary sigh. *Lark, I taught you what I could, and what I thought would be helpful. Certainly I had no idea you would ever encounter someone powerful enough to use the sort of dark magic you have described. But I will tell you what I can.*

Ironic that a father's love and desire to protect his child might have the very opposite effect. But I could not fault him for that—after all, I had no children of my own, and so did not know what I would have done in a similar situation. *Please, Father. I do not know how much time I have.*

Again the sensation of him drawing in a breath, and he said, *This Maldis has seized control of the Mark's body, but his own body must be elsewhere, in a state close to a living death, but not dead. There is the subtlest of threads still connecting him to that body. You must find that thread and sever it. The jolt will send his consciousness back whence it came, and the Mark should be freed.*

Will it—will doing so kill Maldis?

Possibly. Lhars told me once, as he talked of the ways in which mages warred upon one another, that the shock alone was sometimes enough to cause the mind and heart to collapse. But this is not guaranteed.

So I may have to kill him myself, afterward.

Lark!

What, Father? I snapped. *I see no point in dancing around the issue. Surely you cannot think that, having come so far, I will not finish the deed if necessary? It would not be murder, to rid the world of one such as Maldis. More like breaking a rat's neck, I should think.*

The silence that met my speech told me all I needed to know of my father's thoughts on the matter. Obviously he feared the ordeal had changed some part of me, made me cold and hard. Perhaps. I could not worry about that now. I could only think of how to break the spell, and return my husband to me.

And if doing so required that I bury a dagger in Maldis' black heart, well, then, so be it. I did not think the world would judge me too harshly for doing such a thing.

Thank you, Father, I told him. *If you hear from me again, you will know I have succeeded. If not...*

I let the words trail off. Indeed, there was not much more to be said.

After that, I did sleep, if fitfully, waking several times an hour, my eyes flying open as if I expected to see Maldis staring down at me with that hateful, lecherous gaze of his. But the snores drifting from the bedchamber where I had shared one sweet night with my husband told me the dark mage slept the slumber of the just, even if he certainly did not deserve it.

During one of those times I wondered if I should simply rise from my bed, take up the fireplace poker, and stab Maldis where he slept. But I knew it would not be that easy. He might give the appearance of drowning in oblivion, but I thought if I even dared to approach him as he slept, he would wake quickly enough. Men such as he generally could not be disposed of that easily.

My mental conversation with my father had wearied me enough that I likewise knew I could attempt nothing until I was more rested. I had tried to reach out with that strange power of mine, the one that told me when spells were being worked and how, and although I did sense something like a dark, gleaming trail moving out from Maldis, I could not detect where it went. Strange stabbing pains burst through my skull and I doubled over, forcing myself not to vomit, knowing that I had exerted myself too much within too short a period of time. My revenge would have to wait until my faculties were completely restored.

So I slept here and there, and tossed and turned, until the sun pushed its way past a chink in the draperies and woke me up fully. I blinked and put a hand to my throbbing head.

"You would have slept better in a proper bed, I think," came Kadar's voice.

Only I knew it was not my husband speaking, but the dark mage. I refused to look up at him. "I slept well enough."

"Indeed." He moved around the corner of the divan and gazed down at me, one corner of his mouth lifting in a smirk entirely unlike any expression my husband would have worn. "I will allow you your tired back and cricked neck for now. But you must rise, and begin your day with me."

"Which will include...what? The assassination of the Emperor of Sirlende? The conquest of Keshiaar?"

"All things in their time, Lark. And ours will come soon enough."

I had no true reply to this, and so I scowled and pushed the bedcovers away. This time I gathered my courage and slammed the door to the bedchamber so I might change in private. Outside the door I thought I heard him laugh. Apparently my weak attempts at rebellion had amused him. So be it. At least this way I could dress in peace.

However, I knew open warfare was not a productive course of action. He had to think me defeated and meek, so I might have more opportunity to bring about his destruction. I chose a gown I had not worn before, of shimmering sea-green silk, and took more than my usual care in combing my hair.

When I emerged, Maldis' eyes took on a certain hungry gleam, and I could see how his gaze strayed to the low-cut bodice of my dress. My very flesh crawled, but I set my jaw and went toward him anyway.

"Very good, my dear," he said, and reached out and took me by the hand. Before I could tear myself away, he had snaked an arm around my waist, dragging me toward him, pressing his vile mouth against mine. I forced myself not to choke, not to splutter or resist.

No, I could not quite pretend I enjoyed that embrace, but apparently Maldis was satisfied that I had not fought him. When he released me, his expression was positively gloating.

"I think you begin to see there are some benefits to being my consort."

Somehow I managed to prevent myself from reaching up and wiping his spittle from my mouth. Indeed, I even smiled and said, "You do kiss very well. Is that more magic?"

"If you wish it to be."

And he reached out to draw me toward him once more, but I put up a hand. "I beg you, my lord, no more. It is not fair."

His eyebrows lifted. "Fair?"

"It is not fair to make me want you, when I cannot...do anything...for some days hence."

A gleam in the golden eyes then, as he licked his lips. "Ah, yes. Well, what is it they say? The good things are the ones worth waiting for?"

Like watching your true body die as it chokes on its own black soul... "We shall only have to hope the wait will not be too long, my lord."

"Indeed, my dear."

He raised my hand to his mouth, and I forced myself not to shudder, for of course I could not betray my true feelings—not now, when he was in an apparently mellow mood. My mind raced. I wanted to know how he had stolen Kadar's form, but I could not be too obvious in my interest. A roundabout way seemed best.

"I am curious, though," I said, in deceptively languid tones.

"Curious?" he repeated, his brows lowering.

A chill touched the back of my neck, seeming to move down my spine, but I somehow made myself smile. "You were so very clever at knowing just the right things to say to Kadar, to get him to accept you as his councilor. How was that? Does your magic allow you to read minds?"

At once his chest puffed out a little. "No, not that. But I learned of his desire to make the North great, no matter what the cost, from a certain young woman who once shared his bed. Apparently they spoke of more than lovemaking, and she knew many of his secrets. And, having been spurned by him, she was all too eager to pass those secrets on to me." He gave an unpleasant chuckle. "Better the fury of the demons of the underworld than an angry lover, eh?"

I managed an uneasy laugh in reply. "She did seem to be a most intemperate woman."

So it was the spurned Tanira who had given Maldis the information he needed to poison Kadar's mind with false hopes of greatness. Of course she could have had no idea of Maldis' true nature when she did gave away her secrets, but even so I found myself hoping viciously that she now suffered in her arranged marriage with the tin merchant even a tenth of the misery she had inflicted on Kadar, and by extension on that poor dead princess, on so many others.

"One might say that. But she is quite the beauty."

I must have stiffened, for he reached toward me again and drew me close, kissed me once more. Closing my eyes helped to feign pleasure at his loathsome caress, although I only did so in order to avoid looking at him.

But he seemed pleased with my reception of his repulsive caress, for he patted me on the cheek, then said, "No need to be jealous, my dear. After all, I am here with you, not her. But now I must be off to begin my day."

I smiled once more and, as he finally left me in peace, reflected on my sudden talent for dissembling.

Then again, it never does to underestimate what one will do when forced into a corner.

What Maldis did with his time that day, I did not precisely know. I could only be glad that he did not spend it with me. Beranne returned to keep me company, but she sensed that

I had little use for conversation, and so kept at her incessant darning, her lips pursed in disapproval.

Tresi ventured out of her basket once Maldis was gone, and I spent some time petting her and throwing the little ball she loved to chase. I suggested a walk, but Beranne gave my silk gown one look and said that she should take care of the dog, as it had begun to snow again, and I would only ruin my dress.

Her absence gave me a chance to focus on Maldis at least. By then I was rested enough that I could sit in my comfortable chair and close my eyes, and reach out to where he was in the castle. The Hall of Grievances, it seemed, and I bit my lip, knowing he had gone there to pass judgment without me. God only knew what dreadful decisions he was making, but I could do nothing about that now except hope that whatever pronouncements he handed down could be rescinded as soon as things were back to normal.

Normal. I wondered if I even knew what that was anymore.

Even so, I made myself concentrate on him, on that dark presence in my mind's eye. From him I again saw that black cord trailing out the back of his head, moving along the corridor. It shone with an oily gleam that showed up even in the shadows, and so this time I was able to follow its path through the hallways and then down the stairs, down...

My breath caught. Could it be?

Yes, it seemed that slick thread of magic worked its way down into the cellars, down at last to the cell which had once held Ulias. And lying on the bed of furs was not that mage's noble winged form, but Maldis' unimpressive body, mouth slack, eyes shut. His hands were crossed on his breast, and I could not see them rise and fall.

I wanted to laugh at the temerity of it, that he should secret himself here in the castle, of all places. Then again, I supposed I could see the logic. After all, people were already used to being warned away from that section of the cellars, so the risk of his abandoned body being disturbed was fairly low. And of course he had no idea that there was anyone alive who could follow the trail of his foul magic to its source. Now all I had to do was discover how to unravel that oily, gleaming thread...

"My lady!"

Eyes snapping open, I saw Beranne standing a few paces off, Tresi panting at her feet. Obviously they had just returned from their walk. She stared at me, the same frown I had seen far too often lately pulling at her brow.

"Are you quite all right, my lady?"

"Well enough," I replied airily. "I suppose I must have dozed off."

Her expression remained dubious, but she merely said, "Of course, my lady. Althan sent word that his lordship would like to meet with you in his audience chamber."

"His what?" I didn't pretend to have familiarized myself with the entire castle yet, but I thought I had a good notion of most of the public rooms, and I had never heard before of an audience chamber.

A sniff. "Well, he's taken it in his head to call it that. The Hall of Grievances, or at least as what it used to be."

"'Used to be'?"

Disapproval flashed in her dark eyes, although Beranne knew better than to utter an open criticism of the Mark. "Apparently he wishes there to be no more grievances spoken. Wants the constables to sort it out, or some such."

Good lord. No wonder Maldis had not taken me with him to the Hall of Grievances today—he'd known I would have protested such a foolish plan. This would be an enormously unpopular decision. I had not spent much time in the North, but I knew the Hall was a longstanding tradition, one that let the people feel as if they had some say in their governance. What on earth did the dark mage think he would accomplish by stirring up his subjects against him before he even got started?

Then again, looking for logic and common sense in a man who thought nothing of draining innocent souls merely to usurp their power, who would steal the body of a man as a means to further his own ambitions, was probably a futile exercise at best.

"I can't imagine what's gotten into him," I said, and rose from my chair. "I'll speak to him right away."

"Thank you, my lady. He does seem to value your judgment."

I could only nod and hurry out the door as she followed along in my wake. Yes, Kadar had come to trust me somewhat, to consult with me on certain topics, but of course Maldis would show me no such courtesy. Why he wanted to see me now, I did not know, but I doubted it could be for anything good.

However, he might have unwittingly played into my hands. For if the two of us could be alone together, then perhaps I would have the opportunity I required to reach out and sever the bond of unholy magic that connected his spirit to his abandoned body.

This thought only caused me to speed up my pace, as poor Beranne huffed and puffed along behind me. When I reached the doors to the Hall of Grievances, she stopped, since the Mark had apparently directed Althan to tell her that I was to see him alone. Well enough. For once I wouldn't mind being left alone with the dark mage.

The guards opened the doors to allow me entrance, and shut them behind me again. The echoing boom with which they closed caused me to start a little, but then I recovered myself—only to stop in my tracks, seeing what changes Maldis had already made to the chamber.

The benches where waiting petitioners and curious onlookers once sat had been removed, and a long red runner traced its path along the stone floor from the doorway to the dais where the throne-like chairs were placed. Or rather, I recognized the one that was my seat when I took my place next to the Mark. His own chair, however, was gone, replaced by a massive piece in carved black oak that made my own rather impressive seat look like a milkmaid's stool. Along the walls hung lengths of red fabric, plain and with no device. Maldis stood on the dais, watching me approach, his face a study in smugness.

"My, you've been busy," I remarked. "I had no idea you could get a woodcarver to make you a chair like that overnight."

Another of those smirks. "Ah, no. All this was kept in a storeroom. Apparently the late Mark had intended to increase her presence here, if any of her own schemes came to pass, but as her plans failed her, these were kept locked away. But I thought it high time they saw some use."

"And no one will mind that there is no more Hall of Grievances?"

"Not when they see the new greatness of this piddling kingdom of theirs." He descended the dais and came toward me, arms outstretched. "Would you not rather be the consort of a great ruler, rather than some trifling fool who hunts with his men and whose plans extend toward nothing grander than a silly exchange that will only serve to fill the purses of his merchants and not his own coffers?"

I thought then I wanted that man very much, the one who considered carefully every grievance brought to him, who knew the names of his servants, who thought nothing of getting on his knees in the mud to inspect the latest repairs to the city walls. It was that man for whom I fought, and not merely for our future together, but the future happiness of all his subjects.

That thought steeled me as I went to Maldis, allowed him to pull me against him, let him put his mouth on mine. Time enough for him to be distracted, for him to run his hands down my arms, to hold me in place so I could not pull away.

Not that I wished to.

No, not because I had gone mad and desired his touch. Not that at all. Standing this close, though, it was almost as if I could reach out and touch that oily tentacle of black magic, the one so strong I could practically see it even without shutting my eyes and reaching out with my mind.

Because I was so close, I could finally see how it was knotted in and around itself, writhing strands of dark power, connecting his will to its anchor in that body, slack and silent many feet below where we now stood. And because I could now see how that spell was wrought, I could also see how to unwind it, to do the work that would forever bind his tainted soul to his abandoned body.

There was nothing but those streams of magic, not his hands on my body, not his mouth on mine—nothing but the strength of my will, ripping outward like a blazing sword of light, cutting through them, severing the strands in one mighty rush.

A keening cry, ripping at my ears, and a rush of cold air around me—and then the hands on me loosened, and the man who had held me just a few heartbeats earlier slumped to the ground. I gathered myself, questing outward for any remnants of that magic, but it was gone, scattered like a morning fog in the race of the rising sun.

I knelt beside him, reached out, turned him over gently. His blank eyes stared up at the stone ceiling, and then he slowly blinked, thought and reason returning to his features. When he spoke, his voice was barely more than a whisper. "Lark?"

It was him. I knew it then, knew it in that one simple syllable, in the open way his gaze met mine. "Oh, yes, beloved, I'm here." And I reached out and pulled him to me, weeping.

His arms tightened around me, but he asked, in firmer tones, "Maldis?"

"Dead." Then I shook my head, and pulled away just a little. "That is, he should be dead. The shock of the spell being broken must have killed him."

"'Should'? 'Must have'?" With a moan, he rolled away from me and staggered to his feet. "Do you know where he is?"

I didn't bother protesting that he had had a shock as well, and that he should not be exerting himself. Instead, I rose and said, "The cellar. Where you kept Ulias."

Only a nod, and then he was moving away from me, his steps stumbling and ragged, but determined. Too determined.

"Kadar—"

"Do not try to stop me, Lark. I will have my vengeance."

There being nothing I could say to that, I merely followed him as he made his way through the hallways, more than once bumping into people, all of whom looked after him with startled expressions but did not protest. Maldis might have thought Kadar a very casual ruler, but he was their ruler nonetheless. After that it was down the stairs, into the cold and the scent of dank, damp cold.

I was not sure what we would find there. Maldis' body, still and unmoving, only this time in death and not the mere semblance of it. Or perhaps the fur-covered cot empty, with him tricking us again at the last.

But I saw neither of these things—the dark mage stood there, the slight form of a woman cradled in his arms, some kind of thin reed, stained with blood around the edges, projecting from her throat. Blood dripped from his mouth, showing the vile purpose of that reed.

Ulias had never told me exactly how Maldis stole his victims' power. Now I knew he had taken it by drinking their very blood.

My stomach coiled in revulsion, even as Maldis sneered, "You are too late! I have taken her power, and then I will take yours, lying bitch!"

Kadar's arm was a blur. At first I could not even tell what had happened, exactly, only that Maldis collapsed, the unknown woman's limp body sliding from his arms. As the dark mage's head rocked backward, the torch light caught a gleam of steel buried in the pale flesh of his throat. And then I looked from the wound in his neck, which had just begun to bleed, to the empty scabbard at my husband's hip.

Our eyes met, and, incongruously, he smiled. "Magic is all very well in its place, my love, but never underestimate the power of a good blade."

I gave a hiccuping little laugh and ran at him, throwing my arms around him, pressing my face to his chest. He held me, his heart beating strong and sure against my cheek. And then I lifted my face to his, and he kissed me, strong and sure and sweet, my love, my husband. I did not want to stop, or let go, because his mouth on mine reassured me that he was himself again, only my Kadar, the one man in the world who knew who and what I was, and loved me for it despite everything.

At length he said, "Not that I don't appreciate you breaking that spell. Magic does have some uses."

I gave him a mock glare, playing along. "Oh, it does, does it?"

"Yes, it does. And do you know what else?"

I shook my head. "No."

The golden eyes gleamed. "I think you will make North Eredor a very fine queen."

"North Eredor doesn't have queens," I pointed out.

He grinned, seeming to light up the dingy room with the force of his smile. "It does now."